The Journey of Simon McKeever

Other books by ALBERT MALTZ

The Cross and the Arrow

The Eyewitness Report

A Long Day in a Short Life

Man on a Road and Other Stories

A Tale of One January

The Underground Stream

The Journey
of Simon McKeever

Albert Maltz

Introduction by Patrick Chura

CALDER

CALDER PUBLICATIONS
an imprint of

ALMA BOOKS LTD
Thornton House
Thornton Road
Wimbledon Village
London SW19 4NG
United Kingdom
www.calderpublications.com

The Journey of Simon McKeever first published by Little, Brown and
Company in May 1949
This edition first published by Calder Publications in 2024

© The Estate of Albert Maltz, 1949, 2024

Front cover: David Wardle

Printed in Great Britain by CPI Group (UK) Ltd, Croydon CR0 4YY

ISBN: 978-0-7145-5080-0

Contents

The Journey of Simon McKeever

    Introduction   vii

    The Journey of Simon McKeever   I

    Notes   235

Introduction

The official release date of Albert Maltz's third novel was 9th May 1949. Several weeks before that date, the book had already created a controversy. Should Maltz, a known "Red" and one of the ten "unfriendly" film-industry witnesses before the House Un-American Activities Committee, be allowed to make money in Hollywood? How had he even been allowed to sell a novel? Shouldn't he be in prison?

These and other questions were effectively addressed on 24th May, when the *Daily Compass*, a New York leftist tabloid specializing in investigative journalism, published its findings:

STORY BEHIND NEW MALTZ BAN

Hollywood liberals will begin tomorrow night a fight to get Albert Maltz's novel, *The Journey of Simon McKeever*, back on the production schedule at Twentieth Century-Fox, from which it was suddenly dropped without explanation five weeks ago.

Robert W. Kenny, former attorney general in California, Carey McWilliams, noted author, and Maltz himself will give "the full story of the book banning" at a public meeting at El Patio Theater, sponsored by the National Council of the Arts, Sciences and Professions. Thirty-five prominent writers and film personalities have signified their intention of sitting on the platform at the meeting, which will conclude with a dramatization of *The Journey of Simon McKeever*, prepared by Arthur Laurents, with Will Geer as McKeever.

Twentieth Century-Fox bought *Simon McKeever* early in April, paying $35,000 for the screen rights. Since Maltz was one of the ten Hollywood writers held in contempt of Congress for refusing to state whether or not he is a Communist, there was considerable surprise in film circles at the purchase. Maltz hailed it as indicating "a change in the policy of the blacklist of the Hollywood Ten by the studios".

Walter Huston read the novel and declared his interest in playing McKeever. Jules Dassin, of *Naked City* fame, expressed a strong desire to direct the film. The novel was given by Fox to Daniel Fuchs and John Collier to read, as potential writers of the screenplay.

Then, two weeks after it had acquired *Simon McKeever*, Fox announced that it would not make it. Who was responsible for the turnabout? Who had authorized the purchase in the first place? Only someone in a very high place could have made the decision to buy *Simon McKeever*, in the face of the ban on Maltz by the studios.

Reporters seeking answers to these questions met only silence from Fox executives. However, informed observers believe that Darryl F. Zanuck, production chief of Twentieth Century-Fox, read the book, and, believing it highly suitable for the screen, went ahead with the purchase despite the storm that might break around it. There were, then, the usual objections from highly conservative forces in Hollywood, but it is believed that Zanuck remained impervious to them.

Finally, it is reported in authoritative quarters, these groups communicated with the board of directors of Fox, and the board went into a meeting to consider the matter. It is generally understood that Zanuck's contract gives him absolute control over production policy, subject only to the vote of the board. It is believed that the board exercised this vote on *Simon McKeever*, forcing Zanuck to drop it. This is, perhaps, the first time that an action of Zanuck's has been overruled.

Though studios occasionally buy stories, they seldom take the trouble to make an announcement about it. They merely shelve the story and forget it. However, it was apparent that the announcement was made in this case to quiet the pressure groups and to re-establish firmly the weakening lockout against the Hollywood Ten.

"This is obviously the last piece of work any of the Ten will ever sell to a studio," one film executive said yesterday, "until they have won their cases and have succeeded in divorcing a man's political views from his right to sell a piece of property to a willing purchaser."

Unfortunately, Maltz and his nine co-defendants did not win their cases. But the *Compass* article was prophetic in realizing that the uproar over *McKeever* would end up strengthening the ban on the Ten. It would be twenty years before Maltz would again sell a screenplay. And Maltz's right to sell books was about to be taken away as well.

The article also alluded to a temporary "weakening" of the blacklist. Today this is an interesting reminder that Maltz was in one way lucky with *The Journey of Simon McKeever*. The novel's release by a prestigious publisher, Little, Brown and Company, took place during a brief period of uncertainty about whether the government-imposed exclusion from film work applied equally to the print industry.

By 1950, when the legal case of the Hollywood Ten reached its conclusion, the publishing ban certainly did apply. Maltz would never place another novel with a US commercial press. His fourth novel, *A Long Day in a Short Life*, was refused by eighteen publishers before Maltz gave up and sent it to a small Communist publisher in 1957; his fifth and final work of long fiction, *A Tale of One January*, was not made available in the US until 2023.

The Journey of Simon McKeever received excellent reviews, made spicier by mentions of the Twentieth Century-Fox fiasco. *New York Times* senior editor William DuBois dubbed Maltz's title character a "spunky septuagenarian" and described the book as "always engrossing and, at times, inspiring". The reviewer also showed temerity, first by weighing in on the central argument of Maltz's famous congressional testimony, and secondly by siding with the artist against the philistines:

> Insisting, with others, that un-American activities committees are un-American, Mr Maltz refused to answer. Anyone who reads Mr Maltz's new novel can imagine what Simon McKeever would have bellowed to the same question. Even a picture-story editor would be hard put to find a more representative American than Simon McKeever, or one less likely to overthrow democracy by violence.

For a major US news outlet to defend Maltz was a rare phenomenon during the Second Red Scare. But the notion that Simon McKeever somehow embodied aspects of the national character was shared by many.

Just what *type* of American did Simon McKeever represent? An immigrant, a soldier, a self-educated manual labourer inclined to think for himself, he is sobered by personal tragedy, but remains an optimist and lover of humankind. In the tradition of Walt Whitman, he is a vigorous man of the people who stands up for the poor and despises riches. Nearly seventy-four, he has lived a meaningful life, but isn't ready to surrender, bodily or spiritually. His unwillingness to "knuckle under" is what leads him to assert his independence and, ultimately, to become an artist.

Near the end of his career, Albert Maltz spoke about the origins of *Simon McKeever* in a series of interviews. As he recalled, on the way home from a week of screenwriting work on a film set in northern California in 1946, he stopped to pick up an old man who wanted a hitch:

> In those days I always picked up people on the road, because it was a chance to talk with varied persons. And when this man picked up his old-fashioned Gladstone bag and began to walk towards my car, I saw that he was unable to take a step of more

than a few inches at a time. His name was William Stevenson, and I didn't know it at that time, but I was to write my next novel about him.

He told me that he was running away from an old-age home and that he wanted to get to Glendale, where there was a doctor that could cure his arthritis. We travelled together (and paused for meals) for about eight hours, as I recall, and I found him an absolutely fascinating man.

In journal notes Maltz made while the controversies of 1949 were raging, he recorded deeper descriptions of Stevenson's character:

In the many hours we spent together, I came to feel that I was in the presence of the human personality at its best. He was old and ill, but he was vitally alive and unconquerable. He was a militant union man who quoted Debs and saw the world in change and knew that only men could change it for the better. He had laboured hard all his life, he was proud of his skills and the usefulness of his labour, but he was keenly aware at the same time that he had been ill used by our economic system. His solution for that was social change through the efforts of men. He had been a union man all his life, and when he got cured of his arthritis he intended to go back to work again and join a union and move the world forward.

The model for Simon McKeever was therefore a figure right out of the great people's culture of the 1930s, a decade when the once-mighty movement for a workers' literature was in full swing. In this ageing fugitive philosopher, the novelist saw an opportunity.

When Maltz met Stevenson, he had recently had a public quarrel with other socialist writers about the form and meaning of proletarian art. Early in 1946, Maltz had published in *New Masses* the essay 'What Shall We Ask of Writers', in which he asserted that Communist novelists were producing inferior work because they were placing political concerns above artistic ones. For creative writers, Party doctrine was in Maltz's view "not a useful guide, but a straitjacket". Essentially Maltz asked that leftist writers be judged by the quality of their works rather than the Party committees they join, reminding fellow Marxists that "where art is a weapon, it is only so when it is art".

A handful of senior leftist critics immediately and harshly rejected Maltz's argument in *New Masses* and the *Daily Worker*. Under withering attack, Maltz recanted his views and wrote a rebuttal to his own "mistaken" article. He was accepted back into the Party fold, but the painful controversy stayed with him.

The Journey of Simon McKeever may be understood as Maltz's last word in the debate. With this sublime and technically flawless novel, he transcended the intra-Party dispute he'd suffered for, satisfying both leftists and literary critics with a story that, in the words of scholar Bernard Dick, "raised proletarian fiction to an art".

One of Maltz's aesthetic methods was to make intentional reference to elements of perhaps the greatest of all proletarian novels, John Steinbeck's *The Grapes of Wrath*. In *McKeever*, Maltz paid homage to the Pulitzer Prize-winning ur-text of the Great Depression, redeploying certain motifs from the 1939 dustbowl epic and novel of the road. The hitch-hiking McKeever, who has just freed himself from a shabby state-run rest home, is a wizened version of Tom Joad, the hitch-hiker just released from the McAlester prison in the opening chapters of *The Grapes of Wrath*.

Thirty years after his encounter with William Stevenson, Maltz's affinity for Steinbeck led to another opportunity.

In the mid-1970s, Jane Fonda made no secret of her search for a film role that would cap her father's long career and put him in contention for the Academy Award he had yet to win. Henry Fonda had come close to winning the Best Actor Oscar only once. At the 13th Academy Awards of 1941, he was nominated for his role as Tom Joad in John Ford's film version of *The Grapes of Wrath*.

Seizing the moment, Maltz got in touch with the Fondas. Henry read *The Journey of Simon McKeever* and loved it. On 11th November 1976, he wrote with news that must have helped Maltz exorcise some part of the trauma of spending ten months in prison and twenty years on the blacklist:

DEAR MR MALTZ,

I can't tell you how excited I am about *Simon McKeever*. I don't wonder that [Walter] Huston and [Spencer] Tracy both wanted to play him. I think he's a delightful old fart, and I mean that only affectionately.

You can uncross your fingers. I am involved.

Cordially,

HENRY FONDA

The *Simon McKeever* film project, starring Fonda with a cameo by Jane Fonda as the Glendale doctor, was announced. But the seventy-two-year-old leading man fell ill, progress stalled, and the chance passed. Devin McKinney's recent biography of Fonda describes the unrealized ambitions of the actor's last years. Prominent among the projects that had strong potential was *The Journey of Simon McKeever*. The biographer's certainty that McKeever "could have been a great Fonda character" makes the loss more regrettable.

Soon after the Fonda deal fell apart, Maltz made a last-ditch attempt, writing to Burt Lancaster to ask him to consider the role. "In 1949 Walter Huston was excited about playing it, and used to go around to parties reading aloud from the book," Maltz explained, "but the blacklist stopped the film from being made." He added that "In 1966 Spencer Tracy wanted to play it, but unfortunately he died." Maltz then shared an opinion first held by Darryl Zanuck: "I believe the character of McKeever offers such opportunities for an actor that the one who plays it will automatically become an Academy Award contender."

Whether or not the seemingly cursed film version is ever made, Maltz's final plea to Lancaster makes a superb case for this new edition of the long-neglected novel: "I want to stress that the story is not about the problems of old people in our society. *It is an adventure story that celebrates man's courage and determination, and life force, at their highest.*"

Patrick Chura, University of Akron

The Journey
of Simon McKeever

To
My son, Peter

"What is man? He is not you, not I, not they... no! He is you, I, they, the old man, Napoleon, Muhammad – all in one! Do you understand? That's... tremendous. In that are... all beginnings and all endings. All is in man, all is for man! Only man exists, everything else... is the work of his hand and his brain. Man! That is... magnificent! There's such pride in the word! M-A-N! You must respect man! Not pity him... not lower him with pity... you must value him! Let's drink to man, baron!"*

MAXIM GORKY, At the Bottom

Chapter 1

On a warm afternoon in May 1947, an old man paused on a street corner in Santabello, California, and stood waiting for the traffic light to change. Simon McKeever was his name – he was seventy-three years old, and at this moment his heart was pounding with both excitement and anxiety.

The excitement he felt was rare to his life, and therefore deeply pleasurable. It came from the fact that an hour before, by the sweet and mysterious grace of God, he had found a twenty-five-cent piece.

In the careless vigour of McKeever's youth, a quarter found by accident would have been spent on a drink of whiskey or a posy of flowers for the girl on his arm or a tattered copy of a Jack London novel.* But now, in the current state of his affairs, a quarter was the handiwork of an alchemist, and it would buy, in preference to everything else, a can of good tobacco. McKeever was an old-age pensioner of the State, and each month his fifty-five dollars' insurance was turned over to the Thomas Finney Rest Home for his board and lodging. They were granted tobacco at the Home – a weekly ration of horse manure or mattress sweepings or whatever else the poetry of old men's bitterness might choose to call it. But this quarter meant a can of *good* tobacco to a man who dearly loved to smoke.

His anxiety lay in this: that to buy the tobacco he had to cross the street to a drugstore. For almost two years now he had not needed to expose himself to the dangers of city traffic. Once a week Mr Finney transported him, and the other boarders who needed medical attention, to a hospital clinic in Santabello, twelve miles from their Home. Truck to hospital, back into the truck – this was the routine of the most eventful day in his week. But on this morning McKeever's clear blue eyes had spied the twenty-five-cent piece gleaming loose on a grass plot by the clinic door. His cane covered it, a crowing bubble of laughter rolled in his throat, and he got down, first on one lame knee, then on the other, to snare it for his own.

McKeever was no less generous than most men, but these days he suffered from a gnawing greed for good tobacco. Although his conscience told him he was being low-down, he couldn't bring himself to share this good luck with his friends. He slipped the coin into his pocket and fretted impatiently through his lamp treatment. Then, as soon as the doctor had tapped him over (advising again the same bitter, useless medicine), he sneaked away from the clinic. He even omitted his weekly flirtation with the pretty nurse he so especially favoured there. He was in a passion to set out – quick, before the truck should leave – on this monumental journey across the street.

McKeever's trouble was arthritis, an affliction he violently resented, because he had been always an active and vigorous man. In the two years past, his knees had grown so stiff they would scarcely bend; the sockets of his hips and ankles seemed to have lost their fluid; all the fine springs and hinges of the inward mechanism had rusted, so that they groaned and cracked and rebelled at every use. At the Home, when he listened to the other men describing their ills, he sometimes interrupted with a gust of uncharitable scorn: "You can *walk,* Percy – now, can't you? What are you beefing about, then, you coot? Why, this plague the doctors call arthureetis – why, it sends a rust and a poison to every last part of your body. And here I was a lad who ran from Belfast to his own gate stile – twelve miles, an' that's not stretching it. Oh, it's a damn, poisonous blight to a thoroughly healthy man!"

Like the others, McKeever was willing to speak candidly about his physical deficiencies, but he owned one weakness he would not reveal. He never confided to his room-mates that almost every night his sleep was disturbed by the same loathsome nightmare:

he was on a road... a car came... he tried to move... and he was run down like a cockroach and squashed; then, most distressing of all, people stood around examining the remains and said: "Why, he was only a cockroach after all – not a man, a bug." He had pondered in vain over the dream; he was ashamed of it, and he never spoke of it.

That nightmare was teasing his mind unpleasantly at this moment. He was standing on a street corner with a silver quarter in his pocket; the traffic light he had been waiting for had turned green – but he was fearful. He was fearful, but he was even more greedy for his can of good tobacco. He spat into the gutter suddenly, chuckled with nervousness and stepped down from the kerb.

It was a wide avenue. Leaning heavily on his cane, he inched his way, tiny step by tiny step, in a manner painful to see. A lank man, over six feet in height, McKeever had a wide, flat back and long shanks and a lean, flat body. Once he had covered ground with great loping strides, but now, as he told himself sourly, he crawled like a tortoise with the clap. The traffic light changed before he had advanced a yard, and a shiver of anxiety ran through his body. His bright-blue eyes darted from side to side; little drops of water appeared at both temples, and his mouth and angular chin worked with exertion.

Actually he was in no particular danger. It was a residential area, and there were signs to motorists warning of a hospital. But the old man was so uneasy that when an auto passed by without waiting, he exploded in a shout of resentment. The driver had drawn over near the opposite kerb, and McKeever had not been menaced in the slightest, but he paused in a tremble, cut the air with his walking stick and cried out, "Fool – you're a fool!" – and instantly felt mortified. Rather often these days, when he was alone, McKeever muttered his thoughts aloud – and now, as he leant on his walking stick and laboured on, a thin grin came to his lips, and he began to whisper to himself with sardonic amusement: "Take a turtle now, Simon – a stubborn, soft-brained thing. Out on the highway it goes, right between the wheels of the ten-ton trucks. Watch it now, you jackass, or you'll be seeing your father and your mother and your good sister before your time."

He was halfway across the street when a voice called from behind him, "Going for a hike, Mr Mac?" The little nurse, who was his special friend at the clinic, was running after him. She reached him, linked her arm with his and glanced up at him flirtatiously. "Take me along?"

Indeed he would, and he was thankful that the rest of the traffic canyon would be negotiated on her arm, but he worked his mouth in silence for a moment and then replied, "Nope, I'm not going to... Not taking you anywhere." His speech was vigorous, the tone strong and faintly shaded by the Irish twist of his childhood, the words clean-spoken. "Just a gold digger you are... chasing after me like all the others. You women make me miserable."

The nurse laughed; McKeever pressed her arm and smiled down at her; his mind was framing a thought important to him, and he wondered if he might tell her, or if it would seem idiotic coming from an old man.

"Wherever you're going," the nurse said gently, "you won't forget your truck, will you? It'll be leaving soon."

"No, but I'd sure like to forget it. It's no home to me, that place." He began to chuckle. "I'd rather be going to the island of Bali. I'd see the naked girls an' drink the coconut milk."

"The girls never hurt any man," said the nurse. "But keep away from coconut milk. Gives you the runs."

McKeever threw back his head and hooted with pleasure. Then he jerked around in momentary alarm at the sound of an auto horn. "I'm just going to the drugstore to buy something."

"Why didn't you ask *me* to get it?"

"Ask *you*?" He gazed down at her severely. "How can a woman buy tobacco for a man?"

"Nuts to you, Mr Mac," she said affectionately.

He grinned and asked, "Where you going?"

"For my lunch."

"Go ahead."

"No hurry. I eat late on clinic days."

"I don't need help, if that's what you're thinking." They had reached the security of the kerb now, and McKeever paused. "You run along."

"Don't be so bossy." She said it roguishly, using all of the coquetry of eyes, lips and tone that a pretty woman employs with a man her own age; this was the invariable play between them, and now, as always, it left him grinning shyly. For weeks he had been longing to tell her how keenly he relished her sauciness. Did she know, he wondered, what it meant to an old man to be dealt with in that manner?

"Join me at the counter, Mr Mac, and I'll buy you a soda."

"Can't stomach it. Not 'less there's rum in it. Will there be rum in it?"

The nurse laughed, took hold of his arm and helped him over the kerb. She was short, not even up to his shoulder, a chunky girl with snapping black eyes and glossy black hair and a lovely, voluptuous mouth. McKeever had been smitten by her since his first visit to the hospital. Living as he did among the aged and infirm, her pert vivacity was hot sunlight to his senses and spirit.

"Got a laugh like a... sheep's bell in a meadow," he said to her suddenly. "Ever heard a sheep's bell? They tinkle sweet, just like you."

"You're sweet to say it."

"I'll tell you something, Sarah. That's your name, ain't it?" His glance rested on her fondly as he began to inch his way forward. "A man gets to be my age an' some things don't matter any more. But he never gets tired of the look of a pretty woman. When I see you each week at the hospital, my heart just lifts up." It was spoken now, the thing he had wanted to tell her.

"Why, thank you." She flushed with genuine pleasure.

"You're better than just pretty, lass," he continued quickly. "You've got spirit. Most people are half scared – did you ever think of that? Scared of what other people will say, scared of their boss, scared of their own hearts even. Oh, there's an awful lot of dying in most people's living. I've seen it. It's a miserable thing."

She looked up at him quietly. "Around the hospital I'm 'that loose Miss Kahn'. I'm twenty-seven and I've been divorced twice." She laughed a little, not quite happily.

"Is that so? Well, don't you mind. Just find the man you like. Grab hold and love him hard."

"That puts it," she said with a laugh.

The pharmacy was several stores from the corner, and McKeever paused to rest for a moment. He shifted the cane to his other hand and winced a little as he flexed his fingers. The nurse waited at his side, glancing up at his face with warm eyes, wondering about him now – what his life had been like, whether it had been good, what he had done with it. She reflected that except for his clothes McKeever looked rather like a country physician or a schoolteacher or even a scientist. He had a narrow, distinguished-looking head with thin, white hair neatly parted on the side, the sunburnt scalp showing through at the crown. The long bony nose, a little humped at the bridge, the keen eyes, the thin, clear-skinned face ending in a sharp jaw point, all contributed to an impressive appearance. She knew he had been none of these imagined men, however, because his speech was of another sort, and because of the way he dressed: invariably in the same pair of drab corduroy trousers and in the same green flannel shirt – no tie, no jacket. She said suddenly, "Tell me, Mr Mac, is it very bad there, at your Home?"

"Bad? No. Only, it's a dreary life for an active man." Wanting to explain, he used the opportunity to boast a little to this attractive girl. "I've covered the forty-eight states, an' you can name them one by one. I worked in most an' left the mark of my work in twenty."

"Were you a salesman?"

"A salesman?" He answered it with scorn. "*I* was always a *working* man: I'm a pipe fitter – an' that's a skill your modern oil industry can't do without. Believe me, when *I* finished a day's labour, the world was a little different... Oh, I get so fidgety nowadays I could jump out of my skin!" He began to walk again, his mouth puckered up resentfully. "What's a man without some useful work?"

Wondering at him a little, she said, "But you're not young any more; you shouldn't *have* to work. People are entitled to rest after they reach a certain age."

Almost with anger he replied, "Rest is a way to spend Sunday, girl, not your good six days. If those damn doctors would cure up my lameness, I'd have no need to rest. Why," he continued with animation, "I was in a mattress factory doing highly useful war work until two years ago, when this arthureetis got me down. I'm a bit old for the oil fields, I'll admit that, but there's other jobs, there's…" He paused, looked at her cautiously, then said, "I'm talking an awful lot. I'm kind of a talky man, ain't I?"

"I like to have you talk to me," she replied fondly. "You're interesting."

He smiled with gratitude, but remained silent.

"How old are you anyway, Mr Mac? Sixty?"

He replied with a gust of laughter. "You've seen my record. Can't butter me that way."

"I haven't seen it." She opened the door to the drugstore. "Are you older?"

"You know I'm a pensioner, anyway. That makes me sixty-five to begin with."

"I forgot that." Amused, she tried to estimate his age as he walked past her into the store. She had noticed a number of things before this: that the backs of his hands were mottled in colour, the skin blotched yellowish brown in a manner characteristic of the aged, and that the blue veins were very prominent at both temples – but on the other hand his voice was vigorous, his mind obviously quick, his eyes clear and free from rheum. "I'll lay good money you're not much over sixty-five."

McKeever chuckled with pleasure and turned to watch her face as she came in after him. "If I don't pass over before the middle of next month, I'll be seventy-four."

Her surprise was marked and genuine.

"Born June 10th, 1873," he continued with pride. "I surprise everybody. It's the lack of wrinkles in my face. An' I'm strong, got a fine constitution. Used to do a back somersault easy as breathin'."

"You certainly surprise me… you look ten years younger – more. I think you're wonderful."

Embarrassed by her praise, he worked his mouth in silence for a moment as he tried to think of something to say. Nothing came.

"You want to know something?" she told him softly. "There aren't many old people who look as though they've had a good life. You do."

McKeever stopped walking. He stared closely at Sarah, with an intensity that rather surprised her. "Good?" he enquired seriously. "What do you mean by 'good'?"

"I don't know exactly."

"My life ain't been easy – no cushions. It ain't always been content either – my, no!"

"That's not what I meant."

"What did you mean?"

"I can't quite say."

"I'd like to know, lass."

Sarah became uneasy. She had intended no more than a passing compliment, and McKeever's intense response was embarrassing. "Just good," she murmured. "Am I wrong?"

He turned away with a sigh. "Well now, I wouldn't exactly know."

They stood for a moment rather awkwardly, and she wondered what she had touched off in the old man. She said quickly, "I've got an idea: my boyfriend has a car. How about we drive out to the Home this Sunday morning and pay you a visit? I'd like him to meet you."

"Visit *me*?"

"Why not?" She smiled with genuine warmth. "I like you. He will too."

McKeever hesitated, unable to accept easily that this spirited girl really wanted to visit an old man like him, a stranger. Then his face lit up. "Why, I'll be very pleased. I've never had a visitor out there. Got no relatives."

"How do I get there?"

"You just take Highway 99 towards Stockton," he said with great animation. "When you pass the Fair Grounds, you clock about eight miles. You'll see a filling station there at a crossroad. You turn down right to the third house, an old museum of a place – brown, it needs paint. An' I'll likely be out on the porch."

"It's a date," she said. "You go buy your stinky tobacco now. And don't miss your truck."

She left him with her bright, sexual smile, and he stood in quiet delight, watching her as she strode to the counter. He took pleasure in her moving flanks, the buttocks graceful despite the starched nurse's uniform, in the glossy, black bun on the nape of her neck. In the mind it was still possible to know a woman like this and recall how one's senses had relished the exquisite skin, the warm odours, the passionate flesh. "God bless you, child," he thought... and then he turned to buy himself a can of good tobacco.

Chapter 2

"Young lady," he said with a gay smile as he reached the cigar counter, "I'm in the market for some Leslie Plug tobacco."

"We haven't got it."

"You don't mean that! How come? You sure you ain't wrong?"

The saleslady was a thin, crabbed-faced woman of fifty. She frowned with irritation and remained stubbornly silent.

"Would you mind looking?"

Silently the woman turned to another customer. "Yes?"

"Two Chesterfields."

McKeever peered over the counter while waiting and observed with pleasure that Half and Half was only twelve cents a can. He didn't favour the brand quite as much as Leslie Plug, yet...

"Young lady," he said with an attempt at humour, "I'm sure you don't smoke pipe tobacco very often, but to a man like me—"

"Listen," the woman interrupted wrathfully, "we haven't got it. And how dare you call me 'young lady' in that sarcastic tone? It ain't your privilege to make fun of me."

"Why, my goodness," McKeever exclaimed in bewilderment, "I had no intention, I'm awful sorry... I'll take two cans of Half and Half."

In silence the woman gave him the two cans and a book of matches. McKeever handed her the quarter, she returned him a penny change. Then she leant over the counter, her bleak eyes suddenly apprehensive. "You gonna complain about me to the manager?"

He replied with astonishment, "I should say not! What for? Guess I talk too much. It's a weakness of mine."

She sighed unhappily, in gratitude and relief. "I'm sorry I bust out on you. I ain't well today – I'm jumpy."

"How's your teeth, I wonder?"

"My teeth?"

"It might be a cavity. Most people don't get good dental care, even doctor care. It's one of the shames of our times." McKeever hesitated, and his mouth worked for a moment. He felt like quoting a line of poetry to the lady, but he was uncertain about its reception. In a lifetime of varied reading, he had found the greatest personal comfort in poetry, and he had spent hours in memorizing verses. He had it in mind to tell her:

> Whatever be thy fate today,
> Remember, "This will pass away!"*

It was a good verse, apt to the occasion – but some people didn't take to poetry, and he had a notion she was that way. He decided against it, nodded a friendly goodbye and started off. He felt saddened by the encounter. During all the years of his life, he had been observing the wretched state of women like this saleslady – of his own widowed mother worn down by work on their farm in Ireland, silent and crusty and bitter even at forty, stingy and quarrelsome so that a boy asked himself: "Why is she living, what does she enjoy in her life, what bit of goodness will she take to her grave?" And the sorrow of his sister – of being married to a drunkard, knowing the hard fist of the man more often than his hand in tenderness, glad when he left her, glad to be a washerwoman for the rich in order to keep up her children, and yet lonely and always longing for the one she didn't have, for the kiss of a man on her mouth and a man's talk as they sat by the fire. What a crime and a shame it was, he thought now, this stony life of toil that these middle-aged women led: the scrubwomen and the hotel maids, the spinsters at the laundry mangles and the farm women like his mother. Poor saleslady with her bad teeth! The world needed a pound of fixing – he had always said it!

Now, as McKeever laboured towards the front door, he noticed that he was being stared at intently by a woman who was leaning against one of the telephone booths. He glanced over at her and found her to be a stranger. The scrutiny continued as he moved along; it became altogether too impertinent for him to accept it in silence. If there was one thing he resented, it was to be stared at as though his lameness made him a freak. Sourly, out of the corner of his mouth, he said, "Take a good look, young lady – won't cost you a cent."

The woman replied with a burst of hearty laughter that left him bristling. The drugstore seemed overrun with difficult females this afternoon. This one was squat, heavy, in her early forties, he judged, with powerful shoulders and a protuberant rump that was tightly sheathed in green slacks. Her plump face was wine-ruddy in complexion; she wore her dyed, blond hair in a boyish cut, and altogether she was thoroughly unattractive. Yet within another moment McKeever was ready to embrace her. The woman took a step towards him and said, in a warm tone that he knew was genuinely sympathetic, "Excuse me... I was just wondering how long you've had arthritis, you poor man."

He stopped where he was, instantly alert and inquisitive. "How do you know I got it? How do you know it ain't something else?"

The woman gave him a tender, fat-lipped grin. "Why wouldn't I know? I had it... had it much worse than you... had it so bad I could only walk on crutches. And now look at me: not a trace of it left... cured... completely!"

A shiver ran through McKeever's body. His pulse began to race with excitement, a spurt of colour stained his thin cheeks. Faltering a little he said, "You wouldn't... make a joke of it?"

"Why, Lord," the woman replied earnestly, "I'd send a person to jail who'd make a joke of a body's suffering."

"That's right!" he muttered. He looked her up and down with hot eyes. "An' you got cured? How?"

"Knock wood!" She leant over to rap her fat knuckles on his walking stick. "Four years I had it, getting worse every day. It curved all my toes in. And my hands" – she raised them for his inspection – "both these knuckles here, swollen like radishes. I couldn't—"

19

"Who cured you?" McKeever interrupted. "Can he work it on me?"

"Doctor Amelia Balzer, a woman. And oh, Lord, is she a whiz on arthritis!"

"Where's her office?"

"Don't rush me, Daddy." She set her hands akimbo on her plump hips and leant towards him with a tender smile. "Why do you think I spoke to you in the first place? Because any time I see a poor creature who's suffering like I did, I want to help him."

"Go on, then," McKeever said eagerly. "I'm listening."

The woman suddenly flung both fat hands up towards the heavens. "Lord, the money I spent trying to get well before I met my Doctor Balzer! I went to doctors in Denver, in Phoenix – I went to Frisco and Chicago. Cost me over seven thousand dollars, and no relief at all."

"And then you found this doctor!" McKeever supplied impatiently.

"Found her in Los Angeles, right in Glendale on my own doorstep – found her through my delicatessen man... he went to her for sinus."

"Does she have a machine? Electric?"

"No, it's some injections – she sticks the needle in here." She slapped her buttocks, then flung both hands heavenwards once more. "And oh, is she a miracle worker! In three months I put away my crutches and started using canes. In six months I put away my canes. And now look at me!" Energetically, delighting in her good health, she wiggled both hands at the wrists, twisted her heavy torso from side to side to show the suppleness of her spine, finally ending up by doing a knee bend, which left her very red in the face. "Course I still got my high blood pressure, but Doctor Balzer brought *that* down from two hundred fifteen to one sixty-five. You got high blood pressure, Daddy? Probably you have!"

"Not a thing wrong with me," McKeever said emphatically. "Clean as a whistle inside. Got my own teeth, eat everything, keep my bowels regular. Used to do a handstand easy as breathin'."

"Ever had a basal?"

"What's that?"

"Oh Lord, you've gotten poor medical care, I can see that already! Why, a basal metabolism is elementary. Every doctor has you take that."

"You're right there," McKeever agreed bitterly. "Those doctors at the clinic haven't lifted a finger for me – they haven't improved me at all."

"Tell me about the pain – is it sharp or an ache?"

Sarah Kahn, the nurse, came up to them before McKeever could reply. There was a streak of mayonnaise on Sarah's upper lip, and she was full of bustle and disapproval. "Mr Mac, you'll be late for the truck! Mr Finney won't let you come in next week."

"Who cares? I'm having an important conversation here. That big Booger can just wait."

The nurse frowned at him, not without affection, and ran to the door to look out.

"It ain't pain I got at all: it's lameness," McKeever told the woman. "My joints feel like they're rusted up. Why do you ask?"

"It's part of the diagnosis. I won't say I know as much about arthritis as a doctor, but there's darn little I don't know by now. When did this stiffness begin?"

"Four years ago. I began to feel it in my hips when I bent over. I was working in a place where the floor was always damp, one of those fly-by-night war factories – that's what did me in. An' two years ago now my hands got so bad I had to quit... What's the name of your doctor again?"

Sarah came hurrying back from the front door. "The truck's waiting, Mr Mac, and everyone's getting in. I'll run across and ask Mr Finney to swing around for you. But you start for the kerb right now, you hear? Please!" She ran out.

"Will you write down the doctor's name for me?" McKeever asked the woman. "An' the address?"

"Indeed I will – that's what I had in mind when I spotted you. I'll write her about you, too. I write to her home every month just like we were friends. She wants to know how I'm doing – that shows the lovely kind she is." She snapped open her purse. "An' she's not one of those money-grabbers, either. Whatever your income is, that's how she charges."

"My, that's wonderful – it's just what I need."

As the woman printed the name and address on the back of the envelope, she said enthusiastically, "Ain't it a lucky thing I met you? I'll say! Life's full of accidents. It was an accident made us sell out the liquor business in LA an' go into real estate up here. An' you might say it's accidental my husband had to go into the hospital today, which is how I'm meeting you. My husband has prostate difficulty – he's having it snipped out tomorrow morning. You ever had that difficulty?"

"Not me."

"You're lucky – my, you're lucky!"

McKeever leant forward on his cane, his eyes very bright. "You're positive this doctor can cure me – eh?"

"She fixed *me* up, didn't she? I've sent her patients by the…" – she stopped as the telephone rang stridently in the booth behind her – "dozen. Oh Lord! That's for me – that's my son in Toledo. Goodbye… good luck." She squeezed hastily into the booth, shutting the door on McKeever as the latter cried out in distress, "Wait – you ain't given me the address!"

Sarah Kahn, running in from the street, called out with some annoyance "Why, Mr Mac!" at seeing him still over by the phone booths. "Mr Finney's turning the truck around and you haven't even started. I promised you'd be ready."

"Just a minute, lass." McKeever advanced a few steps closer to the phone booth; he reached out with his gnarled walking stick and rapped on the glass pane of the door. The fat face turned, a fat hand gestured towards the phone, waved him away. McKeever rapped again. Annoyed, the woman jerked open the door. "Please – it's a long-distance call, it's expensive, it's Toledo!" she said, her voice rising with each word.

"But you haven't given me the doctor's address!"

"Oh Lord!" She called "Hold on a second" into the phone. The envelope was in the hand holding the receiver, and she muttered to herself impatiently as she untangled things.

"You can write your doctor I was holding down a good job until two years ago," McKeever said animatedly. "Paid me thirty-two fifty a week, not counting overtime." He accepted the envelope with a smiling nod of gratitude. The door closed again, but he was too excited to stop. "Would've been working still, if it wasn't for the damp on that floor."

Sarah tugged at his arm. "Mr Mac, you'll get in trouble. Mr Finney says he'll leave without you."

McKeever looked down at the envelope with the precious name and address on it. "I'm coming, lass," he said, and his voice quivered with elation. "An' as for that Booger outside – why, he can just wait." He began to chuckle and started his slow crawl for the door. His eyes were bright; a flush coloured his cheeks. "He can wait, or he don't have to wait. Won't be the first bus I've missed in my life. Won't be the last."

Chapter 3

As McKeever moved slowly out of the drugstore into the warm blaze of the afternoon sun, he kept one hand in his pocket. His fingers were gripping the paper with the doctor's address on it as though it were a wild bird that might escape him. He felt tipsy; he felt like raising his head to the sky and howling his joy like an animal.

It was not the sheer fact of growing old that McKeever ever had minded. There was a rhyme and a reason to that, like night and day. There were some men in the Home whom he deeply pitied; they were spirit wanderers, he always maintained, pining uselessly for the time when they were thirty or forty or even a boy. As for himself, he knew beyond argument that each stage of life brought its own adventure when a man wasn't dead in his heart. There was a profound satisfaction in observing life in a sixty- or a seventy-year-old way; it was quite different from any other way, or so he had found. And there was an extraordinary new pleasure he had found in doing things all alone – in watching the stars from a park bench or in taking a Sunday bus trip into the country to spy out birds he had never noticed before. And oh, there was a terrific satisfaction in managing your own affairs at seventy, in earning a living and carrying on a useful work. It wasn't at thirty that he had designed a new drill for the oil fields, but at sixty-two. He had never got anywhere with it, true, but then neither had Thomas Edison with many of *his* inventions. Anyway, there was nothing at all a man had to regret in growing old... provided it wasn't *that* – the only thing he did fear – the horror of having to lie twisted and helpless in a bed, endlessly, day and night, without function or purpose, while life passed him by. When a man was like that, he was nothing, he was... garbage.

McKeever raised his eyes to the Finney truck at the kerb and then asked himself whether it was fool's gold his heart already was chasing. He decided firmly that it was not – the woman in the drugstore was evidence enough. But in that case, his mind asked, very practically, how would he get down to Glendale... where would he find the money... where could he stay? He didn't know the answer to any of these questions, but he suddenly thrust all doubt aside in a burst of impatience. There was only one thing important to a man: the road he decided to travel. Any problems that arose were no more than hills to climb. His situation was clear: four hundred miles away there was a doctor who had a special cure for him. Four hundred miles was a huge distance when a man was no longer young and had no means – but even ten thousand miles wouldn't count if it meant getting well. He had known for months that the highfalutin young interns at the hospital had secretly given him up. He knew – he had smelt out the meaning of their looks and grunts; in their eyes he was a "Terminal Case". But he had met ignorance and incompetence before in this world, and had never truckled to them. Why should he now? He knew absolutely that the sickness from which he suffered was not the product of a fatty heart from too much fat living or of syphilis or of anything else that was a part of *him*. It was the effect of factory damp – a rust, a mould, and he had always been positive that when he got hold of the proper doctor, he'd come through exactly as he was before the blight put its mark on him. He'd be a few years older, of course, but essentially the same: a skilled man with strong hands and a limber body who had always been able to make his way. It wasn't age alone that counted in this world – what counted most was a man's spirit. There were some men who were licked at twenty – he'd seen them by the dozens. And even if it proved that this doctor couldn't cure him as she had cured the woman in the drugstore – nevertheless, why shouldn't he have a damn good whack at it?

There is nothing worth the doing that it does not pay to try...*

It was a good verse; he had fixed it in his mind years ago as something fundamental. It showed him now the path to travel.

McKeever thought this and felt a moment of exquisite elation, as though he were already in Glendale and already cured – and then the doubts he had cast aside rushed out from the corners of his mind like hungry mice. The doctor was in Glendale... it was four hundred miles... how would he manage? As his mood darkened again, he recalled what Sarah had said to him in the drugstore – that he looked like a man who had had a good life. It had depressed him to hear her say that, it had left him restless and uneasy. Why? And why now did he think of his damn nightmare also, seeing himself helpless on the ground with those buzzards all around him croaking, "He's only garbage... a cockroach"?

McKeever sighed. A man's mind sometimes was like a train without a driver: it ran on a set of iron tracks all its own. He didn't understand any of this, and he wouldn't try. And yet – he *would* go to Glendale. That he would!

Sarah Kahn was purposely walking a little ahead of McKeever towards the truck at the kerb because she was so anxious for him to hurry, but McKeever was quite oblivious of her urgent glance. Sarah had her eye on Mr Finney, who was leaning against the cab with an impatient glare on his face. She knew suddenly why the old man referred to Finney as "the big Booger". It was only partially his size – even more it was a flabby grossness, the lack of any solidity to his tall, fleshy body. And knowing that McKeever was altogether in his hands, that Finney could, if he desired, make the old man's life dreadful at the Home, she wished McKeever would at least try to hurry.

In her anxiety Sarah was misjudging both men. McKeever would not have hurried for anyone at this moment. And Finney was not so formidable a personality as she feared. Soft of body, he was even softer in the fibre of his heart, and he was not indifferent to the pensioners in his charge. For the past ten years he had witnessed intimately what old age meant when it was lived in poverty. Within the limits of profit and loss he tried his best for his boarders – and he lay awake nights with the grim fear that he might end up like them. If now he was impatient at McKeever, it was only because returning McKeever to the Home was his task, and all tasks worried him dreadfully until they were completed.

"For God's sakes, Simon," he bellowed suddenly, "do you think I got all day? Snap it up there – what's the matter with you?"

McKeever shook himself out of his reverie; he paused and eyed Finney with a grin that masked his pain. "Ever watch a crab out walking, Thomas? Walks sideways, don't it? Can't walk any other way."

"All right, but don't stop," Finney whined in exasperation. "Keep moving."

Seated in the truck, watching McKeever, were two old men and two old women, a small load for a clinic day. McKeever knew what was in their minds: no matter their own ills, they were thanking their stars right now that they didn't have to crawl through life like a bug. He suddenly didn't care that they would be having this thought: he had his own secret to comfort him now. At this moment, he didn't even care about the truck itself.

Like the others at the Home, McKeever hated the Finney pick-up truck and resented the Booger for selling his broken-down station wagon, even though it had been a constant expense to him. Finney answered their complaints with an argument they only partially believed: there was an inflation – costs had shot sky-high, yet their pensions had remained fifty-five a month. He was losing money, and the only reason he didn't shut down the Home altogether was out of pure charitable consideration for them. Furthermore, he had sweated to make the truck comfortable for them – what honest complaint did they have?

What his guests could not explain to Finney – or what Finney chose not to understand – was that their resentment of the truck had nothing to do with comfort. The truck was unusual as a passenger vehicle, and therefore conspicuous; twelve old men and women, lined up side by side on benches in the back of a Ford pick-up, knew that they spelt INSTITUTION to passers-by... spelt all that they resented most about their pensioner status in life. And perhaps it was McKeever who hated the truck most deeply of all of them, since his was the final indignity: he had to submit to being lifted to his seat by the Booger. The truck was outfitted with a set of movable steps by which others climbed to the tailboard. Given enough time, McKeever also could have managed them, but Finney never would wait. Each week, despite the old man's mutter of protest, Finney would boom heartily, "Come on, now, Simon, I ain't got all day, upsy-daisy" – and, laughing, he would thrust his meaty hands under the old man's armpits, lift him up and set him rump down on the tailboard; then, getting up on the truck himself, he would complete the job by hauling the shamefaced McKeever to his feet as though he were a wobble-kneed drunkard. Oh, the indignity of that moment! And yet today, for the first time in a year, McKeever didn't mind. He felt so eager about the future that he couldn't be deeply upset by anything – even at being handled like a sack of meal before his friend, the pretty nurse.

"Goodbye," Sarah called to him. "I'll see you Sunday, Mr Mac."

"So long," he replied, and quite forgot that he was already hoping to be in Glendale by Sunday. "You know what?" His gaiety bubbled out of him. "If it wasn't for that mayonnaise on your lip, I'd throw you a kiss."

Sarah laughed, wiped her mouth with the back of her hand, threw him a fat, exaggerated kiss. The truck moved off.

"Coming to visit me on Sunday!" McKeever explained proudly to the others. "A friend of mine."

"*Hm!*" said one of the women. She was Amelia Jackson, originally from the Carolinas, a snuff-chewing, vulgar woman whom McKeever liked best of the ladies in the Home. "Simple Simon, ain't you? Your feathers all ruffled by a swish-assed nurse." Amelia paused appreciatively as the others burst out into rocking laughter. "You men beat me down. You can be a hundred an' four an' you still act like you had some pecker left in you."

"That's what makes you like us, ain't it?" asked McKeever.

"Like you?" Amelia spat over the side of the truck. "The one thing I'm grateful to my old age for is that I'm shut of you men for ever."

"Is it now?"

"I suppose a swish-ass like your nurse don't think so, but that's only because she's young an' don't know no better."

"Amelia," McKeever said, "there's two kinds of females on this earth: there's them that swish and there's the other kind. I always figured you were once a hell of a swisher."

"Oh my," Amelia exclaimed with a hearty burst of laughter, "from thirteen on I wiggled my rump like a dog with fleas."

"I always knew it." He added with a delicate grin, "I wish I'd been around, Sweetie-Pie. I'd 'a' pinched you good."

"Would've got your face slapped for it."

"The first time, maybe – but how about the second?"

"The second you'd 'a' been sittin' on my lap."

They laughed hard over that one, and McKeever knew it was an exchange that would grapevine the Home and be repeated at his expense for days to come. He didn't mind that, but he recognized the poverty of their situation: that all of them, isolated and inactive, had nothing better to do than chew over the bones of an old conversation. It was not the life for him.

During the twelve miles home he knew he was being foolish, but he couldn't help himself. He allowed his rambling mind to drift into one tender fantasy after another, in which he was cured, at work again and part of the doing world. Once his body was limber, he'd never return to the Booger's. Jobs wouldn't be so easy for him to get, maybe, but who would know he was seventy-four when he looked only sixty? There was a timekeeper's berth waiting for him somewhere, or something in the oil line, or sorting mail in a post office... or a hundred other useful jobs a skilled man could handle. "God helps those who help themselves," his mother had always told him. It took a woman who had seen the famines of old Ireland to say that the way it was meant to be said: with a stone between the teeth, looking up at a black sky. When you said it that way, you meant it deep down – you looked after yourself and you didn't leave much to God.

It was four o'clock when the truck swung into the Finney driveway. With that the world became real again and Glendale far away. The blunt questions could no longer be avoided: How? In what manner? With what? McKeever hawked and spat and waited for the truck to stop. And then, gripping the envelope in his pocket, he recalled the advice of his top sergeant fifty years back, "Head up, gut in and don't bleed till you're shot." It made him laugh all over again. He waited in hot excitement for the Booger to approach him.

Chapter 4

As Finney lifted McKeever down from the tailboard, the latter plucked his sleeve and said gaily, "I need a business conference with you, Thomas. You'll have to skip your flowers today."

"Skip nothing," Finney replied genially. "You can see me tomorrow."

"Won't do! It's got to be right away. It's a vital matter."

"Man of affairs, ain't you?" Finney observed with his hollow, booming laugh. He started off for the side of the house where he kept his flower garden. "Make it tomorrow, Simon – you know my schedule."

Indeed everyone at the Home knew Finney's schedule. Each day at four he stopped work. Supper time was at five, and it was his task to help carry the food trays to the rooms. But the hour between four and five was inviolately his, and he devoted it to the cross-breeding of flowers. For a number of years he had been in the florist business in Santabello, but during the Depression of the Thirties he had gone bankrupt. The only thing he salvaged from the failure was the dream of one day developing a new species of aster that would bear his name. He had clung to this dream through the lean years of unemployment and through the several revolting years in which he worked as a ward attendant in the County Hospital. He was no closer to success now than when he first conceived the idea – in fact, he was not even a skilled gardener. But no man was ever more passionately devoted to a hobby than he, and since everyone in the Home knew it, he was rather surprised at McKeever's insistence. He paid him no mind, however, and had already left him some yards behind when he heard McKeever say: "Wouldn't you like to wish me goodbye, Thomas? I think I'm leaving tomorrow."

Finney swung around, looked closely to see if he were joking. "What's that?"

McKeever remained silent.

"Where do you think you're going?"

"Los Angeles."

Finney sighed. It was this part of running an old folks' rest home that caused the most trouble. Whenever strangers heard about the nature of his work, they always exclaimed, "My! Cooking for thirty-two old people! What a problem!" But the least of their problems was that: a meat grinder and some large stewpots took care of that. The real difficulty lay in the things that never occurred to outsiders: in keeping sixteen idle old women out of the kitchen when each one of them was dying to do a little cooking or baking; in seeing to it that Timothy Wright, aged eighty-five, was always assigned to a cot beside a light sleeper like Marcus Peake – so that when Timothy rose up in the middle of the night with his incorrigible urge to visit in the bed of one of the old ladies, Marcus would be there to order him back to sleep; or in seeing to it, as now with McKeever, that the wanderlust that overcame some elderly men from time to time was slapped down hard and quick. It didn't take many pensioners found wandering around the countryside to give a bad name to a Home and result in the County Welfare Agency's revoking a licence.

"Now, look here, Simon," he announced flatly, "don't start talking nonsense. What do you mean Los Angeles? You gonna fly? You got a thousand dollars in your wallet to feed you with? Or maybe you've been invited to spend the summer with some movie star in Hollywood?"

A bit acidly McKeever replied, "Why don't you take a few minutes to hear about it? You might know what I got on my mind before you run off at the mouth."

"But you can't leave here, you know that!"

"You running a prison?"

Flustered, the big man replied, "You ought to be ashamed to say a thing like that to me. I just mean you're on the County Welfare

34

list, you're drawing a state pension. It took a social worker to get you into my Home, and it takes a social worker to close you out. You know that."

"That's just why I need some talk with you, Thomas. You're my banker, sort of... my cheque's sent to you, ain't it? I need an accounting."

The Booger flushed. "Accounting? What do you mean, 'accounting'?"

"Oh, I'll explain. Just sit down with me." He added mildly, laughing a little, "You've got more time in your life than I have, you know."

Finney regarded McKeever in silence for a few moments; the tall figure of his antagonist was very erect in spite of the cane, the long face was stubborn and determined. "Oh, provoking," Finney muttered absently, "always things provoking." He scratched at the thick flesh of his neck, then said abruptly, "Meet me in my office. I got something to do till you get there."

He walked off, leaving McKeever with a thin grin on his face. McKeever knew exactly what Finney had to do. When problems arose in the Home, the Booger ran like an adolescent to the bony strength of his wife.

Slowly, a glow of excitement on his face, McKeever moved towards the railing that Finney had built alongside the front steps of the house. The Rest Home was an old-fashioned, dilapidated mansion of three storeys. Forty or fifty years before it had been a rich man's dream, but time had worn down its splendour until now the gables and the little towers and the cupolas seemed quite ridiculous to all of them. The women especially, since they were banished to the second floor as a means of keeping them out of the kitchen, never ceased complaining about what an old barn of a place it was; in the damp and foggy wintertime it was hard for the furnace to heat the rooms on their floor. But all of them loved the porch with its rocking chairs and its view of the vineyard across the road, where they could see the vines being pruned and tied and watch the grapes as they grew purple and heavy and luscious.

Only two of the Finney guests were enjoying the view at this moment. One of them was a newcomer to the Home – Mrs Rumley, a heavily built, diabetic woman of seventy, who had seated herself at the farthest corner of the veranda and whose pudgy, wrinkled face wore a morose look. The other was Percy Fuller, one of McKeever's room-mates, who was rocking himself comfortably with his feet up against the porch railing. A stocky, bald-headed, homely man of sixty-seven, he wore a workman's canvas apron and had a kit of watchmaker's tools on his lap. Fuller was an amiable man, fond of laughter, quietly wistful over the turn of his fortunes. In his early sixties a heart condition had ended his career as a grocery clerk. For several unhappy years he had been an unwelcome boarder with his two sons, and finally had come here. Unlike some of the others in the Home, who complained bitterly about their ungrateful children, Fuller never criticized his boys. But it was an act of pain rather than pride – he never mentioned them at all.

As McKeever hoisted himself up the front steps, Fuller held out an alarm clock and called loudly, "Sell it to you for a dollar, Simon."

"Can I eat it?"

Fuller laughed, and McKeever laughed, and the jest was not the less pleasurable to both of them because it had been repeated many times. "What do you mean, 'eat it'? It's not a steak, you rummy."

"A clock, eh? Does it work?"

"I'm the one who's done the repair job on it, ain't I? Guaranteed," Fuller said with satisfaction. "Listen." He pressed down the alarm button, and the old clock rocked as the bell hammered shrilly.

"God in heaven, tell him to stop that," Mrs Rumley cried. "He's been doing that for the past hour."

Fuller guffawed, shut off the alarm and winked at McKeever, who was pushing slowly past him on his way to Finney's office. "I figure if I make enough noise she'll buy this fine clock to get it away from me."

"And why would I want a clock in this place?" Mrs Rumley asked McKeever archly. "No place to go, is there? Nothing to keep time about."

"He'll tell you," McKeever replied with a grin. "He's the clock-maker around here."

Fuller laughed, "Advise her what a clock can mean, Simon. Why, it's magic – makes you feel you're in your own home."

"It's sure the truth," McKeever added. "An' if you give Percy a dollar, he can buy three more of those beat-up carcasses and slap together another clock."

"And then what?" she asked with disdain. "More noise?"

McKeever grinned and stepped through the door into the front hall. He heard Fuller yell after him "Damn you, Simon, you ruined a good deal", and he burst out in a hearty laugh.

"Haven't got a dollar anyway," Mrs Rumley's voice said with satisfaction. "So you can save your energy."

Smiling, McKeever moved down the hall to Finney's office. The door was open, and he sat down. With a comfortable sigh he took out his pipe. It was a straight-stemmed, Italian briar, a fine pipe mellowed by twenty years of smoking. One by one his other pipes had gone – lost or burnt out, stolen from coat jacket or locker, some of them exchanged for a meal during the evil days of the Depression. As he fingered the smooth grain of the wood, McKeever thought with amusement, "One pipe, one razor, two pairs of drawers." It was more or less the sum of his worldly goods. But nothing new, his mind added – he was a man who had always travelled light. Books, for instance – why, he had bought over a thousand in his life. Read them, relished them and then sold them as he moved on to the next job. That was the oil game; a man clung to his tools and his union card and left the refrigerators to others.

In a ritual that was now automatic, McKeever sniffed the clean, dry bowl of the pipe; then he rubbed the wood against both wings of his nose, shining the dark plum with the oil of his skin. He opened one of the cans of Half and Half and stuffed the bowl slowly with a practised thumb. And then, as he heard footsteps in the hall, he lit up quickly, knowing that he was inwardly tense, just as in the old days when he had gone into a foreman's shanty to ask for a raise. There was something about dealing with authority that always made him knot up a little inside. He wondered why. It had never caused him to hesitate over what had to be done, but as a child in old Ireland facing his father, and still now at seventy-three, it was the same – a sense of tightened stomach muscles and of prickles rising slightly along his spine.

"Now, what's this I hear, Simon?" Ada Finney asked with a laugh as she burst into the office. She was wiping her strong, red-knuckled hands on her immaculate apron. "Leaving us? What's the idea? What sort of talk is that? And you my favourite, my very best favourite in the Home."

Ada Finney never did anything quietly or with a low energy current. She walked, spoke, cooked or cleaned with great vigour and a sense of zest. She was a square-shouldered, big-boned woman just turned forty, rather squat, with heavy-muscled legs that were slightly bowed. Her square face was womanly and attractive, and she had lovely, silken blond hair that she kept neatly braided no matter how busy she was. McKeever despised her. To his mind she was always pretending an affection for the people at the Home that she couldn't genuinely feel. She had a way of exclaiming "Gracious, we're all a big, happy family, ain't we?" that left him nauseated. The Finneys were running a business, and it was one thing to be friendly about it, but quite another to pretend that it was a labour of Christian love in which profit and loss played no part. He hated hypocrisy, and this chatter about "my very best favourite in the Home" was revolting to him. He smoked his pipe, stared Ada in the eye and remained stubbornly silent.

The Booger, looking a bit sheepish, sidled into the office, wedged his bulk around the desk and sat down heavily. He leant back in the creaking chair, thrust his fat hands into the front of his trousers and said heartily, "Well, Simon, what's it all about? Spill it!"

"We're your very best friends, you know," Ada added in a chirping tone. "We only want what's best for you." She patted her silken braids, smiled, sat down close to McKeever. The latter took a long drag on his pipe and leant forward. The Booger leant forward to listen to him, and as he did so his chair squeaked loudly.

"It's this way—"

"Thomas," interrupted Ada, "I told you yesterday that chair needs oiling. It squeaks awful, gives me pimples."

"I forgot."

"It's this way," McKeever began again.

"I want you to oil it tonight, you hear?" Ada interrupted.

"I'll do it, absolutely," her husband muttered.

"Will you leave the damn chair go for a minute now?" McKeever asked in great annoyance.

"Gracious, you're upset about something, you poor dear, ain't you?" Ada said brightly. "Tell us about it now."

McKeever swallowed; with a glitter in his blue eyes he began a third time: "I've got hold of the name of a doctor in Los Angeles – a woman doctor – who cures arthureetis. I'm thinking of going down there to get her cure. I need your help."

The Finneys exchanged glances; the Booger showed instant distress, but his wife turned back to McKeever with a gentle, patronizing smile.

"Now, Simon, that's very interesting – very. What did the doctors at the hospital say?"

"I haven't talked to them."

"You haven't?…" Ada shook her head in benign reproach. "Well, naturally, we'll want to hear first what they have to say."

McKeever's face set in a stubborn mould. "Ada, I never bother my mind with what fakers have to say."

"You call those hospital doctors 'fakers'?"

"They haven't cured me, have they?"

"And how do you know this doctor in Los Angeles won't be a worse kind of faker?"

"Because she cures people!"

Ada laughed out loud. "She sounds like a quack to me, she positively does. I think we'd better have her investigated first."

"How'll you do that?"

"Oh, we'll find ways."

"I've got my own way, Ada. It won't take so long as yours. I'll just go down there an' see for myself."

"Now, Simon, I'm surprised! You've always been so clear-minded for your age. Go down there – what a silly idea!"

McKeever flushed angrily, swallowed. Quietly he said, "It's *my* arthureetis, ain't it?"

"But we're responsible for you. You're in our charge."

"I ain't in *nobody's* charge," he burst out angrily. "I'm in charge of myself! Don't talk like you're a prison keeper an' me a criminal."

Ada became genuinely upset. "Simon! Gracious… why… what a mean thing to say! We're only giving you our friendly advice."

McKeever bit hard on the stem of his pipe and waited until he could control his tone. Then he spoke very softly. "Now just hear me for a minute. I'd like to keep this friendly too. I'm a boarder here, right?"

"One of our best," the Booger said heartily. "We're here to give you service."

"Thanks, that's all I'm asking. Now, look… Most of your other boarders are permanent. But I've only been marking time here, waiting to get well. Don't you know that?"

"*We'd* like you to get well too," Ada said kindly. "We drive you to the clinic, don't we?"

"Sure, but I've been waiting two years now for those clinic doctors to improve me. They can't, they're incompetent."

The Finneys smiled and exchanged glances. For the first time McKeever became apprehensive. There was a delicate play between them that he didn't like, a cold watchfulness in Ada's eyes, a sullen determination on the face of the Booger. It frightened him, because he had been counting on their cooperation. In a tone that was almost beseeching he said, "You don't seem to understand me. I'm a strong man still, I got a lot of vitality, I ain't through my working days. All I been needing is the right doctor, and now I've found her."

The Finneys remained silent.

"Listen," he said hotly, "I may as well let you know... I ain't told anyone yet, not anyone... but before I pass over there's a piece of work I need to accomplish. It's the one thing in the world that's most important to me, it's..." He stopped abruptly. He didn't want to tell them. It was a mistake to have gone that far.

"What?" Ada enquired gently. "You can tell us, Simon."

He was silent, and then his voice rose a little. "There's a book I want to fix up. A big one. I want people to read it."

The other two stared at him. "I don't get it," Finney said with genuine perplexity. "What's that? You want to write a book? Like Dickens or Shakespeare?" He began to laugh.

"Not write it," McKeever explained irritably, knowing that it *had* been a mistake. "Just put it together. I'm intending to collect other people's writings that I like."

"Who ever heard of a book like that?"

"People who read books, that's who!" McKeever retorted tartly. "Didn't you ever hear of *The Cry for Justice* by Upton Sinclair?* There's a lot of books like that."

Finney raised his eyebrows, shrugged at his wife, waved his big hands in the air. "What's it gonna be about, Simon, cooking recipes?"

McKeever tasted bile in his mouth. He said quietly, "Never mind what it's about. It's vital to me, that's all you need to know. Maybe it's a bad idea I got... but it's a vital one to me. You don't have to go to college to have good ideas, do you? Jack London never went to college, *did* he?"

"How do I know?" asked Finney. "I only read detectives myself. Say, Ada, by God, how about *I* do a book on flowers? Everybody's doin' books around here, why not me?"

McKeever's eyes blazed. He turned to Mrs Finney. "But before I do this book or anything else, I need to get well. Getting well comes first. After that, a job. And then my book." He gazed at her beseechingly. "But don't you see... it's the whole thing I'm after. I'm like a man..." – his mouth worked – "like a man who wants to get out of prison... into the living world... where there's people... an' sky... an' the good life."

"Well, that's fine," Ada said absently. "You know it's supper time soon. I got things on the stove. You ain't told us yet—"

"It's only a bit of cooperation I want from you, Ada," McKeever said eagerly. "The first thing is to save me some time. After I leave tomorrow, I want you to arrange with County Welfare to have my cheque transferred. I'll send you an address. That way I won't have to hang around to arrange things."

The Finneys were silent. McKeever studied them, then continued more quietly, "And the second thing is some money. I need the balance of my cheque for this month. There's five days gone, and May has thirty-one. But we'll say you owe me only five sixths of $55.00. If you give me a pencil, I'll figure it out."

Finney's plump face quivered, and a stricken look came into his pale-grey eyes. "Why, we can't do that!" He glanced over at his wife for support. "It's not allowed."

"Not allowed? Why?"

"It's not, that's all. Out of the question."

For a moment McKeever was stumped by the bluntness of the lie. Then, looking closely at the Booger, realizing the bluff for what it was, he kept his patience and said lightly, "Now, watch what you're saying there, Thomas – it might turn and bite you."

"Gracious," Ada remarked sweetly, "I don't understand you, Simon. You have a home here, a warm, comfortable nest – why, there are dozens on our waiting list just asking to take your place… dozens. Three good meals a day, and you know how I keep my icebox, spotless, and did you ever get spoilt food here?"

"Too much chopped stuff," replied McKeever irrelevantly. "I'm so sick of hash and ground meat and mashed potatoes and custard and junket, I don't know what to do. Baby pap! And getting skimpy these last couple months too, smaller portions."

"But how else can I cook for thirty old folks without their teeth?" asked Ada.

"Skimpy?" Finney interjected. "You taken any look at prices recently, have you, hey-hey?"

"Maybe you can't, maybe that's it," McKeever replied to Ada. "I ain't blaming you. Only I got *all* my own teeth – that's the point, see? I'm a vigorous man. I belong out there, where I can do a day's work and get my teeth into a beefsteak or a loin of pork."

"How in hell are you going to work when you're all crippled up?" the Booger asked excitedly. "*You* can't work – you ain't vigorous. That's old-age arthritis you have. You're crazy to talk like that. A trip? A cure? You've gone loony."

McKeever turned white. "Loony, hey? I'll crack my stick over your fat head."

"And clean sheets every week," Ada interrupted. "Clean rooms – warm in winter, cool in summer. And a can of tobacco every week."

"Don't you talk to me about your tobacco now," McKeever retorted peevishly. "That doesn't sit good with me. Tastes like the sweepings off a barn floor. And I wouldn't be boasting about the clean sheets either. It ain't clean sheets you're putting on Timothy Wright's bed – don't tell me that!"

"He's a wetter, ain't he?" the Booger protested. "You want us to give him fourteen new sheets a week?"

"A warm, comfortable, friendly home," Ada repeated, "with people who like you and respect you. Where will you find another like it? Who knows if you'll even get into a rest home down in Los Angeles? All of them with long waiting lists just like ours, I'm sure. Sleeping on park benches in the rain – that's what it'll turn into. Oh, I'm warning you before it's too late. I'm your best friend, dearie. Once we close you out here, there'll be another one taking your place. There won't be no room when you come back to us. Oh, it's a terrible thing you're setting out to do. It just curdles my blood to think of it."

McKeever felt drowned in words... and frightened. If he had not been certain before Ada spoke that it was the right thing for him to pick up and go down to Los Angeles, she was making up his mind for him now. He knew what she was trying to do; he had met this type of seduction in a hundred ways before

– met it with his first foreman on his first job in London, who had yapped into the ear of an Irish greenhorn that he'd have a lifelong job if only he didn't join the union. Sometimes they gave you the finger sweetly and sometimes they swung a club, but it always came down to this: they wanted a man to knuckle down; they stroked your ass the way a cowboy with a knife stroked a calf – and to the same purpose. It was the wretched little crumbs of life Ada was offering him – a bed for his bones, a roof over his head, three meals a day – so that she could have his fifty-five a month for her own wretched little profit. And if he yielded to her now out of fear of the unknown, then the clean sheets once a week would be his winding sheets, and he was already in his grave.

"I want my money!" he cried suddenly. "Figure it up and hand it over. Quick now."

"It's not allowed!" the Booger told him again in great excitement. "Anyway, you certainly can't leave without permission from the doctors. And there's County Welfare, too. We'll have to get the social worker out here. We can't break the rules. She supervises you, and she supervises us. It'll have to be done official – it'll take weeks. Don't ask us to break any rules now – don't you do it."

With scorn and anger McKeever asked bluntly, "Is it cheating me you have in mind? Don't mix me all up in red tape. I see right through you. Whose money is it the State sends you every month? It's mine! They been paying it to you because I said so… Well, I've changed my mind. Our deal's off. So hand it over quick – stop your cheating."

"Why, dearie," Ada interrupted tensely, "we're using such bad language, ain't we? Cheating!" She laughed in a loud, brassy, unhappy manner. "And who's asking us go behind the back of County Welfare and embezzle State funds? It's you, ain't it?"

Raging, McKeever shook his finger at her. "Embezzle? Do you know what that means? Ain't it my money – my insurance that I worked for, fifty years? By Jesus Christ I'll have the police on you both – I'll have you in jail, I'll send you up."

Mrs Finney burst into sobs. Her strong body shook under the force of her weeping, her mouth went slack and her teeth gnawed her lower lip as the hot tears coursed down her cheeks. "Oh, what a thing!" she blubbered in a heartbroken fashion. "What language."

The Booger jumped to his feet. His face had become swollen, gorged with blood. Like a child in a rage of fear, he flung both arms out wildly, while the words poured out of him in a disjointed, passionate flood. "I'll have a writ on you... they'll pick you up, they'll send you to the booby house! You can't give us a bad name! Ten years I've worked... up at five – five to ten – a dog's life, and for what? You damn old fool, you've got one foot in the grave already – do you wanna pull us down with you?" And then, suddenly, as the Booger continued, his arms flailing the air pathetically, the true state of his economic position became clear to McKeever. "Everything's gone up – food up, gas for the truck, coal, repairs on the house, telephone... I took twenty-two dollars out of savings last month to make up the deficit. I *won't* give you any money. I've *spent* your money already for this month." He banged a huge fist down on the desk. "You're a bloodsucker! What'll be left if the Home goes broke? Hanging on, all my life we've only been hanging on. And now you leave me with an empty bed. It may be two months till we get another man. Shame on you, that's all I can say, shame on you!" He stood trembling, the loose flesh of his face and body shaking all over. "Oh, crap," he said, "crap, crap." He sank down into the swivel chair and wiped his nose on his sleeve. "I'll oil it tonight," he muttered to his wife, who was still weeping. "Don't cry, honey, we'll make out."

There was a long, hot silence. Then, slowly, McKeever pushed himself to his feet. He laughed a little, rather sadly. "Why now, it makes us all like animals, don't it?" he observed softly. "It's the dollar bill that stretches until it's a rope around our necks. You're a poor Booger, you are, and that's the truth. You're just a little mouse in a little rowboat on a great big economic ocean, and all you got to eat is a little bit of cheese an' you can't hardly eat it, 'cause you're so scared of being drowned. God Almighty, what a pitiful situation. The way that old dollar bill can twist a man out of shape. It's the shame of our civilization!"

"And there's another thing," Finney said petulantly, "it's that name you've given me behind my back. Everybody calling me 'the Booger'. I don't like it. I resent it. You're the cause of it here."

"I don't want that money," McKeever said softly. "I'm not needing it half so bad as you are." He turned towards the door. "But I'll be leaving you tomorrow. I've made up my mind – you won't stop me from that. An' I'll take care of my future cheques. I'll write to the County Welfare."

"They'll pick you up, honest!" Mrs Finney warned earnestly. "They'll put you in the booby hatch like all the old men that's found wandering around. And you certainly can't leave without the hospital doctor's permission! I won't let you. It'll get us in trouble."

McKeever crawled out.

Chapter 5

There was a game going on in McKeever's room when he entered it, one they had all played many times. It was called "Going to the Movies", and it involved Timothy Wright, the eldest man amongst them.

This last half-hour before supper was always the sprightliest period of the day in the Finney Rest Home. When the pleasures of life are few and small, the human heart quickens at every excuse – and so mealtime was very important here. Usually the men gathered in the room sometime before their trays were due. They took turns at the washbasin, as once they had scrubbed up on returning from work, they changed into slippers, they prepared variously for the evening meal. John Hanbury, the farmer, just turned seventy, put on a snap bow tie and spent some time in brushing down his bushy white hair. Stan Pavlovsky, who had been a railroad-section hand, rinsed out his dentures. Percy Fuller stowed away his kit of watchmaker's tools, took off his shoes and scraped with a pocket knife at the stubborn corns on both toes. And since topics of conversation exhaust themselves when men are too much together, they were not infrequently at a loss for talk. At such times they turned their attention to Timothy Wright, and they played "Going to the Movies".

Timothy was the willing fool of McKeever's room, a witless and eager court jester. The game they played with him might have been malicious – but it wasn't, and Timothy himself always begged for it. He was eighty-five, small and very slight now, stony bald, with a wrinkled, hollow-cheeked, grinning face and the little pug nose of a dog. When he was all dressed up, as he was at this moment, he wore a Stetson hat, a gaudy bandanna around his scrawny neck and cowboy boots with silver spurs. At one time

Timothy had been a cow hand in his native Montana; over the years he had drifted into working on dude ranches and performing in rodeos, and finally he had become a cowboy in the Hollywood film industry. He had spent the last twenty-five years of his career pounding the saddle before a camera, and nowadays he was rather confused about his life. The real events of his past and the movie stories he had played were inextricably woven together in a fabric of great deeds, admirable suffering and exquisite triumph. "Timothy," one of the men would say, "is it true you once stood off a whole Apache band all by yourself?"

"Gospel-true," Timothy would reply eagerly. He would sit up on his cot, his pale-blue eyes catching fire, his little pug nose wrinkling with eagerness – and the game would be on. Timothy required no further stimulation. He would ramble on as long as he was permitted, enjoying the laughter his stories evoked, accepting it as appreciation. He would dress himself quickly at the beginning of each game and stand posturing on spidery legs before one of the full-length mirrors that lined the walls of the room. All of the men with the exception of Timothy hated these mirrors; why and how the room had been built with so many damn mirrors they never knew. They had speculated over it a great deal, but their only conclusion was that the original builder of the house had been a nut like Timothy. The mirrors were a great boon to the cowboy. He loved to stand, as he was doing now, with an imaginary lariat in his hand and a phantom enemy before him.

"And there I was," he was saying in his rather high, piping tone as McKeever came into the room, "there I was with that damn herd of wild horses racin' down at me an' that damn beautiful woman behind me, holdin' on to me an' tremblin' with fear – an' me with only a rope to defend ourselves."

"What was her name?"

"Whose name?"

"The girl's name?"

A pause. "Why, Percy, I forget."

"Didn't you marry her – and her that beautiful?"

"Hell, no. I ain't the marryin' kind. None of us frontiersmen were."

"So how did you get out of it?"

"Get out of what?"

"Out of the way of the horses that was coming at you?"

"Horses? What horses?"

Laughter – in which Timothy joined, his nose wrinkling in pleased bewilderment.

"Damn you, Timothy, you get yourself in a pickle, and then you don't tell us how you got out."

In an injured tone: "Sure I do."

"How did you?"

A pause. Then, eagerly: "Say, did I ever tell you about the time I was captured by rustlers? The Bar-B gang it was. They got me one day at sunrise an' tied me to a stake. Stripped me clean naked and put honey over me so the red ants would eat me. But at the last minute Tom came and saved me. That's Tom Mix.* You've heard of him? A great rider, great with the rope."

So it would continue, and the men rarely wearied of listening. Timothy never lost his brave tone; his tales had a way of ending happily – and a half-hour with him was like their one-time visits to the nickelodeon. McKeever enjoyed the cowboy quite as much as any of the others, but sometimes he was left uneasy by their sport. Timothy was not only a diversion, he was also a delicately frightening spectre: who among them could be certain that in a few years he too might not be a senile bed-wetter like Timothy, a poor noodle who spent hours each day fingering in a shoebox for the woebegone remains of his life – a dim photograph of a boy on a pony, a pair of tarnished cufflinks, a woman's bed slipper? Sometimes it chilled McKeever to watch him... and it provoked him to a great wonder about life – about why a man was born, and who decreed his particular destiny, and whether it was written down somewhere that at sixty-seven Percy Fuller would be forgotten by his own sons or that Timothy Wright would be a clown.

Slowly, lending only half an ear to Timothy, McKeever came into the room. He worked his way to his cot, took off his shoes and eased himself down with a sigh. His spirits were troubled. He had spoken bold words to the Finneys at the close of their harsh conversation, but where was he now? He had a four-hundred-mile journey before him, and his capital consisted of a copper penny. Even worse, suppose the Finneys wanted to be vindictive about his leaving – suppose, as Ada had threatened, they notified the police that he was out of his head? They were the licensed proprietors of a rest home, they were taxpayers and property owners... and who was he? The police would find a lame old man on the highway without a dime in his jeans. It was not a good situation – in fact, it was a real predicament.

McKeever lay quiet and studied the problem over. He wanted badly to consult with his friends, but he dared not utter a word until after five o'clock. At that time John Hanbury, the farmer, would be leaving the room. Until then anything he said would reach the Booger by direct pipeline.

Five o'clock came when Marcus Peake carried in the first of the supper trays for their room. Timothy Wright stopped raiding an Indian village and scurried to his bed as fast as his legs would take him. Percy Fuller snapped his pocket knife shut; all eyes in the room fastened eagerly upon Peake.

"Hey, Jop, what kind chow we got tonight?" Pavlovsky asked.

Peake – who came by the nickname "Jop" because he had spent most of his life as a lead and zinc miner around Joplin, Missouri – had learnt to prepare a precise answer to this inevitable question. "Got potata soup, crackers, creamed cabbage, bread puddin', cocoa," he replied quickly. He was the baby of their room – a short, thin, wiry man of sixty-three who was not yet eligible for an old-age pension. Alone of all of them he was in perfect health. He had made a deal with the Finneys by which he paid them only twenty-five dollars a month in exchange for considerable porter work around the Home. He lived now in a race with time – always figuring, adding and wondering whether his savings would last until he was sixty-five. He was the only man among them who was eager to grow older.

"Cocoa, always damn cocoa slop!" said Pavlovsky. For a coffee addict like him cocoa was not only an unsatisfactory beverage, it was a cutting indignity, a reminder that he had lost his independence. A coarse oak of a man, even at sixty-nine Pavlovsky could not accept idleness, although cataracts in his eyes made it impossible for him to work at his trade. Half blind as he was, he tramped miles each day along the Southern Pacific railroad tracks in search of any maintenance gangs that might happen into the vicinity. Whenever he located one, he watched the men at their labour for as long as he could, and then came back to supper exquisitely happy. "Cocoa," he said again bitterly. "Who invent cocoa?"

"Cabbage!" Fuller muttered amiably. He glanced up at a fly on the ceiling, laughed with gentle resignation, muttered to the fly: "I lived sixty-seven years in order to eat cabbage twice a week."

"Hey, Tim — how's the potata soup?" Pavlovsky asked. The cowboy, as the eldest man in the room, had the privilege of the first tray.

"*Mm*," Timothy replied with his nose in the soup, "it's fillin'."

And now that this query, too, had been asked, and this familiar answer returned – now the interesting part of the meal was already over; from now on there was nothing to anticipate. After one, two or five years at the Finneys' each man's tongue knew in advance the taste of each dish, as his stomach knew its weight to the last milligram. It was all right... it wasn't so bad as food went... but it was dull and commonplace. Only on rare occasions was Ada Finney's cooking either inventive or savoury.

One by one they were given their trays. Since the six beds, with a small aisle between each two, used up all of the floor space, there was no room for chairs. They sat on their beds with the trays on their knees. And when each of them had been serviced, Marcus Peake came in with his own tray. This was the moment for which McKeever was waiting – because now John Hanbury would leave the room to take his dinner with the Finneys.

As usual Hanbury left quietly and without a farewell, his right leg dragging a little, a cramped smile on his leathery, hard-boned face. He departed in silence, and malice remained behind him. Hanbury was the rich man of the Home. No one knew how much money he had cached away, since he drew his pension like the rest of them, or what he paid Finney for the extra services he received, but the extras were there for everyone to observe. Each Saturday night the Booger drove Hanbury into Santabello, undoubtedly to a movie. Three times a day Hanbury ate at the Finney table. There were always sharp eyes to detect a spot of egg on his vest, sharp noses to smell chops frying or a chicken stewing. Hanbury had his own radio; Hanbury had two pillows on his cot, so that he could read his *Western Stories** in comfort; Hanbury snuggled his feet against a hot-water bottle on damp nights.

In truth the men did not envy Hanbury his bank roll or his special privileges as much as they resented him as a man. They all agreed that inequities were to be taken for granted in this life, so why not in a home for the aged? The rich and the poor we always have with us, Percy Fuller was fond of saying in his good-natured way. But… why did the farmer have to be so damn crabbed about things? No one wanted to deny him the pleasure of a movie – but why not come home and share the experience with them? And why was it necessary for him to buy earphones for his portable radio so that in the long, dull hours out on the porch no one else could listen to it?

The men heartily despised him, and McKeever was not so foolish as to discuss his problem in the farmer's presence. It was from Hanbury, he was sure, that Finney had learnt who had nicknamed him 'the Booger'. "I can smell an informer a mile away," he had told his other room-mates more than once. "I don't like farmers anyway – never did. Farmers and foremen and Pinkertons.* They're the worst products of our civilization."

As soon as the door closed on Hanbury, McKeever set his tray down to one side on his cot. He felt too excited to eat. With his eyes on Timothy Wright, he called softly and cautiously to the three other men in the room: "Hey there, lads... I need some advice – I need a council of war."

The others looked up from their trays and gazed at him with mild curiosity. Timothy, he saw with relief, had his nose in his cabbage and had not been diverted. Timothy worried him. One could never be certain what the cowboy's addled brain absorbed from any general conversation or what his leaky mouth would later give out. Yet any attempt at holding a private talk in their room would make Timothy avidly curious. It seemed best to McKeever to trust in Timothy's usual self-absorption... and in the fact that Pavlovsky, Jop and Fuller were on the cots nearest his own, forming a little rectangle. Lowering his voice now, he began to tell his story.

"I'm in a predicament, lads. When I went into the hospital today, I met a lady – a fine lady, a sterling type. She gave me the name of a doctor who can surely cure up this lameness I've got, a woman specialist down in Glendale, LA. But when I got back, the Booger put obstacles in my way. Him and that woman."

"The Booger!" exclaimed Percy Fuller. He laughed with amiable scorn, showing ugly gaps between his yellow stumps of teeth. "That poop!"

"Gasbag," said Pavlovsky. "Stick him wit' pin sometime, he blow oop. Ha-ha."

"Now, let's try an' keep this a quiet kind of talk we're having... eh – eh?" McKeever asked, nodding significantly towards Wright.

The men glanced over at the cowboy and turned back with nods and grunts of understanding. Marcus Peake cocked his head to one side. In that posture, with his wiry shock of grey hair, his soft brown eyes and his thin face, he looked rather like a friendly old terrier. "What obstacles, Simon? What'd they say?"

As succinctly as he could, McKeever recounted his dispute with the Finneys. He underlined the threats that the couple had made, and then asked the question that was agitating him. "I need to get something straight: what's the legal rights of men like us?" His voice began to tremble a little suddenly as the indignation welled up inside him. "Suppose I start off to hitch-hike to Los Angeles? An' suppose the Finneys get mad and notify the cops? You think maybe they'd pick me up – put me away somewhere?" His face turned beet-red, and he answered his own question cholerically, without giving the others a chance. "Jesus Christ, no! This is a free country, ain't it? Why can't I go any damn place I want to?" He paused, and his forehead creased in an anxious frown. "But suppose they said I was an old loony – irresponsible? Who are the cops going to believe – them or me?"

"Cops pay no attention, old man!" Pavlovsky said instantly in his solid bass voice. "All they give you is kick in ass. Oh, he's a bad one, that damn Booger. I'd like smack him just once. Clop-clop! I kill him, that big fart." Excitedly the Pole began to crack the knuckles of his strong, thick fingers, bending back one after the other with a pop that was like the splitting of a hazelnut. "You better be scared," he warned McKeever earnestly. "The Booger wants you stay here, you better stay. Better you don't do nothing till you fix oop with social worker."

"He's right, Simon," Percy Fuller said emphatically. "That big poop's got it in for you now. He's scared you'll make trouble for him."

"Trouble?" asked McKeever. "Why, I'm willing to let him make off with the balance of this month's cheque! I told him so. What's *he* got to be afraid of?"

Fuller showed his yellow teeth in a pitying grin. "Simon, ain't you had the lesson yet that your worst enemy is the man who's done *you* a bad turn? That Booger's scared you'll report him to the social worker. On account he's got no right to hold back your money. So if you go off, he'll report you. That's his opportunity. If he can make out you're an old loon, then the right's on his side!"

There was a moment of silence. McKeever was very disturbed by the suggestion. He rubbed his hands on his knees, squinted his eyes, tried hard to think his way through the problem. Finally he turned to Marcus Peake. "What've *you* got to say, Jop?"

"Is there anybody don't want his bread puddin'?" Timothy Wright asked suddenly, loudly. "I'll eat it!" No one replied. Disappointed, the cowboy began to lick his saucer with his tongue.

Peake ran his fingers through his hair, thoughtfully rubbed the iron-grey bristles on his jaw. "I'm worrying over something else. I'm scairt to think of you out on the road without no money, Simon. You're not a well man!"

"Of course I ain't, you coot," McKeever retorted with amusement. "That's what this is about – so I can get well and be going on my business."

"But why be in such a hurry?" Peake argued. "The social worker'll be coming back here around the first of next month. When you tell her what's on your mind, she'll fix it up for you, likely."

McKeever shook his head, suddenly and very firmly. "No – no, I'm not going to wait! You just made up my mind for me. Now, look here – how do I know I won't get a run-around from Miss Stark too? First thing right off, she'll say, 'Let's ask the doctors at the hospital.' And what'll they say? Why, naturally they'll have to protect their own ignorance, won't they? So they'll put thumbs down. Then where am I?"

"Maybe it won't happen that way," Peake argued. "Maybe she'll help you."

"Even if she does," McKeever replied in the same stubborn tone, "I'm certain to be here for months till she gets things arranged. Oh Lord, I can just see their red tape twisting me all up." He began to chuckle scornfully. "First she's got to ask her supervisor. Then they got to hold a meeting. Then they write down to Los Angeles for another home. Then somebody puts the letter in the wrong pigeonhole. Oh Lord, it'll be next winter before anything's done! You think I got that much time? All those people signing papers, making up their minds, making arrangements – they won't be in a hurry. They're all youngsters – they can burn time like a millionaire burns dollar bills. No sir, I'm starting for Glendale tomorrow morning."

"Glendale?" echoed Timothy Wright, suddenly becoming aware of them. "You telling about Glendale? You ever live there? I had a little house all to myself – what street was it on now? – with a fig tree in the back. A sweet house – and there was that girl, what was her name? A sweet piece. Oh, I had a lot of girls in my time, lots of them, sweet pieces. I was a killer, I layed 'em right an' left." He began to cackle shrilly, with delight in himself. "Doctor told me once: 'It starts when you're borned,' he said, 'an' it goes right on till you're dead.' That Mrs Scroggins upstairs, she keeps giving me the wicked eye…"

"Here we go," said Fuller with a laugh.

"Figs and cream, figs right out of the back yard I had," Timothy continued. "That was in Glendale." He suddenly noticed McKeever's tray. "Don't you want your bread puddin', Simon?"

"I do, I do," McKeever replied. He set the tray in his lap and began hungrily to spoon up the lukewarm potato soup.

"Bread puddin' I always loved best, and one thing else," said Timothy. "What was it?" He got down on his knees and reached under his cot for his old shoebox of mementos. "What was it now?" he murmured. He sat on the floor, rummaging in the box.

"So then you're really going off tomorrow?" Peake asked McKeever anxiously.

"Made up my mind! I pack my suitcase, go out on the road and thumb my way. I figure I ought to make Los Angeles by night if I have any luck."

"I think you're nuts, Simon."

"Now, Jop," McKeever said good-naturedly, "I got that line from Ada, I don't want it from you."

"But it don't make sense. You meet a strange woman in a drugstore an' you're ready to fly off to Los Angeles just on her say-so? It's reckless, it's horrible."

"What's reckless about it? What've I got to lose? I'm playing a hunch here, Jop. Some of the best jobs I got in my life came from a hunch, or a tip from some oil man I passed on the street. Now, here's a woman had the lameness worse than me. She got cured. She gives me the name of her doctor. What's reckless in that?"

"How you going to pay for all those injections? You thought of that?"

"Sure I have. This doctor's no money-grabber, that's the first thing."

"How do you know?"

"She told me. I'll get the money somewhere. There's State Welfare might arrange it, or I can delay till I'm working again, or I can look up some old pie-card* at the A. F. of L.* an' borrow it maybe... There are ways – I'll handle that part of it."

"It still don't make sense. Not hitch-hiking. Does it, Percy?"

"Not to me," Fuller agreed. "Like I was off to swim the English Channel... ha-ha."

"You'll just keel over on the road somewhere," Peake continued excitedly. "You'll end up in the morgue."

Calmly McKeever took a spoonful of cabbage, gazed at each one of his friends in turn. "Got a morgue in Santabello too, haven't they? Nothing tried, nothing gained. Only, I hoped you lads would help me out a bit."

The others were silent. They stared at his quiet face, his stubborn jaw. Then Peake, always the worrier, said in an angry whisper, "But where will you stay, even if you get down to LA? How you going to eat? It's almost a month before your next cheque's due."

"Got that semi-figured out already," McKeever replied easily. "There's the Presbyterian Church I used to go to in Montebello, and the Methodist Church when I was working the oil fields around Seal Beach. One of 'em will maybe give me a little loan on my next cheque."

"Maybe."

"Nothing tried, nothing gained," McKeever repeated. He quoted a bit loftily:

There's nothing worth the doing that it does not pay to try...

"I tell you something," Pavlovsky interjected eagerly. "I got idea! Maybe Timmy here got some old friend in Glendale – he put you up little while?"

"Hist on that," McKeever said quickly. He peered over at Timothy, who had fallen into a doze, his shoebox of mementos on his lap, his head resting against his cot. "I don't want the old feller to know what's up. He might spill it to the Booger."

"But is good idea I got. I tell you what: I got 'nother idea. How about I tell Timmy *I'm* gon' to Glendale next month? I ask him for me?"

"Well," said McKeever thoughtfully, "wouldn't hurt, maybe. Try it."

Pavlovsky shifted his bulk around on the cot. "Hey, Timmy. Wake oop."

"Hm? What?" asked the cowboy. He rubbed his eyes with both hands. "What's happening?"

"Listen, Timmy – you live long time in Glendale, ha?"

"Glendale?" A sleepy little smile crossed the old man's lips. "Oh, I'm fond of Glendale. Know every street an' avenue."

"You got friends there?"

"Everybody in Glendale knows me," Wright said with sudden liveliness. Still sitting on the floor, he took off his Stetson hat and flourished it. "Ride my horse in the parade every July Four.* Boots and spurs and shootin' off my guns. I'm the best friend Tom Mix ever had. You heard of Tom Mix, haven't you? A great rider, great with the rope."

"Listen, Timmy," Pavlovsky said patiently, "you listen careful now. Next month I'm gon' take lil' trip to Glendale. You got friend there I can stay wit'?"

"Loreli Hines," the cowboy replied instantly. He scrambled to his wobbly legs and teetered a little from side to side as he spoke. "Oh, that Loreli, that sweet pigeon! What a good heart she has. Do anything for me. Any pal of mine is a pal of hers. Got the sweetest little house, little grape arbour in the back, little orange tree an' a ping-pong table. But don't try to lay her now. Don't take advantage of me."

"Don't you worry," Pavlovsky said reassuringly. "You just tell me – where she live?"

"In Glendale! An' she'll put you up sure. Oh, she's a lively jane, a comfortable jane."

"What *street* does she live on?" asked McKeever.

"Now, let's see." The cowboy frowned, gripped his little pug nose between forefinger and thumb, studied the question. "Where does she live now?" he wondered aloud. "I don't hardly remember the exact address. But it's a sweet little house, white, costs her only twenty a month – it has a picket fence."

"Forget it, Simon," Percy Fuller advised *sotto voce*. "Take you all night, an' you won't get nowhere."

Timothy snapped his fingers with excitement. "I know! She used to work at the railroad restaurant, where the trains come in, a table waitress. Just ask for Loreli Hines." He paused, frowned. "Darn it – what was it I heard? Did I hear she quit there? Yep, that's right. I heard she quit that restaurant. Where's she workin' now, I wonder?"

"Say listen," Fuller enquired suspiciously, "when did you last see that jane?"

"Who, me? Loreli? The other day. When the war ended. We had a celebration."

"Now, why you talk so foolish?" Pavlovsky asked severely. "You been right here on day war end. I was here too. You tellin' lie again, Timmy."

"Hah?" Timothy exclaimed. "What? I did too celebrate." He became quite excited. "They had a parade. They burned the Kaiser. On my honour. It's clear as crystal."

McKeever burst out in a guffaw. "He's talking about the end of the *last* war, thirty years ago. Ain't we dumb?"

Percy Fuller opened his mouth weakly, looked up at the ceiling, laughed with soft delight. "Oh, that cowboy. He's our treasure."

"Loreli Hines," said Timothy. "I can see her in my mind right now. She liked to bite me sometimes." He giggled a little.

"All right now, Timothy," said Peake. "It's time you were getting your rest now. Go to the toilet, wash your face and hands, wash out your plates, then come back here."

"OK, Jop," the cowboy said.

"Don't leave your plates on the sink."

"No, Jop," He started out of the room.

"And come right back *here*. Don't go upstairs."

"Yes, Jop," He went out, yawning.

"Damn it, Simon, I don't like it at all," Peake said with great anxiety. "I don't like your goin' off without any money! An' I don't see how anybody so crippled up is gonna hitch-hike. An' I don't see… It's plain reckless, that's what it is!"

McKeever laughed. The laugh was a partial lie. He was not without his own anxieties, but he knew that he had to resist the pessimism of his friends. And in addition… he was determined. As a fish leaps towards the sun, so he intended to make this journey whatever its result. "Lord, I hitch-hiked from Santa Fe, New Mexico, clear to Santa Barbara once in a single hop. I'll make it. The road's a friendly place." He paused and rubbed the hump of his nose delicately with a forefinger. "There's one way you coots might help me, though. That is, if you wanted to?" He eyed them expectantly.

"What do you mean?" asked Fuller.

McKeever began to laugh. "That Booger… you got me a little worried over him. I'd like to skip out without his knowing."

"How you gon' do that?" asked Pavlovsky. "He be on watch for you sure."

"How you even getting out to the main road to start your hitch-hiking?" Peake added. "It's almost a mile. You can't walk it. Don't many cars come past here in a day. It's a pipe dream."

"Now, just hold on a minute," McKeever said softly, still laughing. "I've been thinking up a strategy, kind of a conspiracy."

The others regarded him in silence.

"You willing to help me?"

Fuller nodded. Pavlovsky popped his thumb knuckles, leant forward to squint attentively at McKeever's face. Joplin looked both worried and reluctant.

"First thing tomorrow morning," McKeever said, "while the farmer is off at breakfast, I'll pack my suitcase. I can't go to LA without some clothes. An' a change of shoes – my feet will need that bad."

"Now, how in hell do you expect to get a suitcase out of here without the Booger knowing?" Joplin interrupted angrily. "It's pure dreamin', Simon."

"Shut up a minute," McKeever said affectionately. "What a coot you are!" He rubbed the hump of his nose, and his voice turned sly. "Right after breakfast, when the Booger's ready to go into town for marketing, I'll buttonhole him. Oh, I'll be meek. I've thought it over, I'll tell him. He's right, and I'm wrong. I'm staying right here at the Home."

"Then what?"

"Then you come along, Percy," McKeever said with a grin to Fuller. "You say, 'Hey there, Tom,' you say, 'how about driving me out to the main highway? It'll help pass the day,' you say. Then I'll say, 'That's a good idea, Percy. I'll go with you. We'll count cars.'"

"*Hm!*" said Percy, beginning to laugh. "You get the poop himself to drive you out to the main highway! That's slick!"

"By God!" Pavlovsky exclaimed. Delightedly he cut the air with his fist. "That make him fart when he find out, that Booger."

"Now here's where you come in, Stan," McKeever continued with relish. "You're a good walker. Soon as we two go off with the Booger, you take my handbag and walk it down to the main highway. You meet us there."

"I do it!" Pavlovsky said with delight and enthusiasm. "I sure do."

"Simon, I got an idea of my own," Fuller put in excitedly. "Who knows what sort of weather you'll run into? Maybe rain, maybe a cold spell down in LA. You need an overcoat with you."

"Haven't got one. Only my sweater."

"I have."

"Aw now—"

"I ain't makin' any use of it till winter. You can send it back. I'll trust you."

"That's sure decent," McKeever said gratefully. "It might come in very handy. Thanks."

"I carry it," said Pavlovsky. "Bag and coat, that's my job."

"Better let me," Peake suggested without enthusiasm. "You'll be carryin' too many things. Suspicious. I'll take the coat. You go out the front way, I'll sneak out the cellar. We'll walk separately."

"Ha-ha! That poop, we're too bright for him," Fuller said with relish.

"Ha-ha!" Pavlovsky echoed. "That gasbag, that dumb Booger!"

The door opened. Timothy Wright came in, very wobbly now that he was tired, carrying his dentures in a glass of water. His wrinkled old face seemed no bigger than a walnut.

"Good boy," Peake told him. "Go to sleep now, Timmy. Take off your clothes. Hang 'em up."

"I will." The cowboy's voice turned querulous. "Will you tuck the blankets in so my feet don't stick out?"

"Don't I always?" Peake asked good-naturedly. "You get in bed."

"My feet get cold in the middle of the night," Timothy murmured in a troubled tone. He began to undress.

"Eh now... there's one thing more," McKeever whispered. He began to stroke the hump of his nose again. "You fellers have got me out on the main highway now. But suppose I don't get a hitch right off? Suppose the Booger comes back from town and I'm still there? What then, hey?"

"*Hm!* That's bad," Peake muttered. "That's where your plan breaks down. He knows you can't *walk* back to the Home. He'll want you to *ride* back with him. There's no excuse you can make."

"We just spit in his eye then," said Pavlovsky belligerently. "He try to make you come back, I knock him down. That settle it. Ha-ha!"

"No, you don't," McKeever replied. "That'll have all of you in the soup. There must be another way." He eyed them closely and waited.

"Well… he's liable to call the police, that's the trouble," Percy Fuller muttered. "He'll get a writ on you, a retainer or something."

"You think he could?" McKeever asked provocatively. "Would it be legal?"

Fuller rubbed thumb and forefinger together scornfully. "When was you born? Five dollars to the right party can get half a dozen writs in any state. You wanna sit in jail or in a mental hospital for two weeks till your case comes up?"

"You got me cornered," McKeever said. "Now I don't know what to think." He eyed them slyly. "If I could only get across the county line, I'd be safe. He'd have to extradite me then." Again he waited.

"I've got it!" Marcus Peake announced brightly. "I've solved the whole thing. We flag the first bus comin' along, see? You take it to Stockton. That's across the county line! From there on, you're safe."

"Oh my, that's a wonderful idea!" McKeever agreed with enthusiasm, quite as though it hadn't been in his mind for the past ten minutes. "That does it all right. No, wait a minute." A glum look came over his face. "It won't work, Jop. No good."

"Why not?"

"It takes too much capital. I'm dead broke. One cent – that's my whole finances right now."

"Oh!" said Peake, very distressed. He fell silent.

"You see? The bus to Stockton, why, that must cost a dollar and a half – two dollars, maybe."

"No," Pavlovsky interrupted. "Bus costs…" He frowned. "I remember now… Santabello to Stockton bus costs… last February I went to Stockton for Polish picnic, you remember? Bus costs…" His frown cleared. "Ninety cents… I remember. From main road, here, maybe only eighty-five."

"Only eighty-five?" McKeever echoed eagerly. "And I got one cent already."

"Shucks, we can scrounge that up for you," said Fuller. "I got twenty-three cents, Simon, got it left from that clock I sold to the garbage man."

"Aw now," McKeever replied with sudden dismay, "but if that's *all* you got, that's to buy new parts with, ain't it? I wouldn't want to be taking *that*."

"You'll owe it to me," Fuller said heartily. He took a dime, two nickels and three pennies out of his pocket and tossed them on the cot by McKeever's side. "There you are."

"I'm a grateful man," McKeever told him softly. "And I'll pay you back from my first cheque."

There was an apologetic murmur from Stan Pavlovsky. "I don't got nothing, Simon, no money, not even a jitney."*

All three old men turned to gaze at Peake. "Jop – what do you say?" asked Fuller. "Simon only needs sixty cents more, sixty-one."

Peake swallowed, looked miserable and muttered: "Watch my pennies like they was God's words."

McKeever felt instant shame. "Jop's right! We're on the pension, but he ain't. If he don't watch himself, his savings'll run out."

"Awful tight now," Peake muttered apologetically. "Anything comes up extra, like a dentist bill or something, I'm sunk. Got two years till I'm sixty-five. Hate to think of spending any time in the poorhouse. That's the horror I'm afraid of, fifty men to a room. Keeps me awake nights."

"Aw sure now," McKeever said earnestly. "Forget it. I'll raise that sixty cents. There's Mrs Jackson upstairs. She'll help me."

"You won't have time to see her," Peake muttered. He jumped up. "I'm a jackass, Simon. What's sixty cents? If I go to the poorhouse, it won't be for that. I'll have it for you tomorrow."

"I wouldn't want you—"

"Forget it. So long as you're going, I'll do my share. But I still think it's a crazy idea – crazy."

"Thank you, then," McKeever said softly. He looked with shining eyes from one to the other of his room-mates. "I wish... wish I had the way to thank you with, you coots. It's like you was helping me out of prison. That's what this damn arthureetis is, like prison bars, locking a man up..." He paused, groping for words. He wanted intensely to express all he felt, but he knew in advance that he could not, that it would be like trying to hold a rainbow in his hand. "First there was this fine, kind woman in the drugstore," he said a little tremulously, "then you men now, helping me plan, giving me comfort and ideas and your good money. You're a damn bunch of good lads, you are. Oh, I tell you there's a lot of brotherhood in this world, I've always known it, it makes up for the bad." He fished in his pocket and took out a little notebook and the stub of a pencil. He found a clean page, moistened the pencil point with his lips. "My debts! I'm writing them down... twenty-three cents to Percy Fuller, sixty-one cents to Marcus Peake."

"Jop..." Timothy Wright called in a querulous tone, "you tuckin' in my blankets?" Timothy lay curled up, a tiny figure now, his eyes half closed, his snub nose poking out over the edge of the sheet. He had hung up his clothes neatly on the wall hooks; the glass of water with his dentures was under the cot. "Thank you, Jop," he murmured sleepily as Peake checked the covers. "You're my friend, Jop. I like you."

"Goodnight, Timmy."

"*Hmmm...*"

Peake began to gather up the supper trays. "Well... got my dishes to wash."

"Simon," Pavlovsky asked eagerly, "you play checkers with me? One game – last game?"

"Sure."

Pavlovsky turned away and pretended to be searching for the checkerboard. He suddenly felt very blue. With Simon gone, the hours of the Finney day would be much harder for him to bear. Simon was talkative, Simon was cheery, Simon often read aloud to him from the newspapers. It was just as though the Southern Pacific were to move its railroad tracks away. There were two good things in Pavlovsky's life – and one of them was about to depart. He squinted over at McKeever now, cracked the knuckles of his big, old hands and thought of the day forty years back that he had entered the harbour at Boston with his young wife, seeing the emerald water with the brilliant cakes of ice in it, the dazzling sky, the great city and the great land. He felt bad.

"Well, I'm off," said Peake, hefting the load of trays and stacked dishes. As he started out, the door opened and John Hanbury came in. His bony face impassive, leg dragging, the farmer walked towards his cot. Pavlovsky said brutally, "How was pork chops? How was steak? How was chicken?" Every once in a while Pavlovsky erupted in this manner.

"Mind your talk, you dumb foreigner," Hanbury replied with chill contempt. "I don't know you're alive."

"One day I'm going hit you once," said Pavlovsky with relish. "Clop-clop. You be dead, you old fart." He burst out into a rumbling laugh as he joined McKeever and Fuller. "Hey, fellers – how 'bout we tell social worker this damn farmer is embezzlemer? He's got no right to old-age pension. He's got *plenty* money."

"Who'd believe a dumb Polack?" asked Hanbury loudly of one of the mirrors. His hard, work-worn body was quivering with rage. "Everybody knows Polacks are liars."

"Next month I'm sure tell social worker," Pavlovsky lied with great satisfaction.

Hanbury spat on the floor. "Foreigner!" He sat down hard on his cot, put his radio earphones over his head and began spinning the dial.

Percy Fuller massaged his bald dome with stubby fingers, laughed softly. He took a corncob pipe and a package of the Finney tobacco out of his pocket. "Here now, wait," McKeever said quickly. He pulled out one of his cans of Half and Half. "It's yours, Percy. Throw that manure away."

"You don't have to do that," replied Fuller, although he was eyeing the tobacco with instant greed. "You'll need it for your trip."

"I got another."

Fuller took the can from McKeever and gazed at it as though it were a diamond ring. "How in the world did you promote two of 'em?"

"Found a quarter near the hospital. Lucky, hey?"

"Half 'n' Half," Fuller marvelled. He opened the package. "Smell it, Stan."

Pavlovsky laughed. "I no like. Candy I like. When I was workin', I used buy pound box candy every Saddy night. Eat it up like kid." He set the checkerboard on his knees and began laying out the pieces. "Now no job, no candy, no noddings." He chuckled harshly. "Goodbye all along line. Last caboose. Ha-ha."

"Better wash my socks out later, hadn't I?" McKeever murmured as he stuffed the bowl of his briar. "An' steal a piece of that Booger's soap. I'll need soap for my trip."

"You move, Simon," Pavlovsky said. "Begin. An' no damn cheatin'."

McKeever smiled at him. In the back of his mind there was a thought that gave him great pleasure: that when he got cured up and had himself a job, he'd buy Stan Pavlovsky a fine box of candy. A gift for each one of the others too. Decent men they were. All his life he'd been learning this same lesson: that the world was made up mostly of good people. Some punks, some mean ones, some crooks, but most were a pleasure to recall. "By God," he exclaimed suddenly. "I'm cocky tonight, I'm sharp. Watch it how you play, Stan."

"Ho!" said Pavlovsky. "Big talk."

"Feel like a champeen; feel like the day I ran from Belfast to my own front yard."

"Big talk, big talk."

"Indeed!" said McKeever. "If you was a few years younger, I'd lay you out with one good punch."

"Ha-ha," Pavlovsky said, "joke."

Smiling, they began to play.

Chapter 6

In the middle hours of the night, McKeever awakened out of his familiar nightmare. He lay rigid, sweating, uneasy in brain and heart. "A bug," the voices in his dream had been saying, "a cockroach... squash him!"

The room was still, quite as usual. Only a soft, wheezing snore from Percy Fuller and the intermittent hum of cicadas in the fields challenged the night calm. A pale wash of moonlight from one of the windows illumined the foot of Pavlovsky's cot, touched his own where his hands lay clenched under the blanket and continued on to gleam back softly from a wall mirror. Everything quite as usual.

Shuddering, McKeever asked himself why he suffered this dream. Until he came to the Home he had been a man for whom sleep was a comfortable thing. Since then, once or twice each week, this nightmare had shattered his rest. There were some people who believed dreams came from the other world, that they bore a message from the spirits of the departed. But if so, why was his dream so cruel? It could only be his mother or his sister or his wife who might be wanting to speak to him. They loved him, they would speak to him only with kindness. He had read magazine articles that said dreams revealed secrets of the mind. Perhaps so, psychology was the newest thing. But in that case what secrets did *his* dream reveal? What the hell was it all about?

Each time it was more or less the same: the dark road... a grey fog... and McKeever groping the lonely night, lost and searching, wanting so desperately to find... he didn't know what. And then, suddenly, a terrifying glare of headlights. He tried to run, but his legs became bloodless stilts that would not move. The truck bore down upon him unrelentingly, the driver without pity or concern. "Oh my!" his heart cried. "How awful, what waste – a man wasn't born to end—" And then he was lying under the wheel of an immense oil truck, pinned down, one of the huge tyres on his chest. He lay there in anguish while people slowly gathered. They chatted idly with one another and occasionally squatted down to peer at him. And presently one of them reached out and turned a petcock in the belly of the truck. Oil spurted down. McKeever twisted his head from side to side, but to no purpose; black and suffocating, the hot oil poured down on his eyes, his chest. There were dozens of people squatting around in the moonlight – dozens, like buzzards – but they would not free him. They only looked at him with tremendous unconcern, with cold and beady eyes. "I'm a man," he kept calling to them, "why don't you help me?"

There was no reply.

"It don't cost anything to be decent. It's only brotherhood – you've heard of that!"

Silence.

Forlornly: "But I'm on my way. It's vital."

And then the voices murmured coldly, "A cockroach."

"What's that? I'm a human being of Christian parents. Baptized in the Presbyterian Church of old Ireland."

"Keep quiet, you bug."

"Born in the image of God. Where's your decency?"

"Where's your union card?"

"What? Why, it's here. The Oil Field and Gas Workers' Union, A. F. of L."

Laughter.

"I swear. Built the pumping station and the refinery at Lebec. Had our pictures in the paper. Laid pipelines from Bakersfield over the Ridge."

Indifferently: "You have no business out on the road. You should have stayed in your hole."

"Hole?"

Contemptuously: "Step on him!"

"Hole... hole?"

Angrily: "Squash him, the old cockroach! He's no good for anything. A parasite. Garbage!"

Garbage! His brain whispered to his outraged heart, "You'll die now. Blackness will come like the wings of black birds, and a black muck will cover your eyes, your face and every living part of you…"

Horror!

Each time the nightmare was no less vivid, no less dreadful. He would awaken with clenched fists and pounding heart.

Slowly McKeever relaxed. He wiped his damp forehead and neck with the sheet. Quiet night, Percy Fuller snoring. The pale moonshine on his cot was pretty. With effort he turned on his side to ease his stiff limbs. He composed himself for sleep again. And then, in the instant, he was very wakeful, his brain flashing questions about the next day's venture. What if he didn't reach Los Angeles in a single day? How would he eat – where would he sleep? He had maintained an attitude of great confidence in talking to the other men. But suppose his nightmare came true and he was caught on the open road with a truck rolling down on him like thunder? How would he escape – he who had once run like a whippet over the green lanes of old Ireland?

He felt hot suddenly. He thrust back the blanket and pushed up to a sitting position. He muttered aloud, "What's the matter with you, lad?" He stared into the wall mirror at the foot of his cot. He saw his face dimly reflected in the moonlight – tense, severe, his sparse, white hair damply tousled. He saw his lips part to frame words: "Skittish, lad? At your age?"

Silence. The lips in the mirror were motionless, pressed together. Then they twisted in a delicate grin. "You coot, there's maggots in your head. Go back to sleep. You're starting for Glendale tomorrow."

He lay back on his cot, feeling calmer and even faintly amused at himself for his moment of panic. The trip might not be an easy one, naturally. Perhaps luck would be for him, perhaps against.

But a man did what he was bound to do whatever the obstacles. And if he said it himself, he was an old hand at dealing with Lady Luck, he was practised and scarred from their combat.

He thought this, and the smile slowly left his face. An old pain lanced through his flesh, a hard scar throbbed in a recess of his heart. Forty-two years before, as he stood in the mud of a cemetery outside the town of Brownsville, Pennsylvania, and watched the burial of his wife and child, he had asked himself a question. He had asked it in anguish, in fury, in vast bewilderment, with the nails of his fingers dug into his palms: *Why were there accidents in life? Who decreed them?* And what sort of God was it who wantonly pronounced that his wife and infant child must be burnt and shrivelled, mutilated and taken from him, by the explosion of a kerosene stove?

Later, as he sat in a saloon in his mourning clothes and quietly drank himself into a stupor, he had pondered the question of accident in the universe. And other things. He had never paused before to examine his beliefs. By the hearth fire in his childhood he had learnt a formal catechism. There was Man and there was the Father of all things, Jehovah – and Jehovah knew when each leaf fell from a tree and He protected a lad on windy nights when the spirits danced. And it was wrong to lie or swear or find secret pleasure between the legs, and He would sternly know, and a lad would feel the whip of misfortune. But now there was nothing at all, not even a universal, mysterious purpose, that could justify to McKeever the evil that befell the harmless and the innocent. It was wanton, and it was not to be justified, and he rejected it.

It was the year 1905, and McKeever was thirty-two, a journeyman plumber drinking cheap whiskey in a small-town saloon, neither a studious nor a reflective man. His mother had wept before him once in regret and apology, saying that the years of his schooling were less than the fingers of her hand. And before this moment of tragedy McKeever had not had much time or need for books or reading or philosophic thought: he had worked hard from boyhood, he had taken simple pleasures as he found them, and knew of little else. But now it seemed clear to his shudder-ing, pain-racked heart that there were secrets to life he needed to discover in order to live at all – and surely it was the learned ones of the earth who knew those secrets, and he wished that he was among them. And slowly, with a consuming need to quiet his pain, he asked himself questions and grappled for answers, and sat stiffly and pondered, and gazed at his long callused fingers twisting a whiskey glass and thought that only three days before they had touched the warm thighs of his child. Why were men born? Was it to no purpose at all? Men struggled and died, and were they no more to this earth than spiders or night-flying bats? And no one caring, the universe rolling on, the pain and the effort no more than the flutter of a wing in an empty sky?

He twisted his whiskey glass and asked a fly on the wall, "Where do I go now... why... to what goal?" The fly buzzed and crawled upon the hands that had diapered a living child.

Lying in the dark, now McKeever smiled a little, sighed. Out of the pain, the defeat, the mystery, he had found a creed, and it had remained with him. It was forty-two years ago that his wife and child had been so early returned to brown earth, but he felt that his life had been lived significantly, in a reasonable universe, and that there was purpose and meaning to man's existence.

He *had* believed this – but did he now, at this moment? He had been sure for years that he was part of a golden endeavour: the shaping of the earth by the generations of Man... But did he believe it now? Now he was a derelict; the world asked of him only that he keep his corpse from stinking up the highways. And now he was no longer so sure about things. He was a bit... confused.

McKeever sighed. He felt the old pain throbbing in the old, hard scar. If a man didn't know at seventy-three what he firmly believed, then when would he ever know? Here was a Pilgrim's Progress if ever there was one,* and why did it seem now to draw him like a magnet to Glendale? He didn't know, he only felt that it was more than just getting well, it was... something... But what?

He lay quiet and listened to the cicadas buzzing off the minutes of their own lives and their own destiny and thought, "Is it possible that I am really almost seventy-four?" Were so many months, years, moments, gone... for ever lost? *That* was a real mystery – surely all men pondered it as they lay wakeful in the middle hours of a night – the twisted mystery of Time. His sinews were tired, Youth had gone, but were all the fine moments also gone – the moments of Chance, sweet and tragic, and the moments of high activity, high triumph and high feeling? He could remember still the crunch and odour of the morning earth as he walked up to Beanie McCarthy in the oil field outside of Tulsa and said to him, "Beanie – I've learnt how to read blueprints!" (Almost trembling with exultation.) "Do you remember what you said to me, Beanie? You said that when I learnt blueprints, you'd raise me from a pipe-liner to a pipe-fitter. Well, I've learnt how, Beanie – I've been studying in night school – you can test me out... and by God I'm a pipe-fitter starting Monday or I quit!" Was that moment of triumph gone? Or was not the mark of it somehow on this earth, inscribed somewhere in Time? There was a fine verse he had memorized because he believed it to be so true:

> There is a saying of the ancient sages:
>   No noble human thought,
> However buried in the dust of ages,
>   Can ever come to naught.*

Was it not so with the actions and the moments of an individual man? He wanted so much to believe it! It took ten million grains of sand to make a foot of shore on which a sea bird hatched its young. So the million moments of each individual man, doing his work for good or ill in the world, marked the land, the earth, the lives of others. Surely it could not be otherwise, it had seemed obvious to the eye of a man like him. He was not important, he was no great thinker or philosopher, yet he was sure that he had been indispensable, and that his moments were written down somewhere, and that they would not die when he passed over. There was the moment he stood on the high ridge at Lebec, pausing in the hush of dusk to listen to the pumps, the first pumps that the golden eagles ever had seen in those mountains. A voice shouted, "Crack a beer, boys. It's finished. We've built a pipeline from Bakersfield to the Ridge, and down again to the Fernando Valley. It's a job well done, you blue-balled* coots." And that moment would not die with him, surely it would not, for the pumps still worked and the pipes were solid. He wanted so much to believe it. And perhaps a man only took to the grave those things that were too private to belong to anyone else. Like the kiss of his own woman.

He could remember still the luminous beauty of his wife's eyes when she told him that she was with child. It was a Sunday, and they had walked out from Brownsville into the hills above the broad, deep-flowing Monongahela. The rust from Pittsburgh's steel mills bloodied the river, and down below, in a valley of smoke, children screamed at play on the slag heaps of a coal camp. But where they lay the grass was sprinkled with clover, buttercups gleamed softly, field birds piped and ran on stiff legs over secret paths. His wife wove a necklace of daisies for each of them. They lay on their backs and stared at an eternity of azure sky, at the slow circling of a hawk. They turned and embraced, lying limb to limb, smiling, lazy on their Sunday holiday, relishing the goodness of unhurried body pressed to body.

She had not been a beauty, this woman of McKeever's, yet she owned what he needed in a woman: a vigour of flesh and spirit that matched his own and a quiet, steadfast tenderness that accepted him for what he was. If not her, then he would have sought another – yet when he lost her, he never found another. Behind their marriage was a felicity of time and place, a coming together by sweet chance that his wandering life never again offered him.

In the summer of 1902, on a sweltering afternoon, a girl of nineteen sat behind the counter of a fly-infested grocery in Brownsville, sat fanning herself with a soiled apron, sat wiping little beads of sweat from her broad forehead and her strong, milk-skinned throat. A man came in, tall and lean and sinewy and pleasant for her to gaze upon.

"I'd like a rye bread, half a pound of baloney,* three eggs."

"Your pals got here ahead of you."

"What?"

"Ain't you a coal miner?"

"I'm a plumber."

"Excuse me. Tomorrow's July Four, and the miners have a picnic. We're cleaned out of baloney and eggs, and that goes for beer, in case you wanted any."

"What are those picnics like? I'm new in town. Any fun?"

"Oh... dancing and eating and firecrackers and some union speeches. They're quite all right."

"You going?"

Pause. "What do you want to buy, mister?"

"If you weren't going to the picnic with anybody else, I'd like to take you. How about it?"

"No."

"Why not?"

"For somebody new in town you mix in other people's business extremely quick."

"I don't mean to be fresh, miss. But I like your looks. I'm a straight talker."

"That's quite all right. I'm quite used to straight talkers. This is my father's store, and I've been working here since I was ten. I can handle a bar fly quite easy – every bar fly that comes in here likes my looks."

"I'm sure of it. But since I'm not that type, I was hoping to make friends with you. I'm just back from Cuba. I'm new in town, and I'm lonely."

"And just because I'm behind a counter, where I have to talk to anybody, you think it's quite a chance to try your wings. Well, I don't make friends with strangers, who are most likely drunkards and who have been over in Cuba wallowing around in dives and dens and catching all the native diseases. Now, what do you want to buy here, mister?"

"My, what a poor creature you are, miss. It strikes me you don't have a friend in the world with that snippy tongue of yours. I've been a wartime member of the US Cavalry under Teddy Roosevelt,* honourable discharge, and I'm proud of it. I'm working for Ollie Johnson, who's the biggest building contractor in the county, and I'm not ashamed of that. And I've never had a sick day in my grown life. Can I have a can of tuna fish and a rye bread, please?"

And in this manner Simon McKeever met his wife, Mary Hinkleman, Dutch Calvinist on her father's side, West Virginia Scotch on her mother's. She was short and broad-shouldered, apple-cheeked, full-lipped and sweet to his eye. She was a stubborn bigot on the question of temperance, and she had a hornet's sting when she was in a temper. But she was quick to laugh and eager about life – she was the girl for him, and she satisfied him.

Under the azure sky on that Sunday afternoon, she opened her blouse suddenly and nestled his head to her breasts. She spoke to him in her father's tongue, saying, "I love you, Simon, Irish Simon, long, thin, strong Simon – I love you, my darling." He knew the words, because their sound was familiar by now. He said nothing, only kissed her softly and felt that his senses were drenched by the beauty of the afternoon, by odours and bird cries, by the taste, shape and kiss of good living itself.

"And what shall we name the boy if he's a boy, or the girl if she's a girl?" his wife asked him.

He raised his head. It seemed to him that his heart would burst from the understanding of all he saw in her eyes: love leaning upon tenderness, tenderness upon passion, passion on confidence... and all fusing into luminous beauty, telling him with exquisite grace of the deep heart's triumph of a fine woman, his wife.

This was one of the moments that Simon McKeever, at seventy-three, wanted in the grave with him. It was too deeply private for anyone but himself, and no man would be jealous of it who had known his own love. It was woven of the broken strands of their short life together, it was fashioned in the shadows of the nights when he lay naked upon her naked body, mouth possessing mouth, limb and flesh and pulse lovingly embraced. And out of all this she had asked, "What shall we name the boy if he's a boy, or the girl if she's a girl?" They named the girl Emily. And Emily died with her mother when she was two years old.

McKeever dozed. In half-sleep he heard Percy Fuller's snore and thought: "It'll be morning soon." He felt a slight cramp in a thigh and moved to his back to relieve it. He thought of finding the twenty-five-cent piece that morning and then he heard Sarah Kahn, the pretty nurse, exclaim: "I think you're wonderful." He smiled a little, feeling warmed by the memory, feeling drowsy and comfortable. His brain whispered, "Why! She's like Mary was, short and chunky and full of spirit like Mary. That's why you like her. She'll be coming to see you on Sunday." He thought: "I'll have to call it off, won't I? I mustn't forget." The big book he was intending to edit came into his mind, and he felt a stir of satisfaction. It was a useful project, he was sure it was, and it was a wonder that it ever had occurred to a man like him. And then he heard Ada Finney's voice and saw her weeping, the sharp teeth biting the lower lip... "They'll pick you up! They'll put you in a booby hatch like all the old men that's found wandering around..." In sudden fear he opened his eyes... and was struck with wonder. There was a strange Presence in the room, hovering near his cot. He could feel it... something... he didn't know what... but something. Then, in the pale wash of moonlight on his blanket, he saw two shimmering lights. They were like coloured discs, and they seemed the size of twenty-five-cent pieces. One was blue with a red circle around it, and one was red with a blue circle around it. They shimmered and moved and came towards him. And he thought, "I'm dreaming, it's a dream again." But the lights were so clear to his eye that he was positive he must be awake. And then he knew what the lights might be: indeed, they might be the spirits of his dead mother and his dead sister trying to comfort him and wish him well for his trip. His heart became swollen with gratitude, and he put out his hand to receive them.

They were gone – suddenly gone. Was he awake or asleep? Had it been only a dream, a fine and wonderful dream?

Chapter 7

At 6.15 in the morning, later than usual for him, Marcus Peake sat on his cot, blinking the heaviness from his eyes and lacing up his heavy brogans. Breakfast was served punctually at seven, and Peake had much to do before then: he had to set out thirty-two trays, each with cereal bowl, spoon, paper napkin and coffee mug; the day being Tuesday, he needed also to open three large cans of tomato juice and pour a precise serving for each tray – not more than four ounces, or Mrs Finney would holler at him, not less than the customary half-glass, or the pensioner would holler; there were sugar bowls to check and cans of condensed milk to be punctured; there was... plenty to occupy him. In spite of his tardiness, however, Marcus paused before leaving the room. He glanced around cautiously to make certain that neither Hanbury nor Timothy Wright were awake. Then he stepped over to McKeever's cot. The blanket had pulled out at the bottom of the cot, exposing McKeever's feet with their rosy, arthritic nodules at the big toe joints, and Peake thought to himself, "Travellin' the road with those, eh? They'll ache you plenty before you see Glendale." Gently he pressed the shoulder of the sleeping man. McKeever stirred, sighed, his lids half opened. Peake gestured for him to be quiet and squatted down on his haunches beside the cot. He whispered anxiously, "You goin' on your trip, Simon?"

McKeever blinked at him, yawned a little, murmured, "Sure."

Excitedly: "Ain't changed your mind?"

In a surprised tone: "Why should I?"

"Oh my!" Peake exclaimed. He ran his fingers through his bushy grey hair and stared at McKeever as might a fascinated terrier, head tilted to one side, brown eyes glistening. "I lied awake half the night picturin' you on that road. Scares me to death."

"Does it? Why, I slept like a baby," McKeever replied expansively. With a sudden pang he wondered where the lie had come from, and how it had slipped out so easily, and why it had felt so good on his tongue. But now that he was committed to it, he decided that it was no more than a tiny and rather innocent exaggeration. The nightmare he suffered was so ridiculous, so unrelated to the man he had been for sixty years, that it would be absurd to accept it as a bona-fide part of his life. "Practically never wake up at night anyway," he added boastfully.

"And here I'm such a worrier," Peake confessed. He laughed awkwardly. "Did you know that, Simon?"

"No." With a grunt McKeever raised himself to a sitting position; it required another moment of directed effort and another grunt to swing his long legs out to the floor. He sat squinting before the bright light from the windows as he waited for the sluggishness of night to drain from his veins. He told himself contentedly that he felt pretty good, not bad at all; his joints were less locked up than they had been for weeks. And the morning air already felt pleasant on his skin; later it would be warm and comfortable out on the highway, and that was pleasing too, another piece of good luck. He heard Marcus repeat, in the same embarrassed tone, "Never used to be a worrier at all, just gone all pulpy inside." He turned in surprise to blink at Marcus; it was not like him to speak so candidly. Peake was still squatting down on his haunches at the head of the cot; he was staring off into space in an absent-minded manner, as though he had forgotten McKeever's presence. He had not. McKeever's imminent departure had stirred his feelings profoundly, although he didn't know why. He was a shy man, never given to intimacies with another, but now suddenly, at 6.30 in the morning, he felt under a compulsion to talk to McKeever from the core of his heart. "Careless as a frog in the moonlight, that's how I was," he blurted out suddenly. "Nothing bothered me. Saw men carried out of the zinc mines a dozen times, smashed to pulp by the rock falls; we just shovelled 'em up, it never cut my wind. Careless... my bachelor nature maybe..." He swallowed, and his

Adam's apple jerked nervously in his thin neck. "Careless – but how much damn fun I got out of living... fiddle the girls... lap a beer... do my day's work..." He fell silent.

McKeever rubbed the stubble of white beard that the night had brought to his jaw. He felt a bit uncomfortable. Peake was still squatting down on his haunches, and now he folded one hand over the other in a manner that was almost prayerful.

"You know something? Seems to me it was some penny candles done my nerve in. You think that's possible? The day I was forty-five my sister had a cake for me with orange inside that I liked, an' all the relatives watchin' me blow good luck. Then I saw those candles. 'Holy Mackerel,' I thought, 'look at 'em all, I'm gettin' old. Where'll I be when I'm fifty-five – how'll I hold down a job then?'" He paused and gazed beseechingly at McKeever. "That finished me! Turned me pulpy inside! Seems to me I been worryin' over every little item since. You think it's possible – some penny candles giving a man a notion like that – change what he is... his spirit, I mean?"

"I don't know," McKeever murmured. "Candles... I doubt it."

"Happened all at once," Peake said helplessly. "In five minutes, no leading up. That's why I blame it all on the candles, some kind of black magic like. You believe in that? Guess I don't myself."

McKeever was silent. The two men gazed at each other. "Like a tapeworm in my gut, the worry," Peake muttered. "Could've had wonderful years." He shook himself suddenly, like a small dog, and with that returned to the reality of his morning tasks. "Say, you're late. It's way past six. You got things to do, Simon. What a morning! I'm crawlin' with excitement. And say – I'll do my part... the sixty-one cents I mean. I'm glad *you* got nerve, even if I haven't."

"Thanks," McKeever whispered gratefully.

As Peake started out of the room, a voice said "Jop!" He turned, and for an instant was baffled – all of the men except McKeever seemed to be asleep. Then, reflected in one of the mirrors, he saw John Hanbury beckoning to him. The farmer lay snuggled under the covers of the farthest cot and had his back turned to the room. It told Peake that for some minutes at least Hanbury had been observing him. He wondered anxiously if the farmer had overheard his conversation with McKeever. He doubted it, but he tiptoed across the room with a stiff face. "Mornin'... You want something?"

Hanbury's pale, stern eyes widened in surprise. "Ain't seen me lyin' in bed so late before, have you?"

Peake felt stupid. In his excitement over McKeever he had forgotten that he himself was off schedule, and that the cause of his lapse was Hanbury. Invariably the farmer was up with the chickens, dressed and no place to go by 5.30 a.m. His failure to awaken Peake at their appointed hour of 5.50 could only mean that something quite serious had prevented it. "What's the trouble?" he enquired. "You sick?"

"About time you asked," Hanbury replied coldly. "A man could die here."

"What's the matter?"

"My bad leg – twisted a nerve or something durin' the night – aches and pains, shootin' pains something awful. I don't happen to be the fussy kind, but anybody else would be layin' here split-tin' the roof. I want a hot-water bottle; I want my breakfast on a tray – two cups of coffee, black and strong, a raw egg pinholed at both ends – that's all. I want Tom Finney to come up and see me. I need to go to my doctor for a treatment – you tell him."

"Right away," said Joplin politely. He left the room thinking, "Why, you crusty old stinker, I hope that leg gangrenes on you. Serve you right, you mangy goat."

Their conversation had awakened both Fuller and Pavlovsky. Fuller began his usual morning cough, hacking and spitting into a handkerchief in expiation of fifty years of cheap tobacco. Pavlovsky sat up in bed very suddenly, like a huge jack-in-the-box, and turned to Hanbury with a rumbling laugh. "You sick, eh?" He scratched the curly mop of grey hair on his chest with great satisfaction. "I'm terrible sorry. I'm afraid by tonight you're dead. I smell you stink already." His heavy body shook with laughter.

"It must be awful to be ignorant," Hanbury informed the wall mirror. He reached for the earphones of his radio, shoved the band over his head and spun the dial.

Pavlovsky swung out of bed and turned his attention to McKeever. The latter was concentrating on getting dressed. As with any physical activity, the act of pulling on trousers was no longer a casual matter to McKeever. Since knees, hips and hands were not the dextrous tools that once they had been, even so simple a matter required attention and some ingenuity. Watching him, Pavlovsky asked suddenly, in a cautious voice, "You go, Simon? Glendale?"

"Provided I get these pants on. Can't go in my drawers."

"Something worry me."

"What?"

The Pole bent towards him. "That damn farmer. He's sick, stay in bed. How we gon' do things? How you pack your bag without him know?"

"*Hmmm!*"

"You think maybe you better put off – do tomorra, next day?"

"No," McKeever answered firmly.

"He find out, he make trouble."

"I'll pack my bag somehow."

"He see you, he'll tell Booger," Pavlovsky warned again.

"There's always some obstacles in the way of things. No reason to draw back."

"Ha!" A tawny flush of colour rose into Pavlovsky's cheeks. "By golly, I better get dressed quick. You depending on me, ain't you?" He grabbed for his clothes, "Hey," he called to Fuller, who was dozing again, "wake oop, what's matter with you? It's late!" He jerked his head so ostentatiously towards McKeever that the latter, passing by him on his way to the washbasin, touched his arm, frowned, whispered, "Keep quiet, can't you?"

"Sure, sure," Pavlovsky murmured, very abashed. "Excuse."

Timothy Wright awakened; he yawned, stretched, farted loudly, announced in a gay tone, "The big, bad wolf's around." He rubbed his eyes, belched, slipped his plates into his mouth, asked plaintively, "Ain't chuck come up yet? I'm hungry." Then he too began to dress. And from all over the old house there came the varied sounds of the awakening pensioners: the running of water followed inevitably by the groaning rattle of the plumbing system; the scrape of warped, old-fashioned windows as they were raised another peg to admit the dewy freshness of the morning air; from the kitchen, at the rear of the house, there issued a hurried clatter and bustle, and from the second floor a sudden, high-pitched titter from Mrs Thomas; and all of the whispers, murmurs, creakings and stirrings of thirty-two old people awakening to another morning, glad to be alive because death was more strange, but wondering what they would do with themselves on this new day, so like the one before. At the washbasin, lathering his face, McKeever listened to all of these familiar sounds and relished them because he was going away. Life was a narrow thing when it was lived in a barracks under the rule of others. He had had a bellyful of it. He thought with satisfaction that this was his first carefree morning in two years.

Seven a.m. arrived as Marcus Peake carried in the first of the breakfast trays for Timothy Wright.

"Hey, Jop, what kind chow we got this morning?" Pavlovsky asked.

"Got tomata juice, Wheatena,* java."

"Wheatena!" Pavlovsky exclaimed in disgust. "Yesterday oatmeal, tomorra farina – whatsamatter, ain't no eggs born in California any more?"

"Eggs?" a voice echoed in plaintive bitterness. "You priced the cost of eggs recently?" It was Finney, standing in the doorway of their room, his face eloquent with resentment. "He wants eggs!" he said mournfully to the others as he strode into the room. "Ha-ha. Eggs for breakfast, trout for lunch, pork chops for supper. I'd like it myself. Only, I can't quite afford it – not in my business. Ha-ha."

Pavlovsky became annoyed. "Ha-ha," he mimicked as insultingly as possible.

Finney paused by Hanbury's cot. "Now, what's the basis for that, please?" He spoke to Pavlovsky via the mirror, as Hanbury had done earlier, not condescending to turn around. "You're a chicken? Lay some eggs for us, please? Ha-ha yourself."

"Ha-ha," Pavlovsky repeated. "An' cocoa, always damn cocoa."

"Nourishing," said Finney; "recommended by the State Board of Health. I don't like to be criticized so early in the morning. It's unfair."

"Ha-ha!" Pavlovsky sneered.

"Hee-hee-hee..." Timothy Wright said in a high cackle.

"Damn it," Hanbury complained furiously, "a man could die from pure neglect."

"Easy to criticize, so easy to criticize," Finney said bitterly to the mirror. And then, in a harassed tone that expressed the genuine bewilderment in his heart, he asked loudly of the walls, "Why can't people be friendly? Why they always demanding from each other?" He flapped both arms. "Demanding... criticizing... He sat down abruptly on the edge of Hanbury's cot, and his face turned solicitous. "Your leg again, John, eh?"

At the other end of the room Percy Fuller and McKeever exchanged glances that expressed mutual anxiety. They had intended to approach the Booger after breakfast, but here he was confronting them, obviously in a temper. What to do? Percy cleaned his reading spectacles and glanced the other way; McKeever honed his razor in preparation for his trip and stared at a fly on the ceiling – and both eavesdropped as hard as they could.

Finney and Hanbury talked in low tones for a few moments, and then the Booger said excitedly, so that they could hear him, "But now wait a minute, John, hold on – there's an auction in East Santabello this morning. I told you I was going."

"Don't care," the farmer replied coldly. "I need a treatment."

Timothy raised his nose out of his cereal. "Auction? Twenty-four, twenty-five... thirty-six, thirty-seven... who'll bid? That's how an auction goes! Ever hear one? I have... lots!" He shoved his nose back into his bowl of Wheatena.

"Army surplus... cots and blankets... we need 'em bad," the Booger explained patiently to Hanbury. "You got to be fair about it, John. I'll be back early."

"Doctor's office opens at nine sharp. I aim to be there. I'm in terrible pain."

"Why, why... why, the beds are all coming apart in the ladies' wing. A terrible situation. We need seven, eight. No replacements since Pearl Harbor – metal shortage."

"The ladies can sleep on the floor as far as I care. Breakfast for everyone except me, I suppose," he snapped bitterly to Marcus Peake, who was carrying in the last of the trays for the other men. "Neglect, I'm surrounded by neglect!" He turned back to Finney without listening to Peake's muttered explanation. "What time you drivin' me in?"

Now, abruptly, Finney's voice lost its firmness; it turned wheedling. "Hurts plenty I bet, eh? By the way, you taken aspirin? When I was working at the County Hospital, a doctor told me once, 'Wonderful medication, aspirin,' he remarked to me, 'two little aspirins—'"

"Damn the aspirin! It's my lamp treatment I need."

Finney snapped his fingers. "I got it! Auction opens at nine. I'll ask 'em to put the cots right up. Why, I'll be back here by 10.15."

"You say 10.15 or 2.15? You think you'll be the only one in a hurry? Why should they favour you?"

"Get those cots two dollars cheaper each one," Finney said wistfully. "Maybe a dollar off on each blanket."

"Been lyin' here all night sleepless. I'll take a taxi. You'll pay."

"Wh-a-at?"

"I sure mean it. One or the other. Settle it right now."

"Let it be," Finney said wretchedly. He stood up, accepting his defeat. "I'll drive you in right after breakfast."

"Too soon! Doctor don't open till nine. I don't aim to wait on the sidewalk."

In a dull voice Finney asked, "What time you want to leave?"

"Eight thirty."

"OK."

"You'll wait around till I get my treatment, won't you? So you can drive me right back?"

"OK." Finney bolted across the room.

"I'll want to come right back to bed," Hanbury called after him with great satisfaction. "A man's entitled to service for his money, ain't he?"

Knowing that the eyes of the other men in the room were upon him, and knowing what they must be thinking, Finney yelled "Sure" and pulled open the door.

"Tom!" said McKeever. He saw Fuller's look of consternation, but he went right on. "I want to talk to you."

Hand still on the doorknob, Finney swung his heavy body around. "Now, what do *you* want?" There was a hoarse bay in his voice. This was one of the moments when life's unceasing combat became so oppressive to him that he was afraid he might explode, literally explode into a thousand anguished parts. "Ain't I got enough without *you* comin' at me again?"

Percy Fuller was clearing his throat, shuffling his feet and otherwise attempting to warn McKeever into silence, but the latter paid no attention. Very blandly he said, "I want to thank you, Tom. For helping me so much."

Finney shivered in his surprise; he stared at McKeever with mouth agape.

"I want you to know I'm taking your advice. About not going off, I mean."

"Well, now!" Finney muttered.

"Got a good berth for myself here. I thought it over, I'd be a fool to risk losing it. Guess I lost my temper, didn't I?"

"You sure did," Finney agreed sullenly. "Said some nasty things, definitely unpleasant."

"I'm sorry. I could've bit my tongue off later. I apologize."

Timothy Wright, coming in late on the conversation, echoed with great interest, "Apologize? What for? You wet your bed, Simon? Ha? Oh, you rascal!"

"Shuddup," said Pavlovsky nervously. "Don't interrup'."

McKeever continued smoothly. He had chosen deliberately to flatter the Booger in a moment of humiliation, and he could see that his fish was hooked. It was wonderfully exhilarating to him after two years of petty indignities. "The fact is, Tom, that you an' your wife do your level best for us, an' we all know it. Don't we, fellers?"

Percy Fuller said quickly, "Sure do, yep, absolutely." Pavlovsky, not quite trusting himself, nodded his head up and down and began to pop his finger knuckles.

"Well, now!" said Finney. A ruby flush of pleasure stained his fat cheeks, and his lips trembled with a timid smile that transformed his countenance. In that instant McKeever saw standing before him a shy, grateful and defenceless boy rather than an irritating adult, and he suddenly felt wretched. It was heartless to deceive anyone so gullible. "Well, now," Finney muttered again, "*hmmmm*... I see." He straightened up, squared his heavy shoulders and suddenly exploded upon McKeever all of the resentment he felt towards Hanbury, his wife, the world. "God damn it, then remember it!" He waved his arms. "I'm calling it to the attention of all of you – stop eating there... pay attention! I've had enough criticism around here, I want this bellyaching to stop. Eggs – hah!" He paused for a moment, and the room lay hushed, deeply and solemnly still. Then, wrecking the impressive silence, there came an offensive, sucking sound, an insolent smacking and popping of somebody's lips. It was John Hanbury, sitting up in bed with a tray on his lap, greedily sucking a raw egg.

Finney sagged as he stood there. His chest caved in, his shoulders drooped, his bulky frame deflated. "There, now," he muttered. "I mean it. I expect some changes around here... cooperation" – his arms flapped out from his sides, returned to their original position – "and appreciation. I work like a dog for all of you... my level best..." His voice trailed off.

"Just what I was telling you last night, wasn't I, Percy?" McKeever said. "They're unselfish. Nothing small about 'em or mean." He looked significantly at Fuller, trying to spur him on to taking up his cue. "Do little things for us all the time, don't they?"

Fuller's mouth gaped open for a moment, like the mouth of a fish that gulps air but hopes for water. He uttered no sound, closed his mouth again. He cleared his throat, rubbed his bald dome hard, said in a stammer, "Say Tom... Tom, now... wanted to ask you something... just a little thing... uh..." Then it came out in a rush. "I got a notion to look at the highway today. How about you take me out? Ha? Hey?"

"What's that?" the Booger asked.

"The highway. Want to count cars. Will you take me out?"

"Why, sure," Finney replied expansively. "Why not? A little thing like that – why not?"

"Percy, that's an A1 idea," McKeever said quickly. "I'll join you, we'll both count cars. Will you take me, Tom?"

"Now listen," Finney said uneasily, "I got things to do this a.m., I—"

"Just going along with Percy," McKeever interrupted. "Just a little thing. Give me recreation. I'm kind of upset this morning. You understand, don't you? Sure you do."

"Why, I guess so," Finney replied, becoming expansive again. "Why not? But don't make a habit of it now. Don't be imposing." He smiled benignly.

"You're a good feller, Tom," said Fuller. "We'll wait for you at the truck."

"*Hmmmm*... OK... Well, get my breakfast now." He started out of the room, paused in the doorway, muttered anxiously, "Friendliness, that's all that's needed in the world, a particle of friendliness." He smiled benignly again and departed.

Pavlovsky, McKeever, Fuller gazed at each other in a glow of triumph. Pavlovsky clapped both big hands together and laughed out loud. McKeever jerked his head towards Hanbury in quick warning, and Pavlovsky, interrupting his laugh in mid-flight, humped down over his breakfast tray. Timothy Wright skittered over to them on his spidery legs. He said eagerly, "You ain't eatin' your Wheatena, Stan? I'll eat it."

"Sure, what you think?" Pavlovsky replied. A look of cunning came over his face. "Why you don't dress up, Timmy?"

"Dress up?"

"You're cowboy, aincha?"

"Won the West from the savages, that's all," Timothy replied eagerly. "Billy the Kid, Tom Mix, Wild Bill...* We all had a hand in it."

"You go outside on porch, show rope tricks, Timmy. The ladies wait for you there."

"Ain't got no rope."

"You look back of house? I t'ink I see one."

"A lariat?"

"Piece clothesline."

"Oh, no!" Timothy protested. "Mr Finney don't allow me."

"This is old piece, layin' around. It's OK."

"You sure?"

"Sure."

"You back me up on it?"

"Sure."

"Oh, Jesus Christ," Timothy said with a happy grin, "what fun!" Chattering to himself he ran back to his cot. Fuller leant over to tap Pavlovsky's knee by way of a compliment. A voice said, "Hey!" Marcus Peake, very excited, strode into the room with his breakfast tray and sat down opposite McKeever. His eyes were glistening. "Did I hear right? Booger says he's takin' you out to the main road to count cars."

McKeever nodded and put up a warning finger. "Farmer's there. Watch it."

"Oh, my!" Peake exclaimed happily.

Percy Fuller turned around to check on their enemy. Hanbury had finished his breakfast and had snuggled down again under the covers. "What about him?" he asked softly. "You gotta pack your bag without him noticing."

McKeever shrugged. He drank the last of his lukewarm coffee, smiled at his friends, whispered, "I don't feel like worrying this a.m. I—" He hesitated, fell silent. He had a strong urge to tell them about his experience the night before. All morning he had been pondering over the spirit lights. It was hard to convince himself that they actually had been on his bed, yet he had been left with such a good feeling in his heart that he couldn't help wondering. After all, many learned people believed in the spirit world, not only old ladies. He had read once about two scientists who had exchanged thoughts when one was in Tibet or someplace. Those things were real, they were brainwaves, and everybody knew that all life was molecules and electrons at bottom. On the other hand, when he asked himself if he believed in ghosts or in spirits roaming the world... no, he didn't. He had swallowed enough of those nonsense stories when he was a boy in old Ireland. It was possibly better to keep his mouth shut altogether. For if it turned out that the spirits of his dead mother and his dead sister were really looking after him, trying their best to aid him on his way – why, that was so much to the good, and events would tell. There was no sense in bragging about it – bragging never helped a man climb any hill.

McKeever felt a hand on his knee. Squinting at him, a grin of satisfaction on his face, was Pavlovsky. "Simon, why don't you eat your Wheatena? You need it, you got trip to take." McKeever looked down at his tray. He knew he had eaten his cereal before he drank his coffee, but there on his tray was an untouched bowl of the stuff. "Aw now," he whispered, "I thank you, Stan, but you'll be awful hungry before lunch."

"Who – me? I eat my cereal already," Pavlovsky insisted with delight. "Go ahead now."

Marcus Peake glanced around quickly at Timothy Wright. Then he leant over, grabbed McKeever's empty coffee mug, set it on his own tray, put his own full cup on McKeever's. "I can get another in the kitchen," he whispered quickly. "Go on now, fortify yourself."

"Bunch of coots," McKeever muttered. He wished, wished, wished he could tell them how grateful he was for this support. For two years they had been living together in this Home, friends by compulsion rather than original choice. Each of them would have preferred to live elsewhere, and now he himself was leaving. He was not prepared for this much generosity... including a bowl of cold Wheatena that he didn't want but would certainly have to eat. A friend in need was a friend indeed – how true that was! He dipped his spoon into the Wheatena, grinned fondly at Pavlovsky and began his second breakfast. His mind flashed back sixty years to the cold mornings on the farm when he would sit before the fire in his nightshirt and his sad, work-worn mother would say, "A second bowl of oats, lad? Have it now, it'll put flesh on your thin body, you're growing." Oh, Lord God, if his old mother could only visit back on earth for one morning and teach Ada Finney how to cook a good bowl of oats!

"I'm all ready," a proud voice said. It was Timothy, wearing his ten-gallon hat with boots and spurs and a soiled white handkerchief around his scrawny neck. "Stan – you want to hear how I ambushed Sittin' Bull?"* He posed before one of the mirrors. "Do you?"

"No, Timmy, you go outside, do rope trick on porch."

"Later," said Timothy. "First I'll tell you about Sittin' Bull. I never told you."

"Yes you did," Percy Fuller intervened. He stood up, took the cowboy's arm. "We'll both go out. You'll show me your rope work."

"I'm good," Timothy said amiably. "Copped a prize in a contest once. Where was it, now?" He pinched his nose between thumb and forefinger. "Was it Laredo?"

"Sure, Laredo," said Fuller. He ushered him out quickly.

Peake glanced at his watch. He whispered to McKeever, "Seven forty-five. It'll take you time to get out to the truck. When you gonna pack?"

"Could you fellers lounge in front of me? Won't take me long."

"I got idea," said Pavlovsky. "Listen – *I* pack for you. After you go out, after farmer goes out. You tell me what you want."

"Why, of course! That solves it."

"I've got good head sometimes, right?" Pavlovsky asked happily.

McKeever grinned at him. "There's some stuff in the bag already. I need my sweater, my change of underwear an' my three pairs of socks. My extra shoes are under—" He stopped talking as Hanbury suddenly thrust up in bed and called loudly, "Marcus – what time is it?"

"Seven forty-five."

"Why didn't you call me? You know I'm goin' to my doctor. I wake you up every morning, don't I?" The words were testy, but the voice was not; Hanbury's tone seemed almost humorous.

"I figured to let you sleep late as possible," Peake explained stiffly.

"Thanks, only I wasn't asleep. Ha!" It was a cold, self-satisfied chuckle, devoid of mirth, and McKeever thought to himself, "Why, you barn louse, what do you mean by that?" Delicately the farmer placed his bare feet on the floor. He winced with pain as he stood up to pull off his flannel nightshirt. "No," he said after a moment, "I never sleep when there's things goin' on." He turned towards McKeever with a bony smile. "Fixin' to leave us, ain't you?"

The silence burned. McKeever felt as though his heart had been impaled on a barbed-wire fence. All three conspirators gazed at each other in awful dismay, then they turned back to Hanbury. The farmer disregarded them. Calmly, not even smiling, although they could feel his inward glee, he began to put on his clothes.

McKeever said uncertainly, "What do you mean by that?"

Hanbury smiled thinly, remained silent.

Did he really know? McKeever wondered. How did he know? He said quickly, "Sure, I'm going down to the highway to count cars" – and instantly felt that it was a stupid remark: it would have been better to keep his mouth shut.

Hanbury paused in his dressing. He sat down on the cot, thrusting his bad leg out straight. It was a thin, white, muscular leg with the blue veins prominent under the skin. From above the knee, almost to the ankle, there was a long strip of unhealthy-looking scar tissue, the mark of the accident that had incapacitated him. He began to massage the leg with both hands, and he began to talk. He talked with the irritating, measured exactness of those who are abnormally taciturn and who have rehearsed in their minds whatever they intend to say, repeated it over and over like an actor his lines, and who then deliver it from beginning to end without hesitation or uncertainty. "Figured it all out," he said in his cold, pleased way. "Last night you had your argument with Finney. Told him you was goin'. This morning you changed your mind. Ha! That ain't why others are givin' you their oatmeal an' coffee. Seen it all in my mirror. Or why Joplin was whisperin' to you this a.m. Or why everybody's so excited. Or why you want Finney to drive you out to the main road. Figured it out in my head. Some folks jabber a lot and some folks don't. Some folks got wind in their head and other folks don't. I know *just* what you're fixin' to do."

McKeever stood up, his face pale, his lean jaw thrust forward in anger. "You've figured it out right: I'm going down to LA to get my lameness cured. I want to know from you... *Are you telling the Booger?*"

"Don't know yet," Hanbury said with relish. "Might... might not. Depends." He pushed himself up from his cot and went on with his dressing.

Silence... Pavlovsky took a step forward. His big face turned black with choler. He raised both arms, the fists clenched massively. He was sixty-nine years old, but after a lifetime of rough living he still found violence the solution for a problem. "You tell Booger, I break you in little pieces, I murder you, I send you to horsepital!"

Hanbury laughed out loud. McKeever stared at him and wondered hopelessly how he could appeal to a maverick like that. Hanbury wouldn't scare, and it was clear that he enjoyed being hated. What made him tick? They had questioned the Booger about him, but all he knew of the farmer's history was the accident that had brought him to their Home. Hanbury had been living alone, and one winter day he cranked his tractor without knowing it was in gear. The machine catapulted forward, ran over him and crushed his leg. He lay for a day and a night before someone noticed – a man too tough to die even at seventy. Had he always lived alone? Had he ever married, loved anyone, regarded anyone else with charity? McKeever would have humbled himself willingly before the man provided there was something to be gained by it. So much depended on Hanbury's silence, but how could he reach in to that flinty heart? He didn't know. And so, quietly, his voice trembling a little, he said exactly what he felt: "Hanbury, I hold a man cheap who'll interfere for spite alone in another man's business. A man like that ain't a man, he's just a barn louse."

"Oh!" Hanbury said, turning. The comment evidently had stung. "That's how you want it, eh?"

"Yes," McKeever told him. "Take it or leave it. I ain't asking you any favours."

Hanbury spat on the floor.

McKeever said, "Stan, lift out my bag, will you? I'll pack it now."

Breathing very noisily, his face still swollen with dark blood, Pavlovsky came over, jerked the battered Gladstone bag* from under the cot. "Pack!" he commanded. "He don't do nothing, that farmer. He be scared of me. You see."

Hanbury laughed again. He was standing before a mirror brushing his fine white head of hair. He took his time over it. When he was satisfied with his appearance, he put down the two military brushes and opened a small box on his bed. He took out a polka-dot bow tie, circled it around his collar band, hooked the catch. Then, still examining himself in the mirror, he said blandly, "Mr Peake, give me your shoulder to lean on. I need to go down the hall before I start out."

Joplin cocked his head to one side. "No, I won't! You're a mean old bastard, Hanbury. If it costs me my job here, I won't lift a finger to help you from now on. You're mean… mean… you haven't got the excuse of a rattlesnake – you're just mean. I never met a man like you in my whole life. You're dirt."

Hanbury's thin lips parted a little. It was hard to tell what he was thinking or feeling, because his bone-hard face remained immobile. "Dirt, eh?" he observed coldly. "What's wrong with dirt? A friend, to me – my best… grew money for me. Then I come here and have to live with loafers. Envied me – from the minute I stepped in here, I could see it. McKeever over there, with his talk about labour unions, and that dumb foreigner with his foreign talk, and you – ha – too lazy to get up in the morning to do your job, got to be waked by a man ten years older. Balls to all of you! I never yet met a man I could trust half as well as the pigs on my farm. Pigs don't envy, they don't plot against you and they don't *talk* all the time. Jabber, jabber, jabber… Oh, the wind that's blown through this room, in the last year, my God!" He started out of the room, limping painfully, his lips set thin and hard. But then, as he reached the door, he paused. "You think I'll tell Finney? Why should I? You don't interest me, McKeever. You ain't worth talkin' about. I'm way above all of you – I don't know you're alive." He went out, closing the door quietly.

After a moment Pavlovsky sat down. He said, "I'm son of gun, I don't unnerstand guy like that." And Peake said, "You think we can trust him?"

McKeever threw back his head and laughed with genuine relish. "We'll find out soon enough."

"What if he does tell the Booger?"

"I'll face it when it happens."

"*I* don't trust him," Peake repeated vehemently. "*I* think he's just turning the knife in you. Oh, he's mean! You wait an' see: when you get into the truck, that's when he'll tell the Booger, at the last minute, just to break your heart. Ain't a drop of Christian spirit in him, born without it. Bit his mother's nipples, I bet."

McKeever laughed again. With considerable irritation Peake said, "I don't see why *you* think it's so funny."

"Just remembering," McKeever replied gaily. "I'll tell you a comical story." He began to pack his bag as he talked. "There was a girl in the mattress factory with me during the war, girl about thirty. A big one, kind of a fat face, big behind to her, big titties, kind of a girl should be human and soft with a man. Not her. Had a spring inside her got sprung on the way up. Hated men, but couldn't stop talking about it, always saying something nasty, make a remark, tell everybody she was above men, too good for 'em." He began to laugh again, his blue eyes sparkling over the memory. "Us men used to sit around lunch hour and talk about her. We hated her. She kind of poisoned the whole floor with her nastiness. But after a while we got to speculating. How come she couldn't keep it to herself, made such a show of it? What was she going after so hard anyway? There was a young feller called Georgie Robinson, a bull of a feller, worked alongside her. He said one day, 'I'll fix her.' He went out and bought some pills, I never did find out the name of them. He got into her lunch box when she was out an' dropped those pills in her coffee thermos. Oh my land! Production slowed down that day while we watched. She took to fidgeting and to sighing and to purring and to wiggling and to God knows what. But if I live another life I'll never hope to see a female more in heat. The foreman was in on it too, so he didn't ask questions when she wanted to quit for a while – or when Georgie followed her out to the yard. Well, they didn't either of 'em come back till two days later, and I want to tell you that was a changed female – polite, quiet, decent to everybody and just purring around." McKeever burst out into a bubbling laugh. "Damn it if Hanbury ain't just like that girl. I'm starting to be sorry for him. He hates everything on two legs – but just tell me now, why don't he go off and live by himself? He's got the money. If we're such poison to him, why does he live in a room with five of us, why does he do all that watching in the mirror, all that figuring out – why can't he leave us alone? Oh, Lord God, what living does to the human race!"

"It's time to go," Peake said gloomily. "I still don't trust that farmer, you ain't out of danger. Oh, the whole thing's just reckless as hell."

Pavlovsky said, "So now you really go! Empty bed, great big hole in house. I'm glad for you, sorry for us."

"There's always letters, ain't there?" McKeever suggested eagerly. "We'll pass the news. I'm damn glad you thought of it."

Pavlovsky popped his thumb knuckles, looked unhappy. "I don't write good. I don't write hardly at all."

"The others can write for you."

Peake said fussily, "Get movin', you crab. We'll meet you at the main road with your things."

"You pack everything, sure?" asked Pavlovsky.

McKeever laughed with excitement. "All my worldly goods." He put his soiled panama straw on his head and began to cross to the door. His eyes were sparkling, his thin face was flushed, he couldn't keep a smile from his lips. "Started many a trip in my time," he burst out happily. "Don't know that I was ever so damned excited. Hallelujah, that's what I feel like saying. So I'll say it: hallelujah, lads! Ha-ha!"

Chapter 8

The ride in the Finney truck from the Home to the main highway was cruel to McKeever. His high spirits departed as soon as the pick-up left the driveway. Before that there had been the pleasant moment of coming out on the porch and nodding good morning to the rocking-chair sitters. Amelia Jackson was there as usual, chewing snuff and spitting into a daisy bed when she thought no one was looking, and he wished he might bid her goodbye. He would send her a card from Los Angeles, he thought, one of those picture cards that show a man and a girl on a beach with a spicy saying above it. Amelia would appreciate that. And then there had been a passing moment of shame when the Booger lifted him up on the truck like a sack of potatoes, everybody to see and pity him, because the Booger couldn't wait while he climbed up himself – but even that moment had an exultant side to it this morning, because he knew it was the very last time, and by God if he ever came back for a visit he would give that Booger a kick in the ass just to show how limber his legs had become. A man like a fumbling baby, the Booger, and one minute you pitied him, but the next you hated him – and there were too many times that he had heard the man say "upsy-daisy" in that hearty, hollow tone, with that hearty, hollow laugh, to ever completely forgive him. And then there was the final triumph as the truck rolled off and he waved a casual farewell to the sitters on the porch. At his side was Percy Fuller, grinning over their success. Fuller whispered, "Boy, we made it!" And very jubilantly he replied to Fuller, "We did, didn't we?" But then Fuller said, "What about that damn farmer up front? Saw him whisperin' to the Booger a minute ago, starin' this way, lookin' awful sly, it seemed to me. What do you suppose *he* could have in that chicken brain of his?"

McKeever didn't reply. He was too appalled to bother explaining about his clash with Hanbury. He shrugged his shoulders and set his lips and tried to keep down the nausea of fear that rolled in the soft core of his belly. Was it possible that Hanbury would betray him now? They were two elderly men in a truck, each of them knowing what it meant to suffer – was it conceivable that Hanbury would block him from his cure?

The truck jounced over the uneven macadam road. McKeever sat still and tried not to think or to feel. And when they arrived at the main highway, he closed his eyes for a moment and said a quick little prayer.

Finney stopped at the gravelled edge of a one-pump service station where he bought his gas. Fuller said with great gusto, "Here we are, Simon, over the hump." And Finney, in a hurry as usual, ran around from the front and shouted genially, "Tell you what I'll do, Simon, I'll ask Harvey to give me a coupla chairs out of his house. Upsy-daisy! Then you and Percy can sit in the sun and count autos comfortable as you like."

McKeever scarcely heard what Finney was saying to him. But he knew from his tone of voice that Hanbury had kept his silence and that he had been granted a reprieve. He felt a hot drumming in his ears, and had the sense that a wave of blood was coursing down from his chest to his toes. Fuller said, "Why, thank you, Tom, that's kind of you." McKeever nodded dumbly; he drew a sighing breath and waited for the nervous flutter in his chest to go away. Then, as Finney hurried off into the station, he leant on his cane and laboured forward to the cab of the truck. The window was open where Hanbury sat; his bony face in profile was like a carved stone. McKeever said earnestly, "I'm thanking you from the bottom of my heart, Hanbury. You played me fair."

The farmer turned, snapping out his words. "I keep my feet out of other men's cow shit." He turned away again.

"I hope your leg feels better."

Silence.

McKeever moved off.

Finney came out of the service station with a backless chair and a Coca-Cola box. He dumped them down and bawled loudly, "Be ready for me when I come back, now. Don't wander off somewhere, or I'll never oblige you again, positive." He jumped into the cab, started the motor with a roar and swung the truck around.

They watched it go; it became smaller on the straight road, then disappeared in a shimmer of sun and sparkling air. Fuller clapped his hands in triumph. "Did we or didn't we? What strategy! Oh, I'm achin' to see that Booger's face when he comes back."

"Provided he don't come before a bus," McKeever muttered. "I'm not safe yet."

"Why, you're almost over the county line. What are you lookin' so worried about?"

"Tired, I guess. There's a lot happened this morning."

"Rest yourself." He set up the stool and box so they could lean back against the wall of the service station. "I'll keep an eye peeled for the fellers. You watch the highway for a bus."

McKeever sat down gratefully, pushed his panama back on his head and rested his chin on the knobby end of his walking stick. "I got an idea about Hanbury." He spoke slowly, thinking about it. "You take a kid that has rickets. Everybody knows what that comes from – bad feeding. It's one of the shames of our times. What's the cure? It's economics, ain't it? Well, that's my point. It's one kind of bad living or another that spoils people. Hanbury wasn't born mean. A baby is born like pure silk. What pulls the threads in that silk, knots it up? It's living, ain't it? Rickets an' meanness, they're just two knots in the same piece of string."

"You think too much," Fuller said irrelevantly. "I don't believe in it. When a young feller thinks, he can do somethin' about it. But not us. Thinkin' starts you plannin'; then you want to do somethin'; then you realize you can't do nothin'; it's only an irritation."

They were silent for a few moments. McKeever asked, "See anybody?"

"Of course not. It's a mile walk, ain't it? An' maybe they couldn't sneak out of the house right away. Take it easy." He brought out his can of Half and Half tobacco. "How about a good smoke? A friend of mine just sent this to me."

"That reminds me." McKeever reached into the pocket of his corduroy jacket and took out the second of the two cans that his lucky quarter had bought. His mind whispered "Don't be a fool, Simon, it'll comfort you a lot on your trip", but he said aloud, "Give this to Jop, will you? After I've gone."

"What'll you smoke?"

"I've got some of the Finney Delight."

"That's not fair. Why not split the Half 'n' Half three ways?"

"Let it go, Percy. I want it like that. It's little enough after what you men have done for me."

Fuller smoothed his bald head and considered the equity of the transaction. "OK, Simon." He hawked and spat idly at a beetle crawling over the gravel. "Sun's nice, ain't it?"

"Nice," McKeever agreed. He rubbed his briar against the wings of his nose. They filled their pipes, tamped them down. Percy said luxuriously, "There was an alley back of the chain store I worked at. Noontime the sun came in. I used to eat my lunch there. When I think back on my life, that's one of the best things I remember – that half-hour every day, back to the wall, sun on my face. My wife used to make good sandwiches." He mused for a moment, then added: "I liked my job a lot. The customers got to depend on me. They'd ask me to recommend things. Like a new cereal or a kitchen soap. I wish I was doin' it right now."

"I loved to work," McKeever said. "My, how I loved starting a new job! An' when we got finished – maybe two months, maybe six – always a big beer party."

They lit their pipes and leant their heads back against the wall. McKeever took off his old panama and rested it on his knee. "See this hat? Bought it the day I went up to be interviewed for the mattress factory. I was nervous kind of – my first real job since the Depression pushed me out of the oil line... if you don't count the WPA,* that is. A snappy hat always made me feel good."

"Ever wear silk pyjamas?"

"No."

"My wife kept wanting me to, nagged me. Funny. I bought some once. Didn't like 'em, felt like a damned female. Went to pieces fast, too, wasn't worth the money. Wonder why they make all that fuss over 'em?"

"Economics, it's the old dollar bill. It was the same thing with the Meat Trust.* Do you remember the scandal? Upton Sinclair exposed it in his book.* Ever read it? He told 'em off. Give me another match."

Harry Kilgore, the young veteran who owned the service station, came outside and said "Hi, there" to Fuller.

"How you doin', bridegroom?"

"Will you mind things for me a while? I need to run up to my shack."

"Sure. How's your wife?"

"Ain't divorced me yet. Holler if somebody wants a hundred-dollar rear-end job, will ya?"

"Holler? I'll scream like an old woman." Fuller laughed, and Kilgore laughed, and Fuller called after him, "Say – you seen any Greyhound bus in the last little while, goin' south?"

"Ain't noticed one." He went off quickly.

"That's a nice boy," Fuller observed. "I hope he makes a go of it. Got a red-haired wife like a little china doll. Must be lonely for 'em here."

"You know something? I should've married again. Greatest mistake of my life."

"Why didn't you?"

"I don't know. Maybe if I'd stayed in one place… But it was a roaming life, that's the oil line, lot of unmarried men in it… Say, I wonder where the boys are? I'm getting awful worried." He stared fretfully down the road.

"Take your time, we only been here a little while." Fuller suddenly became loquacious. "*My* biggest mistake was to stay put in that chain store. Thought I was smart to snuggle up to a big outfit, have security; had a hope of becoming a district manager.

1932 came along, an' they curtailed expenses. I was curtailed all right, cut my nuts off me, lost my house with only eight months to pay on it. If I had those years over again, I'd set up my own grocery store, independent, I'd take a gamble. I had a dandy tool-room in the cellar of my house, Simon, used to build lovely garden chairs, lovely, an' rabbit hutches for the kids in the neighbourhood. Could've been workin' in the toolroom right this minute. That's what comes from not havin' enough nerve. I could've been a prosperous man, I bet. Say, Simon" – he opened his mouth, laughed a little, showed his yellow, broken-down teeth – "you ever find yourself thinking it'd be nice to lay on a woman just once more?" A flush of colour rose in his pasty cheeks. "Do you?"

McKeever rubbed the hump of his nose, grinned a little, looked sly. "Think about it most every day. I like to."

"Think you could?"

"Not any more. Too much exercise involved, ha-ha."

"I could. At least I think I could. In the early morning sometimes when I just wake up."

"How old are you, Percy?"

"Sixty-seven."

"Don't see why not, then. One year durin' the war, that was when I was sixty-nine going on seventy, I had a steady woman twice a week, my landlady, Wednesday night and Sunday afternoons."

"Honest? You braggin'?"

"Not braggin'!" He looked at Fuller, whistled quickly, said with a laugh, "Braggin' a little. It was once a week more often than twice. That factory job tired me."

"How did it come about?" Fuller asked with excitement. "How'd you make the grade?"

McKeever, pursuing a memory, said with a chuckle, "You know something? Once I worked for a building contractor called Ollie Johnson. He got married a second time when he was your age. Woman under thirty, a pippin. Ollie had three grown children already, an' got himself four more. I heard lately he lived to be ninety-seven an' died in swimming."

"But you, now," Fuller insisted, "how did it come about? With that landlady?"

"Just happened, you know how those things are. I gave her the eye an' she gave it back, an' one thing led to another till we ended up snuggling."

"Ain't happened to me for nine years, not since my wife died," Fuller said ruefully. "How old was she?"

"Oh... forty-five or so, quite young, a widow. Always favoured older men, she told me, some females are like that. Say, is that Stan off there? Oh my, I'm sure relieved! But I don't see Jop."

"He'll come. Was she nice, Simon?"

"Who? My, yes! Cheerful woman, good cook. Used to give me Sunday dinner. I liked her a lot."

"I mean in bed?"

"Well, no complaints. Kind of thin." He glanced slyly at Fuller. "Don't know about you, but I always liked plenty of woman. I wonder where Jop is?"

"Oh," Fuller said. "Oh, if I could only have a piece of luck like that! Them old bags up at the Home, they don't raise me up at all. I get so ashamed – you know what I want? Why, them sixteen-year-olds you see prancin' down the street. They're just so sweet an' lovely they put a lump in my throat. Even if I could, I wouldn't touch one of 'em – it'd be wrong, wicked, wouldn't it? Oh, Lord, guess I have to be resigned, don't I?" He laughed suddenly. "I'm a jackass. Got a weak heart, sixty-seven years old, oughta be deep-ashamed of myself. Old Harry* oughta be dead in me. Wonder why he ain't? Wonder if it's just mental? I read about that. Gettin' senile, maybe, like Timothy. It's a curse. Everything was quiet for a while, but now it ain't. Worries me to death."

McKeever said fondly, "You're a damn fool, Percy. That isn't anything to worry yourself about. It's nature."

"You think so?"

"There ain't no regular time for a man or woman to give out." He slapped his knee with satisfaction. "There's Jop now! I see him, down the road by those trees."

"There ain't? I always heard so. I thought by the time I was sixty it'd all be over an' done with."

McKeever burst out laughing. "You got some bad ideas, Percy, unscientific. You ought to go to the library, read a book on it."

"On what?"

"On sex. Ain't you ever done that? Biology's a big interest of mine. Always wished I could've studied it in school. How things reproduce themselves, it's wonderful. Certain female spiders, now, they eat the male once the job is done, imagine. That's what's tickling you, Percy, just natural sex. Your heart's weak, but your Old Harry ain't."

"Oh my, yes," Fuller said severely. "I'd like to see myself walk into some library, ask some young girl for a book on sex! Ha-ha! Wouldn't have the nerve in a thousand years. At my age?"

"You never can tell the outcome," replied McKeever, laughing again. "Might be some soft-eyed widow there get interested in you, give you the bedroom look. Oh Lord, Percy, I always knew you were ignorant on labour unions; now I find you're ignorant on sex too. Why, they're two of life's fundamentals!"

"Ain't ignorant about labour unions at all," Fuller retorted peevishly. "Don't like 'em. Rackets. Pay dues for nothing."

McKeever stood up, laughing hard, as Stan Pavlovsky approached them. Pavlovsky was walking fast, his body hunched over so that he could squint down at the road and see where he was going. "We're right here, Stan," McKeever called to him. Pavlovsky looked up eagerly; he blinked against the bright light and swung the Gladstone bag up and down as though it weighed half an ounce. "Got'm here," he boomed. "Ada Finney don't see me. Sneak out good. Ha-ha!"

"Godsake!" Fuller yelled sharply. "There's a bus coming!"

"Where?"

"There – half a mile maybe – by that patch of trees."

"How do I know it's mine?"

"It's sure a Greyhound. They all go your way. I'll run out an' flag it."

"I can't go without my money," McKeever reminded him excitedly. "Jop's got it. Sixty-one cents. My fare."

Fuller waved his arms. "Yell to him. Make him run. Next one might be two, three hours – the Booger might come back." He rushed out to the roadside and began waving his arms at the still distant bus.

Peake was three hundred yards down the side road. McKeever funnelled his mouth between his hands and shouted his loudest. "Jop – oh Jop!… Jo–*op!* Bus coming. *Bus! Run!*" Peake heard only the voice, not the words; he waved back amiably but continued at a walk. Stan Pavlovsky took it up, in instantaneous anger at Peake. His bass voice, issuing ferociously from the great cavern of his chest, rocketed over the landscape. "Hey, you dummy – bus come! God damn it, *run! I* bust your head – *run!*"

Peake heard, and he broke into a dogtrot. He was carrying Percy Fuller's overcoat, and he wrapped it into a bundle so that he could carry it like a football. Pavlovsky strode up to the highway and squinted against the bright sunlight. He couldn't see the bus as yet, but he could hear the whine of its heavy tyres in the distance. "Hey, Percy!" he suddenly commanded Fuller. "Go out in road. Stand in middle. Don't let goddamn bus go by."

"The hell you say," Fuller retorted shrilly. "You think I'm crazy – think I'm a friggin' squirrel?"

Frustrated in this direction, Pavlovsky turned around, yelled fiercely, "Hey you, Jop, why you no *run?* God damn it, whatsmatter you?"

"He's running – take it easy, you coot," McKeever said with a laugh. "Nothing to worry about – all on schedule."

The bus driver had seen Fuller's animated gestures, and he was slowing down. But despite McKeever's optimism, it was clear to Fuller that the big Greyhound would arrive before Marcus Peake. He turned around and yelled anxiously, "Can you make it any faster, Jop?" Peake, two hundred and fifty yards away now, didn't quite get the words. He gestured with his free hand and continued his steady dogtrot. Then he heard Pavlovsky's booming voice: "Faster, God damn it! Run, you lazy son'mbitch! Whatsmatter you?" Peake became very angry. He was in good physical condition for a man of sixty-three, but he had not had the occasion to run a distance like this for years. The moment he started running, it occurred to him that it was back in a sandlot football game in 1916 that he had last run more than a few yards. He made a quick decision that a dogtrot was as fast a pace as he could manage without risking a collapse. Pavlovsky's uncomplimentary remarks, rocketing over the whole countryside, became more and more exasperating to him. He was doing the best he could, indeed he was already wheezing and pumping, and why couldn't the damn fool let him alone? He remembered something then that complicated his anger. The last time he had done any serious running was not in 1916, but in 1919, during a strike. He had thrown a rotten tomato at a company policeman, and the man had chased him with a swinging club for half a mile, yelling in a booming voice just like Pavlovsky's. Hearing his friend now made him angry at that cop all over again, and angry at Pavlovsky, and he had an impulse to throw down the overcoat and quit. But he continued his little dogtrot, and Pavlovsky continued to spur him on with his boilermaker's voice.

The Greyhound braked to a stop in front of the service station, almost a dozen yards from McKeever, and he started his slow crawl for the open door. Percy Fuller, quite forgetting his heart condition, ran on the double quick to speak to the driver. "Passenger for Stockton, you going there?" He waved one arm towards McKeever and pointed the other down the road.

The driver was a blond young man of thirty, thickset, amiable. The old man standing in the road with sweating face and waving arms looked funny to him. He said with amusement, "Couldn't hardly miss Stockton, Pop – not 'less I flew over it. Hop up!"

"Not me – him!" Percy replied, waving both arms back towards McKeever. "Take him a few minutes to get here."

The driver stepped to the doorway for a look. He asked softly, "Is that his best speed?"

"Arthureetis," Percy explained. "Goin' down to LA for a cure."

"Thought you said he was going to Stockton?"

"Gonna hitch-hike the rest."

"Him?" the driver asked. "Hitch?" He returned to his seat, shoved in a gear and ran the bus slowly back to McKeever.

"Why, thank you, young man," McKeever called. "You're very kind." His mouth worked for a moment as he tried to think of something else to say that would eat up a little time, but the driver asked "Want any help up the steps?", and it broke his train of thought. "Why, no, thank you, don't need help," he replied with airy confidence. "Just stiff in the legs." He made no move to enter the bus. Instead, prompted by the same thought, all three old men turned to see how Marcus Peake was doing. He was not doing well. A hundred and twenty yards away from them still, he was perceptibly slowing down.

McKeever muttered quickly, "Stan – run out to him. Relay it."

"Run? I no can run," Pavlovsky muttered in return. "Can't see damn thing when I run – fall flat on puss."

"*I* certainly can't run," Fuller muttered defensively. "Like to kill me."

The driver, slightly perplexed by these antics, called impatiently, "Say mista – you coming or aren't you? This ain't the pony express." A number of passengers laughed at the remark, and he grinned back at them in appreciation, indicating by a helpless shrug that he was not responsible for everyone they met on the road.

With sudden craft McKeever said, "Why, of course I'm coming. Didn't stop you out of foolishness. But my bag now – it goes in the baggage department, doesn't it? You have to stow it away, don't you?"

"Not if you're only going to Stockton," answered the driver. "I'll keep it in front with me. Hand it up."

"Now, ain't that an important piece of information! I never knew that before, did you, Percy? Well, go ahead, Stan. Hand up the bag. Don't waste the gentleman's time. He's in a hurry."

Pavlovsky turned cunning. He carried the bag up the steps. "It goes in back someplace?" he enquired eagerly. "I put it away for you?"

"Just drop it right there."

"You don't want I put for you somewhere? Is heavy – get in way."

A look of bewilderment played over the young man's face. In a final gesture of patience he asked courteously, "Are *you* going to Stockton too?"

"No – only him."

"Then, please, just put the bag down. Thank you. Now you go out and let the other man come in."

"*Hm!* Not many peoples in bus today," the half-blind Pavlovsky said comfortably as he stepped down. "You get good seat, Simon." In point of fact, the bus was almost full, and the driver began to feel he was dealing with idiots. He said firmly, "Pop – I've wasted too much time already. Either you come into the bus right now or I'll throw your bag out."

Joplin was still eighty yards away, pushing himself in a kind of jerky walk rather than a run. "Listen, young man," McKeever said in despair, "you see that poor old man running so hard down the road?"

"What about him?"

"He's got my money – that's why we're delaying you."

The driver stared. Then he threw back his head and laughed with delight. "Why didn't you let me know? Tell him to slow down before he kills himself. Oh, my God!"

"You're a very decent young man," McKeever told him with enormous relief.

"Well brought up," Fuller added. "Stan – quick, help Jop out."

Pavlovsky started off instantly, head down. "One jiffy," he yelled, "right back, driver."

"Can't see well, poor feller," McKeever explained. "Got cataracts – that's eye trouble."

The driver grinned. "Is that so? Suppose you come in now, Pop. We'll get that over with, anyway." He stood up to give McKeever a hand.

"You're doing a great thing by waiting, young feller, a small thing to you, maybe, but very important to me... I don't need any help, thank you. Just take my stick." He handed it up and began hoisting himself with slight grunts from step to step. "Very important I make this bus, you see. A later one might be too late. I can't explain, but it's so. These steps ain't bad at all. Some steps are, but not these."

"Take that seat by the door. It's empty."

"Thank you, I will." Instead McKeever turned around to peer down the road. Fifty yards away Pavlovsky and Peake were at the point of meeting. Peake stopped where he was and held out the overcoat in speechless fatigue. His face was milky white, covered with runnels of sweat.

"Whatsmatter?" Pavlovsky asked. "You tired? You no run so fast, you damn slow. Almost lose bus."

Peake was not so weary that he couldn't express himself. "Go crap," he said with simple bitterness. Pavlovsky wheeled around, offended, and went off haughtily. Ten yards down the road he stopped, yelled frantically, "Money! You dope – you forget money."

"In the pocket," Peake replied. He waved him on again, with infinite disgust. Then, pulling himself together, he followed on trembling legs. He wanted urgently to say goodbye to McKeever and he wanted thanks from somebody. It seemed to him that he had run pretty well for a man of sixty-three.

At the bus McKeever was having much the same thought. He could see that the driver might pull out before Joplin arrived, and he said to Percy Fuller, who was sitting beside him, "Listen now – you tell Jop I thank him a million times. Not just the money, that I'll pay him back, but everything. All of you now, you been friends in need."

"Have a good trip," Fuller said emotionally. "Get cured up, we're betting on you. An' come back to visit us sometime."

"Oh, I will," McKeever replied fervently. They shook hands with tremulous excitement. "I will that."

The driver said to Fuller, "Let's go, Pop," as he saw Pavlovsky approach. He started his motor and raced it a bit by way of making things clear. Fuller ran down the steps in time to let Pavlovsky climb in with the overcoat.

"Money in pocket," Pavlovsky whispered, "Jesus Christ, I hope you get cure, Simon, I hope." He squeezed McKeever's hand in both of his. "You been a good friend, Stan," McKeever told him very emotionally.

"Here we go," said the driver. He shoved in a gear and started the bus. Pavlovsky scrambled down and the driver shut the door.

McKeever pressed his face to the dirty window. He could see Joplin waving to him. He waved back and muttered tremulously, "Bye, fellers… thanks." And then, as their faces were cut off from his view by the movement of the bus, he leant his head back against the cushion and shut his eyes. He listened to the hum of the tyres as the bus picked up speed, and he thought of his three friends back there on the road, and he felt as though he would burst at the seams with gratitude.

Chapter 9

The bus driver said amiably, "Well, Pop, let's pay the fare now. Santabello to Stockton is ninety-five cents."

McKeever sat erect and blinked his eyes. The night before Pavlovsky had told him the fare would be eighty-five cents at most. He had not thought to check the information. Obviously there had been a rate change over the year, and now he was ten cents short. He reflected that his adventure was turning out to be quite lively – oh, very lively indeed.

"You hear me, Pop?"

McKeever's mouth worked for a moment, then he said, "I wonder if you could spare me a road map? Might happen I'd make a stopover before Stockton. Got some business to handle."

"What town?"

"If you'd let me have a map—"

"I know the road like my face. You tell me where you want to get off and I'll tell you the fare."

McKeever's mouth worked again, and he was silent for so long that the driver half-turned to look at him. "You're not trying to do a job on me, are you?" he asked with soft amusement. "I can't let you ride for free."

"Why, certainly not! Just trying to remember the name of that town." His forefinger rubbed the hump of his nose, and he peered at his young antagonist out of the corner of his eye. "I recollect it was just the other side of the county line."

"Lodi! Is that where you want to go?"

"You sure it's the other side of the county line?"

"This is Santabello County, Lodi's in San Joaquin County." He grinned a little. "You sound like the sheriff's after you."

McKeever grinned back, although the hackles were rising on his neck. "Robbed a bank. Ain't paid my alimony neither. I'm wanted on two counts."

The driver laughed. "Santabello to Lodi is fifty cents."

Lodi! There flashed into McKeever's mind an image of a large building, a rainy day during one of the Depression years of the Thirties and a stout man with a liquor-veined nose who had refused him a job. He said to the driver, "Ain't there a big winery near Lodi?"

"Just the other side."

"Exactly where I want to go!" To make his story more plausible, he added: "I have an old friend there. Fifty cents, eh? Have it for you in a minute."

The driver half-turned around again. He asked softly, "Just between me an' you, Pop" – he turned back to the road again. "How in hell do you figure to hitch-hike to LA?"

"Well, why not? I've hitched all over the States when I had to."

"When?"

"Right down the years."

"Since you been crippled up?"

McKeever's voice turned peevish. "What's the difference between sitting in a bus or a private car? You tell me that!"

The driver didn't reply, and McKeever stared with sudden annoyance at his wide back. He was familiar with the stupidity of the young towards the old, but he never could accept or forgive it. He recalled the nosy lady in the Los Angeles zoo during the war. She had spoken to him as though they were old friends – such crust! "My, it's a hot day for you, ain't it, Grandpa?"

"No hotter for me than for you," he had replied as civilly as he could.

"Oh, but it is! You're *elderly*! Why don't you sit in the shade for a while? My grandmother died of a sunstroke, so I know. Elderly people can't take the sun."

"I may be elderly," he replied in a pleasant tone, "but I don't have to wear a heavy girdle around my fat ass. That keeps me nice and cool." Ha-ha! Such a face as she skittered off. The idiot!

He unfolded Percy Fuller's overcoat. In one of the side pockets there were some hard bulges... oranges. He muttered, "Oh my!" How like Joplin to walk into the kitchen under the cold eye of Ada Finney and snitch oranges for him. Three of them – now he would have his lunch for the road, and oranges were high in vitamins, too. In the other pocket he found an envelope pinned to the cloth. He opened it – there was a note, some change and a dollar bill. The note said:

DEAR SIMON,

I figur you might as well owe me a dollar more. You need some eatin money. Get fixed up. Come see us sometim.

MARCUS

McKeever counted the money. There was a dollar and sixty-one cents. He sighed and felt a lump forming in his throat, and swallowed and sighed again. It was just as well that he had been unable to say goodbye to Joplin. What could he have said to him? Not "thanks" – it was not the word. Behind this dollar bill was Joplin's fear of the County Poorhouse, and Joplin writing two letters a week to big corporations, asking for a job, only to get back the same polite answer that his name would be put on a list – and Joplin glad each morning that he was a day older, because in two years he would be sixty-five. A hundred pennies in this dollar bill, and each one heavy with sweat and worry. And what could you say to a man who gave you a gift like that? You could only feel it with your pores. "Got my fare right here," he called.

The driver leant towards him and held out his hand. "You want to get off at the bus station or the winery?"

"The winery. That's where my friend is."

"Right."

"How far to LA from there?"

"About three hundred seventy-eight."

"Ain't much at all," McKeever exclaimed with satisfaction. He felt quite triumphant; he wished the boys had been there to see him handle the driver. "I made nine hundred miles once in a single hop."

The driver remained silent.

"Ever do any hitch-hiking?"

"I'm not supposed to talk, Pop."

"A good rule, too many accidents." McKeever turned around to the passenger sitting behind him. "How far you going, neighbour?"

The man shook his head, pointed to his ear.

"Can't you hear?"

The man smiled woodenly, and McKeever turned forward again thinking, "What a misfortune!" He had always wondered about such people, how they felt about life. Those who were born crippled, for instance. Life was very sad sometimes, and there was no way to whistle about it or to make it right... The bus slowed down abruptly, and he leant forward to peer out of the front window. Ahead of them a dilapidated truck, the rear jam-packed with lambs, was turning slowly off the road to a gravel lot. A number of cars were parked on the lot before a two-storey building that had a sign across its façade: AUCTION EVERY TUESDAY. As they passed, he saw a young calf trussed up in the luggage compartment of a car, its eyes enormous with fright. "Why, you poor thing," he murmured aloud. "Scared to death, ain't you?"

The bus driver said "What?" and McKeever didn't reply. He sat very still and felt a warmth rising into his cheeks. He had become aware, recently, of his habit of talking aloud. He was deeply ashamed of it. "You say something?" the bus driver asked again.

"Nope."

The driver nodded and stepped on the gas. McKeever looked back at the pens along the side of the building. Horses and cows, pigs and sheep. And inside were men at work, men come to buy and to sell. He envied them, he envied anyone who had a good day's work to do.

He stared at the even rows of vineyard. The wide field slipped by fast against the speed of the bus. Old vines, he thought. They were gnarled, thicker than a man's fist, and it made him wonder how many grapes those vines had borne and how many times a man had bent his back to snip and prune and pick the harvest, each little grape juicy and perfect, money in his hand. It made him glow to think of it. There wasn't a spot on earth that didn't have a man's fingerprint on it. Run along a road, and it was men who laid the road and drilled the oil to keep the tyres humming fifty miles an hour; and right ahead there was a motel that men's hands had built; and now an old graveyard built by men for men to lie in; and a goat tethered by one of the stones that a man milked twice a day for his kids to drink their nourishment – oh, Lord, what a monument to the bent back and the skilled hand and the quick brain this old world was! A man could feel proud of being part of the human race, even though it included a farmer like Hanbury. McKeever laughed a little over the thought and said to himself, "Good joke." And then he remembered that he had not yet written down his additional debt to Joplin. He fumbled in his pocket and brought out his notebook and pencil stub. He found the page. The night before he had written, "Marcus Peake, 61¢." He wrote now $1.00, drew a line under it and put the sum, $1.61. Bless Marcus! He had paid his bus fare, but still he had a dollar and thirty-five cents. It occurred to him that the sum would pay his way a hundred miles further down the road. He considered this for a moment, but then dismissed it. He would need a bus fare in Glendale and money for his supper and fifteen cents to telephone the Church at Seal Beach on the matter of a loan. "Much better to hitch," he murmured aloud, "make it by tonight surely, an' see that doctor..." He became aware that he was talking aloud again, and he winced with embarrassment. It was an awful habit for a man to pick up, he would have to watch himself. And thinking this, he remembered his appointment with the nurse, Sarah Kahn! He muttered "Oh, damn it!" and resolved that the minute he got into Stockton he would send her a postcard. Lovely girl. It was too bad he would miss seeing her.

The tyres whined, the bus rocked easily, the countryside slipped past. He wondered what this Doctor Balzer was like and what she would say to him. And presently he slipped into a daydream of the moment when he would throw away his cane and walk down the street like a human being. What joy! Somehow a man never relished his health when he had it. Or the real goodness of living. How many, many times he had walked a hillside, checking a line of pipe in the earth, and never once had paused to breathe deep, to look with pleasure at a racing cloud, to watch a busy ant carry its white egg up a tree. It was another of the mistakes he had made – like not getting married a second time. A life seemed full of these errors, and a man wished he could live a few years over again just to live them right. Very well, he suddenly decided – although it was not likely that he would ever marry again, he could certainly open his eyes and savour the world through every waking minute! He *would* do it! Here and now, he was making a resolution. It was never too late for a man to improve himself.

He pressed his face to the window and stared hungrily at the countryside. There, he thought, that peach orchard, lovely trees in straight lines, their branches so heavy with green fruit. Thinning season was about due, men climbing ladders and swarming all over, tearing off half the peaches. Nature was wasteful – let all the fruit ripen, and its weight would break the limbs. But oh Lord, the man-made waste he had seen that August up around Goleta! Measuring the lemons for size with that little gadget, the foreman rejecting half of them because they wouldn't bring a high price. There must have been half a million good lemons rotting on the ground of that one ranch alone. And Europe so hungry, children getting the scurvy because of a lack of lemons. Or was it the lack of fresh meat that caused scurvy? Or was that pellagra? Anyway, the world needed a pound of fixing, and he'd always maintained it… That pussy cat there, standing in that field, cute. When he got working again, it might not be a bad idea to get himself a cat. They were easy to keep in a room.

McKeever leant back and closed his eyes. It was hard to keep watching a racing landscape, but he had no complaints to offer. He had been travelling mighty slow for two years. "Oh, damn it, my medicine!" he muttered aloud. Was there anything else he had forgotten to pack? His reading spectacles? No, he remembered putting them in the bag. And that book to read. He would have to check over his things at Lodi.

He reflected now that in a curious way the story of his life lay in the reasons he had packed a bag for trips. After his mother died, that was the first time: leaving his sister on the farm, and off to London at sixteen... Oh, what an exciting journey, the world so big and him so ignorant of it! And packing again three years later to come to America – 1892 that was, golden year; glad he did it, still glad to this day – a better land than there was anywhere on earth, with only the sorrow that he hadn't left children to walk on it. And packing six years later to join the army, sailing all the way to Cuba. But a bad war, the hand of Wall Street at work, he'd seen it. Ah, if a man were only ten years younger, he could ship out on a freighter and see if Luis, the saloon keeper, was still alive, and look over what was stirring. But he had no trust in the sugar interests, he'd tell anybody that, he'd take no promises from those robbers even on a stack of Bibles. And then the time he had packed up his single life for a walk down the aisle with his sweet darling Mary. There was sunlight through the stained-glass window behind the altar, and Ollie Johnson for his best man, and Mary's upturned face, her cheeks flushed, her eyes so radiant as he put the ring on her finger. But oh, later, the ache in his heart when he packed up again in the shambles of his home, his sweet ones lying scarred beneath the muddy brown earth. And packing to roam the land from job to job, following the derricks and the refineries and the smell of oil, Pennsylvania to Oklahoma and across to California, Seal Beach and Signal Hill and up and down the Valley – packing to get jobs and packing when the job was done. Lord, what a life of memory there was in a few old suitcases! He leant his head back and smiled a little. He listened to the whine of the tyres and presently he was asleep.

* * *

The driver called "Here we are, Pop, here's your stop", and McKeever awakened with a quick-beating heart. He was over the county line! That Booger could go whistle now: Simon McKeever was safe from writs and sheriffs and legal skulduggery. Sweet, sweet, sweet the grapes of victory! He only wished he could see the Booger's face when he returned to the service station. Perhaps it was cheap of him to feel so pleased, but it was his own good money the Booger had spent, money that would have taken him right down to Glendale. Now he was even, and he was damned if he'd feel sorry for the Booger. Him and his "upsy-daisy!"

The driver picked up McKeever's bag and carried it down to the road. He waited with decent forbearance while McKeever moved towards the door. "Want to give me that overcoat, Pop?"

With a nod of gratitude McKeever handed it down and extended his cane as well. Grunting, he swung his stiff hips from side to side and lowered himself to the concrete.

"I've lost time, Pop, otherwise I'd carry this stuff over to the winery for you."

"You run along. I'm much obliged to you – much."

The driver gave him his cane and dropped the overcoat on the grassy bank that ran alongside the road. He said with a grin, "You been an awful nuisance."

McKeever smiled back. "I didn't do you any solid harm, did I?"

The driver laughed and jumped the steps.

"What time is it?"

"Nine forty."

The door shut, a gear scraped and the big Greyhound went off, saying farewell in a cloud of smoke. McKeever watched it go. He jingled the coins in his pocket, grinned and felt wonderful. Three hundred and seventy-eight miles to LA, and it was not yet ten in the morning. The sun was warm, the blue sky clear, and his legs felt good. Those spirit lights he had seen the night before might have been the work of his imagination, but something was smoothing his way. He certainly didn't believe in magic, but when the stars were on a man's side it was pure vanity not to feel grateful.

He heard the hum of an approaching auto. It was going in the wrong direction. He watched it pass and said aloud, just for the fun of it, "Going the wrong way, mister – turn around for me." He laughed and pushed his panama back on his forehead. He wondered if the man who had once refused him a job at the winery was still there. By the memory of his cucumber nose he was long ago in a grave from cirrhosis of the liver. He had always pitied men with a habit like that. It was one more problem that a grown-up society would handle, like rickets and meanness. The winery looked prosperous, he thought. It was early in the season, and it appeared to be shut down, but it had been making money, he could tell by its new coat of paint. A good job, smooth finish – he liked a job like that.

A car hummed, coming his way. He faced it eagerly, holding out his hand, thumb upraised. It came close, running fast, a shabby Ford with a dent in one fender. It passed by without slowing down, and the driver kept his eyes on the road.

"Number one," McKeever said aloud. He decided it would be interesting to count the number of cars that passed him by. He would give himself ten, perhaps twelve, before he was picked up.

A bird piped suddenly – a high, clear note – and McKeever turned to search for it. He spied it on a fence post just behind him, an odd bird, new to him. It was plump, the size of a large robin, with a brown body, black speckles on its brown wings and a yellowish, fat breast. He wished he knew its name. It was a saucy, darling bird with a flirting little tail that kept wiggling up and down as it chirped. "Morning," he said aloud. "A nice day, ain't it?" The bird flipped its tail, pecked with its long beak for the lice in its wing.

He turned and stuck up his thumb. This one was an oil truck bearing down like thunder, and he didn't have much hope of it. He stepped back in a sudden fret of anxiety as it rolled past. Two yards seemed small security against a monster like that. Well, that was number two.

He turned back to the bird. It was gone. The wide field behind was covered with tomato vines, the supporting sticks marshalled in rows like soldiers at drill, the tomatoes green, hard, small as marbles. They would be bursting with juice by August, he thought, red and heavy if they let them vine-ripen. Tomatoes were a hard crop to pick, all of the stoop crops. City people didn't think of that when they bought tomatoes or peas in a store – he never had. Testaments to the bent back, every little pea. Ha-ha – every little pea means a pain in someone's ass. Not bad. He had awakened on his witty side this a.m.

Number three was coming up. This one was his, he felt sure, a salesman's coupé – those fellows were always glad for company. The young salesman glanced at him with vacant face and turned away. Oh, well, he thought, it was only number three.

For ten minutes or so the cars were northbound. McKeever took off his hat and his corduroy jacket and placed them with his overcoat. The day was becoming warmer, and he could feel the good heat seeping into his marrow. He felt grateful for this clement weather. It had been a long winter, damp and windy; he needed to bake out for a few months.

A string of cars swept down on him. He held out his hand, thumb jutting, and muttered eagerly, "Going down?... Los Angeles?... Bakersfield?" Four, five, six... The cars passed him by. He felt keenly disappointed, and it occurred to him that he had made a mistake in not getting off at Lodi. It was always better to thumb a car on the edge of a town; traffic moved slowly there, and a driver was more inclined to stop. Out here the road was straight and flat, and they went by like thunderbolts. Live and learn. He would stuff his pipe with some of that Finney Delight and enjoy the sun. Plenty of time, only ten in the morning or thereabouts.

He smoked and he raised his thumb – he was alternately eager and disappointed. Traffic was slow. He remembered the Depression time in 1934, when he had decided to try for work in the Oklahoma oil fields. He was sixty-one then, but limber and quick on his feet, and he knew he could handle any pipe-fitter's job that came along:

underground or a hundred feet up, he'd spit and take over. He had thumbed his way across Arizona into New Mexico, but there he bogged down in a jerkwater town* in the middle of nowhere. It was blazing hot in the day, raw cold as only a desert can be at night, and his money dribbled away on hamburgers while he waited two whole days from dawn to midnight in the hope of a car. There were others waiting with him – single men, couples and families – all of them strung out along the road, afraid to walk because the next town was forty desolate miles away. No one of them ever got a lift. A state trooper came along finally, and they found out there had been a murder on the road, a woman raped and cut up by a hitch-hiker. It had been a headline case in the papers all the previous week. McKeever went off into the brush, changed his good suit for a pair of jeans and hopped a freight train. He was afraid of freights, because he had travelled that way once, and a railroad dick* had kicked him off at twenty miles an hour. But he knew that if he didn't get out of that town by rail, he'd starve to death, and sometimes he wondered what had happened to the other poor suckers, and whether they weren't buried there. He hoped he hadn't run into a situation of that sort now.

He smoked and swore pleasantly at the bitter sharpness of the Finney tobacco. The cars passed him by, and time wore on, and he began to feel weary. He crossed to the bank of grass and sat down.

A brown field mouse, with something white clamped in its jaws, ran across the road towards him. When it was almost upon him, it veered off in a burst of fear. McKeever laughed with pleasure. "No arthureetis there," he murmured aloud.

He looked up at the rumble of a truck and waved his cane towards Los Angeles. The driver gestured that he was turning off. "Thank you," McKeever said, "friendly anyway... Lots of sourpusses this morning."

He sat for a while, and then he stood up. And after a while he sat down again. He plucked a weed and cleaned his pipe with the stem. He wiped his face on his sleeve and put on his hat. When cars passed, he raised his cane, and each time he felt a surge of eagerness followed by disappointment. He reached into his pocket, took out the first coin that met his fingers and looked at the date. It was 1931. He said to himself, "Well now, what were you doing in 1931, lad? It'll help pass the time to think about it." And then he murmured aloud, "A good idea. Yes. *Hm!*" He pondered the date. His brain remained vacant. He had found, before this, that the years between 1930 and 1938 were not always easy for him to sort out. In 1930 he was on a refinery job outside Los Angeles, and construction was shut down in the middle, the men laid off, the pipes and girders left to rust... He remembered *that* date all right! He could remember the events of 1938, also, because in the spring he had settled down in Santabello on a WPA park job. But the years in between were a blur – rootless years, scrounging a job here and a room there, a hundred small jobs and a hundred small rooms, and sometimes no job at all and only the earth and the sky for his room. He had sold his car, eaten up his savings, pawned his goods – but he had never gone on the relief dole, and never once had he stood shamefaced on a corner and begged for a handout. "Never," he murmured now at a passing truck. He was willing to admit that it was a false pride, because ten million good men had been forced to do one or the other; but he was proud of himself anyway. And he had accomplished a lot of good reading in those years too – they weren't all waste. He had always wanted to read every word Jack London ever wrote, and that was exactly what he did, page by page and book by book, *The Call of the Wild* twice and *The Iron Heel* three times. And Upton Sinclair and Mark Twain... And now, suddenly, McKeever murmured the name "Caroline", and with that he remembered a day, a month and a year.

Cars passed as he sat on the grassy bank. He raised his thumb automatically, and automatically turned his head to watch them as they shot away towards Los Angeles, but his mind had drifted back sixteen years. He stared at the coin in his hand. He had driven over the Ridge Route on that day in February 1931. He had pulled up his stakes in Los Angeles, and he was out on the road to change his luck. For the first time in years he was unemployed, but he was not perturbed by it. He had good clothes and money in his pocket; he owned a savings account of eleven hundred dollars and a second-hand Hudson coupé. He felt fat, happy and optimistic about turning up a job.

Although it had been sunny when he left Los Angeles, he had rolled down from the ridge into one of the dense fogs that burden the San Joaquin Valley in winter. He had switched on his headlights, slowed down to a crawl and passed the dull time by reciting bits of poetry. After ten minutes of this, his headlights picked out a figure on the roadside. He was pleased at the thought of company, and tooted his horn. The man did not turn. He carried a small suitcase in his left hand, and he seemed to be holding a package of some sort in his right. McKeever rolled down the side window, tooted his horn once more and shouted, "Want a lift, buddy?" The man turned, and McKeever was startled to find that it was not a man at all, but a young girl, who was wearing a man's slouch hat and a man's overcoat – and carrying a baby. The girl hesitated for a moment, and then walked to his car. She was rather tall, quite pretty he thought, despite the deep pallor of her thin face. He opened the door, and she lifted her suitcase to his outstretched hand. As she sat down and settled her baby in the crook of her arm, her large grey eyes fixed on him briefly, then shifted away. He could remember still how her eyes had intrigued him. They were wrong for a young girl, without the slightest spark of animation, like the weary eyes of a dried-out old woman. The girl said nothing to him, not a word of thanks at being picked up. Her exhaustion was so obvious, however, that he couldn't resent her lack of courtesy. He swung her suitcase back to the wide shelf behind them, and said, "How far you going, miss?"

She muttered "Stockton" without turning to look at him.

"Too bad. I'm stopping at Bakersfield." The girl remained silent, and he added, "Well, that's part way." He started the car and headed slowly into the fog. She remained silent, and he kept wondering about her – how long she had been travelling, and when she had last eaten if she had no money for a bus ticket.

After a bit the girl removed her hat, a shapeless man's felt. She leant her head back against the seat cushion and closed her eyes. He could see now that she was no more than nineteen or twenty. Her hands were filthy, and there was a dirt smudge on her cheek, yet her russet hair was neatly braided, as though she were normally fastidious, and her eyebrows looked pencilled. He felt sad for her – it was wrong for a young thing like that to be so woebegone, a lost Mary without her Joseph. The child in her lap was asleep. It lay snugly protected from the weather in a blue coverall that was spotted and grimy from the road. What would it have been like, he wondered, to have his own grandchild now? He didn't even like to dwell on it.

The girl slept, and McKeever drove cautiously along the flat ribbon of highway, his headlights on, his window wiper clicking. As night came on, the woolly fog began to thin. He speeded up. It started to rain then, on a sudden and hard, and he began to worry about his passenger. It was more than two hundred miles the girl still had to travel, and how could he let her off on the highway in a pelting rain, a baby in her arms?

The girl sighed and murmured something in her sleep. Then she awakened and spoke to him. "Where are we?"

"Getting near Bakersfield. You want me to take you someplace so you can spend the night? It's raining."

"Will you let me off at a gas station? I'll keep dry till I get a hitch."

"Suppose someone picks you up and only goes a few miles? He might let you off on the highway somewhere."

The girl didn't answer.

"You got a baby to think of," McKeever said with anger.

There was no response.

"Now look, you're broke, I suppose. A cabin only costs a dollar. I'll give it to you."

The girl muttered, "I've got to get home, mister. If you want to give me something to eat with, OK. But I have to make Stockton."

He said in exasperation, "But you can't expose a kid like that to the rain. What's the matter with you? That blanket'll get soaked, and she'll get pneumonia."

The girl didn't answer, and McKeever wondered fretfully if she were mentally defective. Then she said, quietly and painfully, "The kid's dead. Rain won't hurt her."

He wondered if he had heard. She wasn't looking at him – she was staring at the dark road. "What did you say?"

Silence.

"How long has she been dead?"

"This morning, about five o'clock."

He muttered "Jesus" and turned to stare at her. "What'd she die of?"

"I don't know. My milk wasn't good for her, I guess."

"Did you know she was sick?"

"She didn't cry. I didn't know."

"How long you been out on the road? Where you coming from?"

"St Louis."

"Well, damn it, we'll go into Bakersfield and I'll connect with somebody, the police maybe, an' you'll bury her. What's the percentage* in going to Stockton? It might take you two days in this weather."

The girl began to weep then, so softly and so wretchedly that McKeever felt as though his heart would split. "I want my ma to see her."

Without reflecting about it, without a thought beyond his urgent need to assuage this child's misery, McKeever said, "Why, I'll drive you, you poor kid. I'll get you there before morning."

The girl still wept, but after a while she fell asleep. She had not thanked him for his offer to drive her, she had said nothing about it at all. And he realized that here was someone for whom grief and fatigue had replaced the very marrow of the bones, that she was capable of thinking about herself and no one else, and that this was what his mother had meant when she told him about Ireland in the black year of '48.

He stopped at a lunch wagon in Bakersfield and bought some coffee and hamburgers. The girl sipped the hot coffee eagerly, but seemed unable to eat. McKeever asked if she was married. She nodded that she was.

"Where's your husband?"

She was silent for a moment. Then she told him. What made her story so sad was that it was so commonplace: no job, no home, and locusts over the land. Her husband had stolen, and he was in jail. She told McKeever this, and her voice went dead and she kept quiet.

They drove until three in the morning. When they came to Stockton, McKeever awakened her, and she directed him to her mother's home. It was a small frame house behind two others, approached by an alley that was strewn with cans and yellowed newspapers. It was old, dilapidated, forlorn.

And so she left him. She had told him her name, Caroline. She didn't say thank you to him, or even goodbye. She merely stepped out of the car and walked up the alley with her sorrow in her arms. And that was the year 1931, as he remembered it.

McKeever put the coin back into his pocket. He felt low now; the world had turned grey. The cars had been passing, and trucks had been passing; it was noon already, or it was later, and the road stretched very long, Glendale impossibly far. He lay back on the grassy bank and thought, "I was a fool to start out!" And then he thought, "For an old man every year is the time of the locust. Why didn't I remember that?"

He lay frowning, deeply unhappy. At moments like this, when he was depressed, he invariably remembered that girl. She had been no more wretched than others he had met in a long life, but she had become a symbol for him. A pretty lass of nineteen with her man in jail and a baby dead in her arms... it represented the waste of a human being, it was the fine dream of an innocent heart turned into garbage. And it took an old man, lying frustrate on a grassy bank, to understand how wicked such waste was. He had had his own dreams. He could count them like beads on a string. Each was different – yet all the same, for they had ended the same. He had buried the first one forty years back beneath muddy, brown earth. And then, slowly and painfully, his heart had moulded a second: he would study at night and learn mathematics and become an engineer. There would come a day when he would point to a map and say in hushed pride, "I wrote my name here. Here is a river and a bridge. Ten thousand people cross the bridge every day. The span is arched like a rainbow. The marble columns are like the milk-white throat of a woman. I built it." But then life did not allow him this second dream either. He took a course in elementary algebra… and the job shut down. He moved on to Oklahoma City, enrolled again in school – and four months later the job moved on. He tried correspondence courses, but how could a man learn when he couldn't ask questions? And it wasn't always possible to sit over a textbook on a hot night: after eight hours in the August sun, a man wanted to drink a beer and glance at a newspaper and shut his eyes.

And so, after ten years, he gave up that dream also. But he found still another. There would be a farm for his later years, chickens on it, ducks and rabbits, security and pleasant work, perhaps a woman. He saved for it. The Depression of 1914 wiped out his savings. He saved again. There was unemployment again in 1920. He saved still once again, and then this dream also shattered against the cold 1930s.

Now he had a final dream. He knew there would be no other. It was different from the dreams of his youth, more impersonal, but no less precious. It was not wholly his own, but still his own. It was to fix up a book, a monumental book, that others could read. He had a title for it already: *The Path of Man*. It would be a book in two parts: the first section would hold all of the material he had ever read about Man's destiny on earth, provided it was sensible – it would describe the world and the changing of the world by men, the golden endeavour; and the second part would have selections from Debs* and Upton Sinclair and London and Whitman* and thinkers like that. This part would tell the role of the forgotten man – it would prove that the common man, as the doer of the world, was not yet understood or rewarded. And it would begin with a quotation from Abraham Lincoln: "God must love the common man; he made so many of him."*

But now he was lying by a roadside, a hundred miles from nowhere... and the dream in his arms like Caroline with her baby. Was his dream also dead? Was he a fool to have started in the first place?

He lay and stared at the peaceful sky. He chewed his dark foreboding until his mouth was rancid with it. And then suddenly he spat, and again spat. And after a while he sat up. "Now, hold the reins, Simon, lad," he muttered aloud, "don't get skittish." He thought about it, and he frowned, and slowly he grew angry with himself. No backbone! Why, the very next auto might pick him up and whisk him down to LA! A man's life held good memories and bad memories; when he was facing a heavy task, it was the wrong time to dwell on the bad ones. He was an idiot and a coward to get so moody. Suppose the hitching *was* a little slow; suppose it was even damn slow?

He heard the hum of a distant car and suddenly pushed himself up from the grassy bank. He inched out to the roadside, held up his hand and spat vigorously at an ant on the concrete.

The car passed him by.

Chapter 10

One o'clock and still no compassionate motorist. McKeever was beginning to suck a wry humour from his situation. He would stay there for ever, by God – he would pine away from loneliness and be buried across from a winery. They might even bring tourists to see his grave: "Here lies Simon McKeever. He died with his thumb in the air for lack of a good Samaritan." Ha-ha! Why, they could build up a flourishing business around him.

One o'clock, the sun high and hot, the white concrete highway beginning to shimmer a little before his eyes. He had eaten one of Joplin's oranges, and he was beginning to peel a second with teeth and fingers. He was hungry, his feet ached, and soon it would be time for his afternoon nap. But no nap today, he was too busy becoming a monument – ha! The boys and girls at the Home would be coming out to the front porch now, starting to rock up and down in the sun. Oh, Lord, how that porch would be buzzing with talk about Simon McKeever! They probably had him in Fresno. Little they knew, *Fresno by 1960*, that was his slogan. Good joke.

A man was striding down the highway towards McKeever, walking with a quick and vigorous step. Catching sight of him, McKeever began to hope that the fellow would pass the time of day for a while. He needed something to break the awful monotony. As the man came close, he saw that he was quite a young chap, but he found it hard to decide whether he was a hitch-hiker. The lad carried a small canvas bag, yet his clothes were unusually slick for the road: brown sports jacket and gabardine trousers, white shirt, striped tie, two-toned shoes. He looked more like a local boy on his way to spark a girl. "Hi, there," McKeever called eagerly when young Smoothie was still a few yards away. "You hitching too?"

The young fellow nodded. He was about twenty-five, blond, chunky, smooth-skinned and good-looking. Altogether a nice-appearing lad, McKeever thought, but he wasn't quite sure he liked him – a little too slick. Smoothie slowed down for the last stretch, and his eyes examined McKeever; then they shifted to the bag, overcoat and corduroy jacket on the roadside. "How's it going?" He smiled in a friendly manner.

McKeever spat out an orange seed. "Not so good. Where you headed?"

"LA."

"Me too. Where'd you start from?"

"Frisco."

"When?"

"This morning."

McKeever stopped eating his orange, and a flush coloured his cheeks. He cried enviously, "Frisco? This morning? What time you start out?"

"About six. Why?"

"I been *hours* right here in this spot. Is that a wristwatch? What time is it?"

"Twelve past one."

"Oh, bugger it! Three hours twenty minutes I been here. Now, ain't that luck!"

The young man pursed his lips, laughed a little in sympathy. "Take you all year to reach LA at this rate, won't it?"

"Sure would," McKeever agreed wryly. "Only, it won't. I expect to make LA by tonight. I got to, in fact. Made nine hundred miles once in a single hop, all the way from Santa Fe, New Mexico, to Santa Barbara."

The young man glanced at him with delicate scepticism, and McKeever felt his gorge rise. This was the look he had come to know so well – the automatic, amused disdain of the young for the old, the healthy malice of those who are in full vigour towards the unfortunates who no longer are. He decided that he didn't like this young buster for peanuts.

Smoothie said with a laugh, "I don't hardly think you'll make it by tonight, pal. Not if I know the road."

"Why not? What makes you so cocky sure?" McKeever's tone was so full of bile that the young man glanced away with a frown. "Of course, nobody can be sure," he murmured in quick appease-ment. "It's the way the luck runs. So long. Hope you make it."

McKeever thrust out his cane, blocking him. In a less angry voice he said, "Wait a minute, Buster. I'm sorry I was sharp with you. But I been waiting here an awful long time. Is there something wrong with me? My fly open or something? If you got anything to tell me, I wish you'd tell it."

The young man hesitated, and McKeever said, "Speak out, will you, laddie?"

Smoothie rubbed his chin in an embarrassed manner. "Look, pal, I was stationed in Frisco during the war. I'm in school there now. I've been hitch-hiking this highway once a month for five years to see my folks. So I've had a lot of experience at it. I don't know how much you've had."

"Not much in recent times, to be honest with you."

"Well, that's it," the young man said with embarrassment.

"Because I'm getting on in years, you mean?"

"Not exactly."

"Speak out, laddie – I want to know. You won't hurt my feelings."

"Well… I get hitches easy. And I know why – I've been told. It's the way a guy looks. I always shave, for one thing—"

"I'm shaved, ain't I?"

"Sure, but… Well, look how I'm dressed. Got my best clothes on, see? A man in a nice car doesn't have to be afraid I'll dirty his upholstery. People think of those things. And I look respectable. They don't have to be afraid I'll hold 'em up."

"Jesus, I don't look like a hold-up man, do I?"

"No, but you're not dressed so hot, Pop. There's no use kidding yourself."

McKeever glanced down at his clothes – the drab corduroy trou-sers, the faded, dark-green flannel shirt, the black work brogans in need of polish. "Guess I ain't," he muttered. "You think that might account for my bad luck, eh? Guess I *was* dressed better when I went hitching in the old days."

"I'll tell you a good angle, though," the young man went on quickly. "Keep walking. It makes a good impression. A man in a car sees you going someplace, it gives him more confidence. I've been told that many times. Especially if you're carrying a suitcase."

McKeever's mouth worked. He said, "I can't walk. I got the arthureetis. That's why I'm going to LA. There's a doctor down there waiting to cure me up."

"Oh!" the young man said. He flushed with embarrassment and turned quickly with raised hand at the sound of a car. It passed them by. He took out a pack of cigarettes and offered one in silence.

"Why, thanks."

Smoothie held up his lighter, spun the wheel.

"Forgotten what these tailor-mades taste like," McKeever said with his mouth full of smoke. "Not as much body as pipe tobacco, are they?"

"Guess you'll surely make LA," the young man said. "I didn't mean to worry you."

"Can't worry me," McKeever replied tartly. "Nothing in this world can stop me from getting to Glendale. Crawl on my stiff knees maybe, but I'll get there." He began to laugh at himself. "Oh, Lord, I'm a boasting man, ain't I? But I mean it, got my mind made up." He sucked hard on the cigarette, laughed again. "Ever hear what the bull said when he knocked down the stone fence with his head? Said: 'If a thing's worth doing, damn the obstacles.' There was a cow on the other side."

The young man laughed.

"Oh, Lord, it's a great life, surely it is. Hot or cold, I wouldn't miss a minute of it. Wonderful trip I'm having – new sights, new people to talk to... grand."

"Good deal," the young man murmured.

Both of them held up their hands as a huge milk truck rolled towards them. It passed them by with a swish and a roar.

"You better get moving, young feller. I'll jinx you."

Smoothie hesitated, glanced at his wrist watch. "I'll try it here for a bit. Maybe we'll bring each other luck."

"Why... that's considerate of you," McKeever said in surprise. "That's real nice."

"Sit down for a spell, why don't you?"

"Why, I will. I can't stand too long nowadays. You're being awful nice to me."

"Skip it," the youth muttered.

Now, why had he misjudged this boy? McKeever wondered. He had been so quick to dislike him. A man was not his face or his clothes, he surely knew that. Was he turning into one of those cranks who resent anyone younger? God forbid! He was developing a lot of bad qualities, if the truth be told, like thinking aloud in the bus this a.m. He would have to begin watching himself. "What's your name, young feller?"

"Chuck," the other answered. He watched McKeever with fascination as the latter moved inch by inch towards the grassy bank. He himself could have spanned the distance in one good jump. "Say, pal," he asked softly, "how old are you?"

"Pushing seventy-four. Why?"

"Just asked." He held up his thumb, but the car passed by.

"I look younger, don't I?"

"Yeah."

"It's the lack of wrinkles," McKeever explained with satisfaction. "A healthy outdoor life, never had a venereal disease. Constitution's sound, that's the main thing. Me an' the United States – we both got sound constitutions... Ha-ha." He sat down, eased his legs out in front of him and began to massage his knees. "What are you taking up in school, Chuck? Learning a trade?"

"No, just an education... college."

"If you don't mind my saying, a man gets along better if he has a skill. I don't mean to butt in."

"That's all right. I'm going in business with an uncle of mine, so I don't have to worry."

"You don't say! Eh... what sort of business?"

Chuck held up his thumb for an old woman in a station wagon. She kept her eyes glued to the road and passed them by. "Second-hand bags. Burlap."

"Your uncle sell 'em?"

"He buys 'em, cleans 'em up, patches 'em, sells 'em again."

"You don't say!" Delicately McKeever began to rub the hump on his nose. "Your uncle now... does he have any men working for him?"

"Oh, sure, twenty-five or thirty when business is good."

"I see... *Hm*... well, now... probably he needs a timekeeper with that many men, don't he?"

"A timekeeper? I don't know. I doubt it. They punch a clock."

"Or a nightwatchman? He surely needs a nightwatchman?"

Chuck turned with a quizzical stare. Each gazed at the other, and the silence between them lengthened until McKeever burst out in hot eagerness, "The fact is, son, I'll be cured of my lameness in a month or two. I'll want work. I'm a reliable man. Experienced. I've earned good money in my time. I know blueprints, I know how to figure – I'm quick at learning, too. Maybe you could put in a word for me. Think so? Ha?"

Chuck swallowed. Then he said, "Jesus Christ, pal, you're seventy-four."

McKeever was too eager to become angry. In a voice heavy with amazement he said, "Seventy-four? Where'd you get that idea?"

"You just told me a minute ago."

"No such thing. You misunderstood me. "I'll be *sixty*-four my next birthday, son, almost a year off."

"Oh!" Chuck said. He turned back to the road and raised his hand for an approaching truck.

"I'm limber as a birch whip when I don't have this lameness," McKeever continued eagerly. "Why – I was working in a factory until just three months ago. I used to do a back somersault easy as breathin'. Look at Churchill,* now. In his seventies. Ever heard of Justice Holmes?* He was on the Supreme Court of the United States when he—"

"Let's go, pal," Chuck interrupted. "We got a hitch."

A battered pick-up truck was slowing down for them. McKeever cried "Jumping Jesus" and broke out into a sweat of excitement. The truck stopped by the time he had pushed himself to his feet. There were two men in the front cab; the open rear had neither sides, top nor backboard. The man nearest them, who was middle-aged and stout, surveyed them with a humorous gleam in his eye. "We're going down to Fresno. That do you guys any good?"

Chuck said, "*Will* it? That's swell!" McKeever said, "Fresno – that's crackerjack." The stout man, satisfied that he and his partner had stopped for men who were properly appreciative, said, "OK, hop up in back."

McKeever picked up his overcoat and jacket. His movements were as quick as he could make them – but they were not quick at all, and Chuck, who had started towards the truck, ran back to help him. He took the coat and suitcase and whispered, "Get going, pal."

The stout man watched, and his broad forehead creased in wrinkles as he saw McKeever's halting locomotion. And then he began to mutter aloud with increasing disapproval. "Have to ride in the back, you know. No room up here. Have to ride standing up, you fellers; the only place to hold on is the cab. And my buddy here, he steps on it, a lot of bumping and swaying." He was silent for a moment, and then he made up his mind. "I'm sorry, you fellers, but it's no deal. If the old man takes a spill off, we'll be responsible. Let's go, Harry."

Chuck yelled, "We're not travelling together. How about me?"

"OK," the stout man said. "Hop on."

Chuck dropped McKeever's things. He vaulted on the back and grabbed hold of the cab side to steady himself. Then he turned back to McKeever with a flushed, uncomfortable face. "I'm sorry, Pop, but I can't miss this."

McKeever stood stiff as a poker; his mouth worked, but he said nothing. The stout man waved his hand, a gesture of commiseration, and the truck started off. Then Chuck yelled, "It's the Alco Bag Company, Pop. A-L-C-O."

The truck shot away. McKeever watched it... truck going to Fresno, a hundred and fifty miles down the road, Fresno in three hours maybe. He picked up his suitcase to get it off the highway. He picked up Percy Fuller's overcoat, brushed it off, folded it over his arm. He found that his head was aching, and he knew that it hurt him exactly as if somebody had jammed his temple with a bony elbow.

For a few moments he stood by the road with a vacant stare, seeing nothing. Then a metallic chatter intruded on his thoughts. He thrust out his hand, but the auto was going the wrong way; it was an old jalopy that rattled at every corner; seated in it, looking utterly ridiculous, was an old fat hog of a man in a battered Derby hat. McKeever smiled, then said aloud, "Why, good for you, Buster. Don't let 'em keep you at home." He laughed, and his head cleared. And then he realized that he was not so disappointed over the loss of the truck ride as he was trying to pretend. To every age its fortitude. No man grew old in a night, and it was only a fool who disputed the laws of nature. It would have been fine to ride that truck down to Fresno, like a cowboy riding a crazy bronc – but it was beyond his powers, and why lie about it? The stout man was right, and Chuck was right to grab the hitch when he could. So bugger it. He would make LA at his own good speed. Glendale had been there yesterday, it would still be there tomorrow.

He took out his notebook and pencil stub. He selected a clean page. Printing the letters carefully, he gave the page a title:

Then, beneath, he wrote:

1. Alco Bag Co., LA (Burlap Bags). Remember Chuck on road by the winery (Nightwatchman?)

2.

He heard an auto. It was coming out of the winery grounds directly opposite him. Before he could get his hand up, the car swung around in front of him and stopped with a jerk. The driver jumped out and came around to McKeever with a dark, unsmiling face. He was a man of thirty-odd, squat and sturdy, with heavy, muscular arms that were spotted with green paint. He said, "You like a hitch, mister?" His speech was soft, the intonation delicately musical, and McKeever put him down correctly as a second-generation Mexican. He couldn't make out if the man were angry at him or not, but he answered heartily, "I should say! If I don't move out soon, I'll grow here like moss."

"I'll only take you a few miles," the other said apologetically. "But I'll drop you at a gas station. It'll be easier to get a ride there."

"That's great. I'm obliged to you like anything."

The man nodded and picked up McKeever's things. He put them on the back seat of his sedan and waited in silence while McKeever moved to the door.

"This breaks the ice," McKeever told him happily. "I been all morning right here."

"Sure, I been watching you."

"You have? You work in that winery? I thought it was closed."

"Winery's closed, sure. But I'm a painter. I'm doing some painting inside."

"Did you paint the outside too? That's a good job, clean."

"Yeah, it's a sure good job – I think so too," the other replied with sudden, smiling loquaciousness. "That's because of my boss: he mixes the paints, that's the main thing. He's a nice feller, square. I told him I wanna give you a hitch, he didn't holler at all. Won't dock my pay, I'm sure."

McKeever paused at the open door of the car. He stared in wonder at the dark, pudgy face of his benefactor. "You mean you weren't going any place – you just quit work to give me a hitch?"

"Well, sure," the other replied seriously. "Why not? Won't kill me to drive you a few miles, will it?"

"No, but there's been cars passing all morning an' nobody else got that idea."

"Maybe they never been on the road. I been on the road, see? Besides, you're an old man. I got my old man in my house right now. I treat him with respect. He's old. He wants to go any place, I take him. I respect him."

"I'm much obliged," McKeever said softly. He felt terribly moved. "Makes the world go round, don't it, the way people deal with each other? I thank you." He bent down to step into the car. Then, with one foot inside, he suddenly became aware that he was facing a problem. It was two years since he had stepped into a sedan. It was no longer a simple matter for him, he could see that at once. A man had to pivot his body around to get into a seat, and he had to do it on bent knees. How was he to manage?

He tried. He slid his left foot further into the car, held on to the door and attempted to turn his bent torso. It was cruelly impossible. His locked hips were incapable of so simple a movement. He tried again. When he stopped this time, a cold sweat was dripping from his armpits. He stood rigid, suffering, while panic and humiliation clotted his veins. Was this the end of his trip? Was he so far gone that he couldn't grab a hitch when it came along?

The man, watching him, asked, "What's the matter?"

"I can't climb in." His voice was sick. He put his left foot into the car again, slid it forward, again tried to turn his body – and stopped. He said, helplessly, "What in hell am I going to do?"

The man came over and stood by him. He studied the opening in the front, then studied McKeever. He observed soberly, "If you was little fellow, it'd be easier. Your legs is sure too long."

"I'll cut 'em off," McKeever said bitterly. "No good to me now – they sure ain't."

"How about ass-backwards? Push in behind first?"

McKeever turned around. His body began to tremble with nervousness. He sat down on the edge of the seat. His lips tightened into a hard line. Laboriously, straining, he inched his rump back towards the wheel of the car, further and further back, until he was sitting behind the wheel itself. And then, his face creased with anxiety, he slowly began to swing his long legs into the car, using his hands to guide them, bending them at the knees as much as possible. There was an inch or two to spare. "Oh, man alive," he sighed happily as he straightened up, "what a damned crazy way to get into a car!"

The other said nothing. He closed the door, came around to his own seat and started the motor.

"Ice broken at last," McKeever murmured. He wiped his wet brow.

Chapter 11

The service station was a disappointment. The Mexican had
hoped that by waiting there McKeever would catch a ride all the
way to Los Angeles. He bought McKeever a Pepsi-Cola, shook
hands with serious, unsmiling face and returned to the winery. But
it was a rather dilapidated station, and few cars stopped. In the
first hour there were only two autos, neither of which had room
for an extra passenger. Half an hour later a station wagon pulled
in, and McKeever got up from his cracker box in high excitement.
The driver was a round-shouldered spinster in her late thirties, and
the service man put the question to her when she was paying her
bill. She looked down her long nose as she slipped the change in
her purse and said, "Why, no, of course not, I wouldn't think of
taking a strange man in my car, I wouldn't dream of it." She spoke
loud enough for McKeever to hear, and he was aching to yell out
"Don't itch so, lady – you ain't worth rape, an' I can't anyway",
but he was afraid it might cost the station man a future customer.
Finally, past three in the afternoon, a farmer stopped. He was only
going to a crossroad ten miles further on, but McKeever was too
fidgety to pass up the ride. The farmer dropped him at a lonely
spot, a dry onion field on one side of the road, an empty meadow
on the other. Then it began all over again – the speeding cars, each
one of them surely bound for Glendale; the legs that took to aching
and had to be rested; the dragging hours. McKeever admitted to
himself glumly that the boy, Chuck, had been right. His luck was
more than a bad roll of the dice: evidently his appearance was
not the kind for getting hitches. He wished that he had borrowed
a tie and worn it. He wished especially that he could throw away
his cane. It was the cane, he felt increasingly certain, that caused
most of his trouble. A cane indicated age or infirmity, and most

people didn't care to stop for a shabby old man who might be dirty or senile, or who might even put a touch on them for money. He murmured to himself with wistful irony, "To them that hath shall be given and from them that hath not shall be taken away."* More than likely those words had been spoken on a hitch-hike from Galilee to Jerusalem. Joke – ha!

Weary hours, but he refused to let his spirits sag as he had at the winery. He was on the way to his own Jerusalem, and nothing else counted. He hummed and smoked, rested when he had to, turned a beetle over to watch its legs wriggle, turned it back again to watch it labour off. As the afternoon wore on, he began to wonder how he would manage the night. He needed to eat and rest a little, and he needed to keep warm. Once the sun departed, the temperature dropped fast in this valley, even in May.

A passing Greyhound offered a solution: he would use a bus station. It only required that he make a town by nightfall. "*Hm! A good idea! Fine thinking*," he told himself aloud. As to food, he had a dollar and thirty-five cents. Hamburgers were the cheapest, he'd concentrate on those. If the trip lasted so long that his money ran out... Well, he'd face that when the time came. There was always the Salvation Army in a good-sized town. Provided he was cautious with them and had a convincing story to tell. Otherwise some snoopy Joe might notify the police, and they'd ship him back to the Booger's.

Cars bound for Glendale – but they wouldn't stop. Thumb up and thumb down. Four o'clock becoming five, five dragging into six... And he was getting tired – quite, quite tired, McKeever admitted to himself. Towards the end of the afternoon he began to worry lest darkness close down on him while he was still on the road. A night on the ground would be the worst thing in the world for him, he knew. Overcoat or no overcoat, he would awaken in the morning with limbs like boards.

The orange sun was dangerously low in the sky when he finally caught a ride. The man who stopped was a liquor salesman; the gilt letters on the door of his coupé announced the fact, and the man himself proved a further advertisement of his product. When he saw with what difficulty McKeever walked towards his car, he stepped out to help him. He was a well-dressed, rather handsome man in his late forties, as tall as McKeever, but carrying a heavy, unbecoming paunch. He was so drunk that he automatically steadied himself against the frame of the car as he walked. McKeever was appalled. It was a horrible choice to make – whether to spend a night on the ground or to risk life and limb with a besotted driver.

The salesman said genially, "Let's have your bag, Dad."

"Brockton?" McKeever asked, playing for time in which to think. "You going there?"

"Brockton, sure, my town." He grasped the handle of the Gladstone, adding with drunken expansiveness, "I'll drive you to your front door like a taxi. That's me, George the poop."

McKeever didn't quite know how to take this last remark, but he murmured, "It's the bus station I happen to be wanting."

"Then it's the bus station I'll take you to," the salesman replied heartily. "I'm your man."

McKeever's mouth worked unhappily. "I'll be strictly honest with you, mister. I appreciate your stopping for me like the very dickens, but I'm scared you'll run your car off the road. Man, your eyes are bloodshot an' you're so cockeyed you can't walk straight. I'm scared to death."

The salesman looked offended, ran a hand through his tousled hair, then burst out in an odd, embarrassed guffaw. "Bloodshot eyes, eh? Occupational disease, that's all. In my line, four out of five have it. Doesn't hurt our family life, doesn't hurt our driving."

"Well, will you drive *slow*, man? I don't like to put conditions, but will you be *careful*? *I* got some business to take care of – I can't afford hospital time."

"You can't, eh?" the man enquired with tipsy delight. "Now you've challenged me, Dad. I'll drive you to Brockton at twenty miles an hour; I'll handle you like a piece of china. How's that? Cross my heart and hope to die." He crossed his heart and stood grinning foolishly.

"I'll take you up on that," McKeever told him seriously. "An' I'm much obliged to you."

The man grinned – a tender, affectionate, drunken grin – and placed McKeever's things in his car. "Need any help?"

"Manage all right." He was pushing his rump in backwards along the seat. "Only take me a minute."

"You live around here, Dad?"

"No, I'm from Santabello way."

"What are you doing on the road?"

"Why, hitching along," McKeever replied with amusement.

"Where you going?"

"Los Angeles." He began to swing his legs in.

"But you're taking the *bus* from Brockton, aren't you?" the salesman insisted.

"Why no, I'm hitching." He straightened up with a grunt. "I'm in. You can close the door. Some system I got, eh?"

"Listen," the salesman persisted in a bewildered tone, "you mean you're hitching *all* the way down to LA?"

"Why, sure. Only way I can get there."

The other stared and nodded silently. Then he walked around to his seat. The drunken gaiety had departed from his face; he appeared thoughtful and vaguely troubled. He took a half-empty pint of Bourbon from the glove compartment and offered it. "Warm yourself, Dad." His tone was gentle.

"After we get to Brockton, eh?"

The salesman laughed a little, without humour. "You're a fox, you sure are. Don't want me to drink any more, eh? OK, watch the speedometer. Twenty miles an hour, a promise from the poop. Don't talk to me now, I have to concentrate."

He kept his word and drove with studied care. After a few miles McKeever's anxiety departed. He let his tired body relax and watched the warm sunset blaze on the far horizon and the purple shadows that were covering the fields like flood water. He said to himself contentedly, "It's been a good day, Simon." He was well launched on his trip, safely away from the Booger. But who would have supposed that hitch-hiking would be so slow? From the winery to Brockton was just under twenty-five miles; a well man could walk that in a day. And if the Mexican painter had not been so decent, he might be eating green tomatoes for his supper. God bless the Mexican, he thought – the sort of man who made the world go round. He only regretted that he had forgotten to ask his name and address. It would have been fitting that when he was cured up and working again he send a man like that a pound of tobacco.

It was dark when they pulled up before the bus station in Brockton. The salesman shut off his motor, rubbed his face absently and turned to McKeever with a wry grin. "Well? Kept my word, didn't I?"

"You did fine."

"Sure – poopy George, the old reliable." His voice was odd, and he seemed tired. He uncorked the whiskey bottle and took a long drink.

What sort of man was this? McKeever wondered. Talking about himself in this way. People could be awfully strange when the good silk in them got twisted, they surely could. He said gratefully, "I'm sure obliged to you. Saved me from a cold night on the ground."

"Glad I did," the other replied. His tone became gentle again, and he added, "That's no place for you, Dad." He offered the bottle. "Have one?"

"Thank you kindly." McKeever took a swallow. "My, good stuff. Ain't had any recently."

"It's on the company. Go right ahead."

"Might keel me over, I'm afraid. Had breakfast early." He took another swallow. "Warms my toes. Thank you."

The salesman asked softly, "You really hitching down to LA?"

"I sure am."

"Broke?"

"Well... I ain't got quite enough for a bus ticket."

The salesman rubbed his face. "Not quite enough for a bus ticket," he repeated thickly, as though he couldn't fix the thought in his head. "Crippled and broke... broke and crippled... a broken-down bastard if I ever saw one. Oh my God!"

McKeever became furious. "Now, see here, you've given me a ride, but you can just shut up – I don't like your manner. A man who can stand on his two feet like I can ain't crippled. There's no call for hooting at me."

"Don't like my manner, eh?" the salesman replied. He laughed a little, very unhappily, and then he said, "There's cripples and cripples, don't you know that? I'm sorry I picked you up, you God-damned old cock. I'm such a God-damned slob compared to you that you wouldn't pee in my soup. Broke... you can't walk... but you're hitching to LA. Oh my God. What a poop that makes me, you don't know."

Uneasy and bewildered, McKeever said, "Thank you, an' I'll be going now."

"Jesus, what a slob I am!" the salesman said miserably. He coughed and began to cry. "Get the hell out of here before I bust a gut."

McKeever worked himself out of the seat. The salesman didn't offer to help him with his bag and overcoat. He sat, blubbering weakly and miserably, both hands clapped over his face.

"Goodnight," McKeever said. "Thank you."

The man flicked one hand in a gesture of farewell. He started the car and drove off.

"Why, you poor, misbegotten lad," McKeever muttered aloud. "I wonder what I stirred up in you, I surely do." He stood musing and troubled, sorry for the man now. What living did to the human race! There was a great deal of mending to be done in this world, he'd always said it.

He picked up his suitcase and started towards the brightly lighted station door. "First day over, first night beginning," he thought contentedly. "It's the best damn trip I ever took."

Chapter 12

The bus station was small and not crowded at this hour – even so, McKeever found an enemy there. He was dismayed but not wholly surprised: this antagonist turned up everywhere. Sometimes he was husky and fine-looking and worked at a man's side with a wrench; sometimes he peered over a counter, pencil in hand, pencil-thin smile on his lips, eyes like two little lumps of cold pork fat. Many faces, but the same man behind all of them – lickspittle and vulture, drillmaster to all who came his way except the boss, all tongue and asshole for the boss. Of all the categories of humankind this was the breed McKeever most despised, because it violated nature at its living heart. Early in manhood he had come to a decision about life, and he had clung to it down the years: that a man who bent his knee to the wrong thing or the wrong person made the biggest mistake of living. The knee would straighten, but the curl in the gut would not. And this breed not only bent to its superiors, but tried to make all others bend to it – a double sin if ever there was one.

Tonight the gentleman looked the part more than was fitting, McKeever thought sourly. He was the desk man and the ticket clerk of the station – a smallish, bald, large-domed slug of a man, putty-skinned and plump, with cold, quick eyes, very quick and very cold. McKeever had only just come in from the lunch counter and was still getting settled on a bench when he saw the man looking him over, taking his size and measure, deciding from long experience that here was a sponger and a deadbeat. *Against orders... Can't sleep in this station... I won't have it!...* McKeever could see the keen glitter of the words in his eyes, and he knew it was only a matter of time before Mr Rattypuss came over to him. What to do?

It was nine o'clock, and his flesh was sagging with weariness. He had eaten a wonderful supper at the lunch counter; his belly was deliciously heavy, and he wanted, needed, craved a quiet snooze. He had made a strategic error, he realized, in the selection of a bench. It had seemed sensible to stake out near the washroom and toilet, but a corner seat would have been less conspicuous. Now he was in direct view of the desk man, and the gent already had him sized up and sawed into lengths.

What to do? McKeever rubbed his bristly chin and bit hard on his pipe stem. He found that he was too tired to think. The desk man was busy on the phone, looking away for a moment... his heavy lids drooped... closed. Instantly he was back on the road, the cars sweeping past him as they had all day, the white concrete shimmering against his eyes. He rubbed his lids and sighed and took the pipe out of his mouth. The desk man was still telephoning. McKeever tried to remember the delicate purple shadows over the land at dusk and closed his eyes again to rest them while he figured out a plan. The hot, white road receded, the cars slowed down... and he was asleep.

A hand on his shoulder awakened him. A thin voice said coldly, "I wouldn't want you to miss your bus. Where you goin'? You wanna buy a ticket?" The desk man stood poised, his plump, soft body alert, a sarcastic smile on his lips. "Well?"

McKeever blinked, sighed heavily. White face, white smile, white rat... the wall clock read 9.18... the station lights felt bitter on his eyeballs. He tried to start his brain working.

"Well?" the man asked again, sharply.

"No, I'm not buying a ticket. Do I have to?" His tone was so sharp in return that the desk man drew back a little. Then he thrust forward once again, confident of his position, angry.

"No, you don't hafta buy a ticket – but you gotta have a reason for bein' here. You see that sign? No loiterin', no sleepin' allowed. Rules."

"I can read."

"I'm in charge, responsible. You can't sleep here. This is no flophouse. On your way, rummy."

The wheels turned in McKeever's head – they turned and stopped, turned again, meshed. A pleasant warmth spread through his chest. He said, with cold offensiveness, "Know the rules, eh? How about the rules on politeness? *Know them?* Politeness to *all* customers?" He leant forward. "Never can tell who's reporting to the main office – now, can you?"

The desk man's mouth dropped open slightly, the tip of his tongue flicked against his upper lip.

"Company dropped two men in LA the past week," McKeever advised him coldly. "I don't know the reason, nobody told me. Peacetime maybe, job competition starting again. Just trying to do you a favour. You mean well, I guess."

The desk man was silent. His eyes shivered with uncertainty. They scanned McKeever from his worn panama to his scuffed shoes, back again, down again, uncertain, angry, fearful.

"Course I might *not* be working for the company," McKeever said. "I might just be a man waiting for his granddaughter who's coming down on the bus from Frisco. What time are the buses due?"

The desk man answered with a slight stammer. "One at 9.53... 1.53... 5.53... You've got someone comin' down on a bus... a bus?"

"Might... might not," McKeever said quietly, with savage pleasure. "I might be a company spotter. Might only be an excuse about my granddaughter so I can sit the night out, look things over, make my report."

"Spotters don't tell," the desk man said quickly.

"Not usually... depends. At my age a man ain't so anxious to put another man out of a job. But that depends, too. On how he acts, of course."

Silence.

"Night work's hard, ain't it?" McKeever asked in a tone that was suddenly friendly.

"Oh no, not for me, I like night work," the other insisted. "I ain't com... complainin'."

"It is for me. Getting on in years. Fall asleep sometimes. What time you go off?"

"7 a.m."

"Then you can wake me up when the bus from Frisco comes in – just in case I fall asleep."

"Rules against sleepin'," the desk man muttered unhappily. "Applies to you even."

"Night work's hard on me. Like to shut my eyes for a while. Don't always sleep. A man ain't asleep who don't snore, don't bother anyone, is he? Give me a restless night an' I'm irritable in the a.m. Make out a bad report when I'm irritable, I always do. There's your phone."

The desk man scurried off, and McKeever sighed with exquisite pleasure. He couldn't recall when he had enjoyed himself so much. Mr Rattypuss would be afraid to act now, not certain whether he was or wasn't a company spotter. Mr Rattypuss was wearing a barbed-wire jockstrap hand-knitted by Simon McKeever. It was a story for the boys.

The desk man had put down his telephone and was staring at McKeever. His fingers drummed on the counter, and his plump face reflected a deep frustration. McKeever nodded to him solemnly and bent down to open his Gladstone bag. He decided that he would stay awake until the first bus came in from Frisco at 9.53. Then he would do two things: he would scribble in his notebook like any hard-working company spotter; he would also remark that his granddaughter must have missed that bus and would be taking the next one. In that way he would keep both stories alive, each one feeding the other.

He dug down into his bag, fingering socks, underwear, shirt, a piece of the Booger's yellow soap... until he found what he was searching for, his reading spectacles and a book. He closed the bag, set the book down on the bench by his side and began to clean his spectacles. A young Chinese lad in army uniform came past the bench on his way to the water fountain. McKeever belched loudly, and the youth turned around with a merry grin. "My, loud as a

Congressman," McKeever apologized with a laugh. "Forgetting my manners."

"Good health," the young Chinese said with a smile.

"Ate too much," McKeever explained with satisfaction. It had been a wonderful, wonderful dinner, and he had indulged in the sin of gluttony all the way round. He had paid sixty-two cents for it, far more than he should have, and five cents more as a tip to the waitress. After two years of pap at the Booger's, he had succumbed without struggle to the temptation of loin of pork. Sweet as honey it had been, too, he reflected happily, tender, chewy, a piece of meat like a healthy man craved. He had always been extra fond of pork. Give him pork chops or fresh ham or pork spare ribs or anything in the pork line after a good day's work out of doors and he had favoured it more than a steak. Cream of tomato soup, boiled potato, apple sauce, a good cup of coffee – it had been a kingly feast. The five-cent tip to the waitress had been an extravagance for a man of his limited means of course; but the girl had slipped him an extra pat of butter and, besides, he always hated to go away from a meal without leaving a tip. He would make up for the indulgence by going light at breakfast. He recalled a poem suddenly, smiled, tried to order the words in his mind.

> But mice and rats...
> ...food were...

How did it go?

> But mice and rats and such small deer
> Have been Tom's food for seven long year...*

Ha! Ha! Very fitting. He hadn't thought of that for ages, a favourite of his at one time, too, a cutie. He'd write it on a postcard and send it to the Booger.

The wall clock said 9.33. McKeever adjusted his spectacles and picked up the book. Once a month the Unitarian Church of

Santabello sent a box of books to the Finney Home, and McKeever had chosen this one the morning before. It occurred to him that the Booger would be sore as a boil when he found it missing. "Fine," he thought, "very good." He would return it when he was ready – the Unitarians wouldn't mind: they were good people, and they would appreciate that a man needed something to read on a journey. This particular book had attracted him because of its title, *The Dance of Life.** It was lively and promising, like Jack London's *Call of the Wild*.

He opened it and leafed through until he found the first page of text. Since it said "Preface", he turned the page without reading it. He had decided long ago that a preface in a book was usually not worth his time. All it said was that the author had depended on his wife and several other people in writing the book. Naturally. No man made his way in this world alone. He might think he did, but it wasn't so. Like no one man made an oil well – although to read Standard Oil Advertisements you'd think it was all due to John D. Rockefeller,* a coyote if ever there was one... kept the union down for years.

The preface was lengthy, and McKeever was annoyed to find that it was followed by an "Introduction". He was at the point of skipping this also when he noticed that it also said "Chapter I". This posed a problem to him. Chapter I was Chapter I, and he knew he ought to begin there. Yet in that case he wondered why it was called "Introduction". An introduction was like a preface, to be skipped. He leafed further, and discovered that the introduction ran for thirty pages. It made him laugh – a hell of an introduction! Nevertheless, it clearly had to be read.

He yawned and pushed his spectacles back towards the bridge of his nose. They were always slipping down, those WPA spectacles of his... they needed fixing. He began to read.

It has always been difficult for Man to realize that his life is all an art...

McKeever studied the sentence, then read it over again. He was not quite certain he knew what it meant. *Was* life an art? This was a new one on him. Art was paintings. What had a man's life in common with painting? He yawned, scanned the sentence a third time. When he was reading a serious book like this, he always liked to study out the meaning of each idea before he passed on to the next. In that way he got the most out of it.

His life is all an art. True or false? Was that a description of his own life?

It was 9.43 by the clock. He was so tired, not really in fettle for a serious book like this. He had ten more minutes until the Frisco bus came in.

...is all an art. It has been more difficult to conceive it so than to act it so. For that is always how...

McKeever's lids slipped shut. The telephone jangled, and it seemed to him he heard the desk man say "Dance of Life." He slept.

Hand on his shoulder. "Frisco bus coming in... coming in..." He opened his heavy eyes, saw the back of the desk man retreating, heard the low grind of the bus in the loading shed outside. With effort he shook himself awake. On the manner in which he conducted himself now depended whether or not he would be kicked out on the street by Mr Rattypuss – 10.23 – the bus was late, he must have slept for a while. He stood up, leant wearily on his cane, laboured over to the fountain for a drink of water. His pores felt drunk with sleep. "Oh, for that lumpy cot up at the Booger's!" he thought wryly. He drank the clear, cold water, patted some on his forehead and eyes. The bus was in and letting off several passengers, all men. McKeever moved towards the ticket desk. The bus driver stepped down, lit a cigarette, exchanged a few words with the desk man. He accepted a ticket from the Chinese lad, took his heavy suitcase. The desk man turned around abruptly, his eyes sharp, "Your passenger on this one?"

McKeever shook his head.

"You said..." He came towards McKeever. "You said..." He stopped uncertainly, and his tongue washed his upper lip.

"What did I say?"

The bus pulled out. McKeever beckoned for the desk man to come closer. "That driver. What was his name?"

"Pepper, James. Why?"

McKeever took his notebook out of his pocket. "He got on the bus smoking. Against the rules. You ought to know that."

The desk man became friendly. His lips parted in an ingratiating smile. "So you *are* workin' for the main office?"

Despite his weariness, McKeever couldn't help extracting as much relish from the situation as possible. "Might be... never can tell. By the way: let me know when the next bus is due. Could be my granddaughter'll be on that one,"

The desk man looked sick with perplexity. McKeever turned around and pushed back to his seat. He placed his overcoat over the back of the bench as a rest for his head. Before he closed his eyes he made a show of scribbling the driver's name in his notebook. This time he didn't try to read. He closed his eyes and held up his thumb for an auto and was asleep before it passed him by.

It was not an easy night. He kept slipping over to one side, his body craving to rest at full length. Each time this happened, he forced himself awake, sat up, sighed, warned himself that it would never do. He could bluff Mr Rattypuss so far and no further.

Once he awakened from his usual nightmare, the people squatting around like buzzards, the black oil dripping down on his face while they called him "cockroach". It was bad, and he felt exceedingly troubled by it.

And once an odd and pleasant thing happened: there was a jangle in his ears, and he opened his eyes to see a girl playing a pinball game on the other side of the room. The girl was laughing, and she was very pretty, very dark and saucy-looking, and so slim it was hard to believe she was grown and a woman, yet a woman indeed with ripe breasts beneath her tight blouse. A young man was with her, a red-headed, strong-looking young man, his eyes fixed on her with the worship of love. He was laughing along with her, because she was happy and it made him happy. And McKeever watched them for a moment before his eyelids drooped again – watched them and felt a surge of great happiness. His mind trembled with half-completed thoughts, each one of them good and comforting, but his brain was too sleepy to trace them out: that here was the fruit of the earth, this boy and girl in love, leaning their bodies together and laughing so… and that this trip of his was somehow like a man's journey through life, somehow it was… he had a goal, and there were obstacles, there were people to help him and others thrusting against him… but a direction, a purpose… His mind went no further.

The desk man awakened him for the 2 a.m. bus. He grinned sleepy thanks at the man, who was obviously angry with him, yet so afraid. This time he didn't bother to get up. He merely scrawled pencil lines in his notebook like an honest company spotter, stretched his aching muscles and fell asleep again.

A bawling infant awakened him a little before six. A placid-faced woman was diapering a boy on the bench beside him. The baby kicked his fat thighs, squalled and several times pulled the diaper out of his mother's hands before she could pin it. McKeever watched them with sleepy amusement. He thought of the book he had begun to read the night before. The baby's healthy, kicking legs were a kind of dance of life – was that what the author meant? It was an interesting subject, deep, and he wanted to keep studying that book and thinking about it.

Second day! How would luck go today? He was three hundred and fifty miles from Glendale with a total capital of sixty-eight cents. And if he cared to be honest about it, he was tired, slack in every muscle. Once upon a time, he would have got up full of beans from a night like this. Now his neck felt stiff, his hips and knees were all locked up, and he yearned for a warm spot in the sun where he could go to sleep. Nevertheless… up and out. A good wash, a good cup of coffee would revive him. And a good long hitch, say of a hundred miles or so, would set him to singing again. Jerusalem, Jerusalem.* His luck was bound to change a little.

The desk man was at the door of the loading shed, checking an outgoing bus. "Here's good morning to you, Rattypuss," McKeever thought pleasantly. He made the washroom with his things, taking them all along for safety's sake. No one entered to compete for the lone basin, and he shaved comfortably. Then he stripped to his waist and patted himself all over with the cool, refreshing water.

As he was combing his hair, he smiled at himself in the ironic way he did most every morning, and murmured with faint pride, "Well, lad, another night gone an' you ain't passed over yet, have you?"

He plucked a silver hair from his comb and remembered how his Mary had cut a lock of his coarse hair to put in a little box with their daughter's first baby silk. Black as night his hair had been then. What had he looked like? It was too bad he had no photograph – not of him nor of his wife nor of anyone else in his family. He couldn't even remember what his father had looked like, except that he was big. A boy had a right to know his father, but he never really had.

He put away his razor and comb. And then, as usual, he took six deep breaths, sucking the air in slowly while he raised his arms, letting the air out slowly as he lowered his arms. He remembered how impressed the army doctor had been with his chest expansion – five inches it was, and not many men with that amount of lung power. But he was a stringy-looking bastard now – he might as well admit it, or else stop looking in mirrors. Used to be he had a belly like a ribbed washboard. The muscles had sunk in, he supposed.

The desk man came into the washroom while McKeever was changing his socks. He came in with a rush and saw McKeever perched on a toilet seat. Only the nickel toilets had doors, and McKeever had not wanted to spend a nickel just to change his socks. He said quickly, before the man could level any charges at him, "6 a.m. bus come in yet?"

"In an' gone," the desk man snapped. "An' don't tell me you're a company man. Changin' your socks, eh? Shaved here, too! Oh, what a job you did on me!"

"My granddaughter on the bus?" McKeever asked joyously. "She's a girl about your size, but not so mushy, has blue eyes an' coffee-coloured skin, gimpy in one leg. Seen her?"

"Why, God damn you, you goddamn deadbeat, I oughta have you arrested!"

"Don't make more of a fool of yourself than you are," McKeever told him happily. "I'm thanking you for a good night's sleep. I always prefer a bus station to a hotel."

"You show around here ever again an' I'll land you in the tank for ninety days," the man shouted. "God damn you but I will." He banged out, his putty-skinned face swollen with fury.

McKeever chuckled, laced up his shoes and put on his corduroy jacket. Then he started out, bag and overcoat in hand, to get his cup of coffee.

Chapter 13

The second day was better in point of mileage than the first, but not nearly good enough. In the course of nine solid hours by the roadside six autos stopped for McKeever, but he found that Lady Luck was still shining her glass eye upon him. Brockton to Manteca, Manteca to Ripon, Ripon to Salida – in each case the destination of the car was the local post office or the nearest crossroad. Seven o'clock in the evening found him out on the open highway and not quite eighty miles further along towards Los Angeles. He acknowledged bitterly that the boy, Chuck, had more or less predicted it. Eighty miles in a day – from any sensible point of view he was an idiot to have started in the first place.

An idiot he was, but an idiot he intended to remain. He had decided this absolutely a little earlier in the afternoon when weariness and a sense of confusion caused him to give up for a while. He made his way off the road and sprawled out under a shade tree to rest. He fell asleep there, as he told himself in advance he must not, but knew in advance he would. The nap was a balm to him. He awakened with an easier feeling in his heart and sat for a while discussing things with himself. It was clear that his venture had fallen into a crisis because he had started with insufficient capital. Five hundred cars had passed him by, and he was still waiting for the one that would take him to Los Angeles. He couldn't wait any longer. Before he got the golden hitch he needed, he was all too likely to fall on his face from exhaustion and hunger. What he needed – what he had to have – was a bus ticket. His choice was clear: to lay hands on some money or return in defeat to the Booger's. He wouldn't go back – that he knew. Nothing, nothing on God's earth, would make him turn around and go back. The only question was: how in hell to go forward?

He worked out a plan that seemed practical. The next town of size was Madera. Surely, he thought, he could dig up an agency there that would give him a loan – Travelers Aid or the Community Chest* or the Red Cross or something. Lord, the number of times he had given a dollar bill to those outfits!... They couldn't refuse him. And it was not like standing on a street corner to ask for a handout. He'd never do that. The only agency he would avoid like the measles would be State Welfare. He wanted no shenanigans about being sent back to the Booger's.

He felt in much better spirits when he had settled this in his mind. He gathered his things and laboured out to the road... to wait and wait... and then wait some more for a six-mile hitch.

Now he was waiting once again. He had been standing in the same spot for almost an hour. It was a flat stretch of highway with empty fields of sun-baked clay on both sides, an abandoned vineyard that was useless now for cultivation or grazing... and unkind for a man to lie upon. He was wretchedly hungry; there had been a cup of coffee and two crullers for breakfast, but nothing since; he was baked out by the hot day and bone-weary – and Madera was still fifteen miles away. He couldn't fly the distance, he couldn't run it, he couldn't walk it. He could only wait.

His mind felt empty as his stomach. He had squeezed his brain dry in the long hours by the roadside. He had hummed the songs he knew and recited the verses; he had marshalled the names and faces of all the years gone by, listed the friends, the jobs, the cities, the rooming houses. And now, watching the sun slip lower and lower towards the horizon, his brain felt like dead pulp in his skull. And yet... not altogether dead: it was idle, but nervous – empty, but troubled.

He shivered suddenly, as though the night chill were already upon him. He put on his corduroy jacket and looked off towards the horizon and said aloud, "It's not dark yet, lad, there'll be a car." And then he said, "You've been tired before." And then he sighed and said, "Sing a little, eh?" He was silent, and he didn't sing, and there was no humming in his heart. And then he muttered, "Read a little, lad. The sun's low now."

Wearily, forcing himself, he bent down and opened his bag. He took out his spectacles and the book. Then, book in hand, he began to feel better. *The Dance of Life* – it was a lovely title. He read with a spasm of weary eagerness, holding the book in a hand that trembled with fatigue, raising the other hand whenever an auto came by.

His eagerness slipped away. It was not the book for a tired moment by the roadside. Hard words and sentences like molasses for a man to push through. He leafed the pages until his eye caught a phrase that he could hold between his hands:

Man is the measure of all things, of those which exist and of those which have no existence.

"*Hm…* Yes !" he muttered. He jerked up his hand. A young couple in a convertible whipped by.

It was by his insistence on Man as the active creator of life and knowledge, the artist of the world, moulding it to his measure, that Protagoras* is interesting to us today.

He raised his eyes from the book and rubbed his chin and said aloud, "I like it… it's deep." He wished he knew who Protagoras was. It was a sound idea… men moulding the world – bottom truth, he had always believed it. He read further, but the language became involved, and he couldn't make whole cloth of it without a dictionary. In irritation he turned to the front of the book for the author's name. Havelock Ellis… Havelock… a damn queer name for a man, he decided. A man with a name like that naturally turned out a highfalutin book. He called his chapters "The Art of Dancing"… "The Art of Writing"… "The Art of Thinking"* – but where the hell was "The Art of Working"? If this was a book about life, where the hell was "The Art of Earning a Living"? A highfalutin bastard who had never worked and had never earned a living – what damn right did he have to write a book on life?

He dropped the book in the dirt. He struck it with his cane. Then he bent down and picked it up; he wiped the dust off it and put it away in his suitcase. And then, slowly, he looked up at the sky.

The sun had gone. A few orange stains lingered on the pale horizon. Blue dusk was moving towards him over the clay fields like a silent, thousand-footed animal. He went hollow inside. He bit his lip and sighed heavily and raised his hand for a car. Black and shiny and full of power it swept towards him, a quick blur in the pale light. He raised his cane, shaking it with anger, and cried out in a cracked, old man's tone, "Why don't you stop?" He licked the caked spittle at the corner of his mouth. His lips twisted and he murmured, "Jerusalem, Jerusalem."

He sat down uncomfortably on his Gladstone bag and held his head between his palms. He was not giving up, he knew; he would not turn back, and he would pass the night – all the same, it had been a good many years ago, at a funeral in Brownsville, Pennsylvania, that he had felt like weeping and had wept.

Slowly, painfully, McKeever walked by the roadside. It was quite dark now, the moon still low on the horizon, the sky a black husk. He was carrying the Gladstone bag, and he wore Percy Fuller's overcoat, because the night had turned chill. As a snail walks, a beetle, a cockroach, he walked with minute, persistent steps, three inches becoming six, a foot, finally a yard. His feet felt swollen, and the muscles of his thighs trembled with strain, but he walked, head down, cane scraping the gravel. He didn't turn around for the cars that swept by; he knew it would be useless, like expecting a hitch from the gleaming passenger train that had hurtled by him earlier on the tracks that paralleled the road.

He was hoping to reach a farmhouse where he could get some food – perhaps he would find shelter there also, perhaps not. He had been walking for half an hour. He didn't know how much longer he would be able to walk, but back there, when darkness first imprisoned him, he had decided that before he lay down with the mice in the field he would try to reach a house.

He walked. Every few yards he paused to shift the bag from one cramped hand to the other, but he was afraid to stop for a rest; he knew too well there would be no getting up from that rest until morning. He was no longer tired as he had been tired: now he was so besotted by fatigue that he was feeling a bit silly, almost light-headed. And whereas earlier his brain had felt like inert pulp, now it was hotly alive, dancing with a hundred varied lightning thoughts and memories that made no particular sense and had no particular connection and seemed like the thoughts of a brain that was swimming in wine: of the way his wife's gums had gone spongy and begun to bleed when she was in pregnancy; and the time his father sliced his foot with a scythe, lying on the black earth cursing and howling, the blood covering his shoe like hot berry juice and a little boy of six running, running for his mother's help; and of the fine big book about the Dance of Life that he was going to fix up as soon as he was fit to walk into a library; and of Paulie Simmons, his IWW* friend, who had borrowed thirty dollars from him once and never repaid him... "How many bus tickets would that buy now, how many?" his brain asked. And thinking this, he suddenly began to compose a light-headed, aimless 'Litany to a Bus Ticket': "Hey there, Bus Ticket, where the hell are you? Ha-ha. O you twenty bucks that Dopey McKeever spent in San Pedro on Millie with the big ass... an' never even got to lay her – where are you? O dollar bills here and dollar bills there – eighteen dollars lost to Beanie McCarthy in that winter of poker playing when we laid that line outside Tulsa. And ten dollars dropped to Moochy Squires on the Willard–Dempsey fight. And, oh Lord, where can I find me a second-hand bus ticket? Ha-ha!"

He walked. The mind commanded sorrowing limbs, and the limbs obeyed. He walked alone and lonely in a crowded world where a young dog barked somewhere off in the distance and a young man drove by fast in a car and a silver moon rose slowly from the horizon to light the night for young lovers. He walked, and thought wistfully, "Jerusalem, Jerusalem!"

* * *

There was a light finally, but it was not a house. It marked a rail-road bridge where the road dipped down and the tracks that had been on the left side of the highway moved over to the right. He laboured up near to the bridge and stopped and sighed and knew that this was as far as he could go. Tonight the mice had taken over.

He remembered something then from the Depression years: that the struts and underside of a bridge provided shelter. It might even be that he would find a bit of kindling down below and build a fire. There were few bridges that had not been host to a generation of road tramps; the brethren sometimes left conveniences for the next fellow – a cooking tin, a stool, a good rock bed for a fire.

He struck a match, cupped it between his hands and searched for the marks of a path. He struck a second, a third and then saw beaten earth lined by dewy grass. He prayed that the path would not descend too swiftly or trip his feet with hidden potholes. He started down on legs that quivered with each minute step. The path was an easy downgrade for a few feet and then it turned sharply. He felt grass under his shoes and paused to light another match. He found the path again, followed it slowly and laboriously, and turned once more as it curved down – and then saw alongside one of the concrete pillars of the bridge a young man, a bright fire within a circle of stones and a steaming pot of supper. He stopped and sighed aloud and wondered if he could tell a stranger that he was a king amongst men.

The youth looked up from the fire and saw his visitor. He was sitting on a seaman's duffel bag, and he jumped up quickly and uneasily. Of medium height, he seemed shorter because he held himself badly, his head thrust forward and his thin shoulders a bit humped. His face was quite handsome, clean-featured, with a lean jaw and large, black eyes and a thick mop of wavy dark hair. In non-committal silence he watched McKeever's tortured gait along the last few yards of the path.

The young fellow was dressed rather curiously, McKeever noted. He appeared to be in his early twenties, but he wore his clothes like a high-school boy. His heavy, geranium-coloured shirt was not tucked into his jeans, but hung down in loose disorder; and the cuffs of his trousers were rolled up to the calves of his legs. By way of breaking the silence between them McKeever said with weary gaiety, "I don't get around so fast, do I? You'd never believe it, I used to do a back somersault easy as breathin'."

"What's the matter with you?" the young man enquired softly.

"I'm stiff from the arthureetis."

"Probably psychological. That means mental." It was said earnestly, with authority. "All sickness is mental!"

McKeever dropped his bag and stared across the fire at the author of this curious and rather insulting statement. At closer range he saw something in the boy's face that he had not noticed before – a brooding quality and a touch of bitter disdain. It was both an unhappy and an angry face, McKeever thought, and his mind whispered quickly, "Easy, lad, don't get snappy an' lose your supper." Slowly, with effort, he lowered himself to the ground close by the fire. He sighed at the relief to his aching limbs and said, in an agreeable manner, "Is that so? I never knew that. McKeever's my name. Simon."

"My name's Harold Malone. I know a great deal about medicine. I could be a doctor if I wanted."

McKeever considered the remark and replied lightly, "A doctor, eh? Don't you want to be a doctor, Harold? It's a good work, useful."

"No, I don't want to be a doctor. I could be a lawyer, too. I was in the debating society in high school – I was their best debater. But I don't want to be a lawyer either." It was all said softly and earnestly in a brooding, rather haughty tone.

McKeever kept silent. He was curious about the young man, but he was too hungry to enjoy conversation. Sitting where he was, he smelt the rich, honeyed odour of a fish stew in the simmering pot. It knotted his stomach and made his mouth run with juice.

"How old are you, mister?"

"Pushing seventy-four. Don't look it, do I?"

"Seventy-four," Harold echoed. He ran a hand through his wavy hair and frowned with intense thought. "Seventy-four... I remember now... With the Eskimos, when a man gets to be your age and is crippled like you, they put him out in the snow to die. Very interesting. I haven't thought about that for a long time."

McKeever felt like slapping his punky little face. He observed coldly, "The barbarians do a lot of things that civilized people know better."

"I'm not sure – no, I'm not!" A tremor of nervous excitement came into Harold's voice. "I'm trying to decide that now, I'm figuring the angles." He began to pace up and down beside the fire. "I used to be blind like everybody else, like you are. But now the scales are off my eyes. You know what I see? I see *reality*! I can see *right* into the heart of things." He paused and clenched a fist and cut the air for emphasis. "The preachers and the politicians and the teachers – they're all liars. The doctors, especially. I'll prove it to you: in a thousand years the barbarians never killed as many people as we did in one war. You see? It's still the law of survival. Same today as it always was. A jungle. Every man for himself. You can't sprinkle holy water on it."

He stared intently at McKeever, as though expecting a reply. When none came, he continued triumphantly, "Gave you something to think about, didn't I? I'm an educated man. Before the war I was in college. Maybe I'll go back sometime to finish up, maybe I won't. They want me all right, but I don't want them. I got things to figure out. You know what I do?" He lowered his voice in a confidential manner. "I sit here and study the fire. Fire is the source of life. All by myself I get comprehensions that are unusual. I see reality deeper and deeper. I mean it! I know!"

McKeever thought to himself with compassion, "Do you, you poor noodle? Or do you see only the dark corners of your own dark mind?" He wondered how he could divert this flood of talk. He was sorry for this boy, but he was too hungry even for sympathy.

"All men are animals!" Harold burst out abruptly, with passionate bitterness. "Aristotle proved it – walking, biped animals.

You don't even know who he is, but I've got it written down. Why doesn't the world admit it? It's time to stop lying about it. Oh, I'm so tired of lies I could cut my own head off! A head full of lies. You know what this world is? A jungle! Everybody eating everybody else – it's logical. Now the atom bomb has come. It's the wild elephant in the jungle, man destroying everything. I predict it. I see things very clear. It's like the Eskimos. They're logical, they—"

"That's real interesting," McKeever interrupted. "You're a smart lad." His voice began to tremble a little with weakness. "That smells like a good supper you got there, too. You're a good cook, I bet."

There was a moment of pause. The excitement faded from Harold's eyes. He examined McKeever, then the stewpot, then McKeever again. His thin face took on a crafty look. "You want some supper, eh?"

"I'm hungry, lad. Only a cup of coffee and a cruller since last night. I ain't begging, I'm just telling you. I never begged in my life."

Harold said slyly, "It's a good stew. Fish I caught today in the Merced River. It's got potatoes in it, celery, onions. But I won't give you any. Not on your life. I'll only sell it. You got any money?"

"I sure have. Got enough for a meal – forty-eight cents."

Harold was keenly disappointed. "That isn't enough."

"Half a dollar? That's a good price for a stew."

"Like hell it is. It's inflation time. I need a dollar – I got something to buy."

"It's all I have, son, forty-eight cents."

"Damn it, I'm no sucker any more." Harold cried with sudden, erupting anger. "Nobody makes a fool out of me. I'd rather cut my head off first. I'm through!"

"I'm sure not trying to make you a sucker," McKeever said as earnestly as he could. "I just don't have any more."

Harold stood up, his thin face troubled and sullen. "I've found out, I'm not blind! It's the animal life. Two can play at the same game, you know."

A dog howled somewhere off in the night, and McKeever thought bitterly: "I walked an' walked an' it would have been better with the mice in the field."

"Well, all right," Harold burst out sullenly. "You can have forty-eight cents' worth, no more." He picked up a spoon and a chipped earthenware bowl from a stone by the fire. He removed the battered lid of the gasoline can that served as a stewpot, stirred the contents, then filled the bowl two thirds full. "Forty-eight cents' worth," he said angrily. "I'm no sucker." His face was dark with hostility as he held out the bowl. It was the equivalent of a twenty-cent helping in a restaurant, but McKeever knew it would be foolish to argue. He handed over the money. Harold counted the coins with his eyes and shoved them into a pocket of his jeans. Then, with a thin, cruel and terrible grin of satisfaction, he began to eat the stew himself.

McKeever watched in stupefaction. With another man he might have thought it was a clumsy joke. But the wolfish grin on Harold's face told him it was no joke at all, that he would not be fed and he would not get his money back.

He couldn't speak, and he almost couldn't breathe under the weight of anger that possessed him. It was not a good anger, because there was nothing to be done with it. He was helpless before this grinning boy, and they both knew it – an insane, vicious punk whom he could have belted across the face only a few years ago. He watched Harold smack his lips over the stew, and felt as though he would strangle from fury and impotence.

And then, as though a strip of film had passed before his eyes, McKeever saw an image: a man lying beneath a truck, the man being himself, and other men who stared at him with cold, cruel faces and would not help him... and among their faces was Harold's. He saw this flashing image, and his brain grew hot in his skull. A memory came back to him. He felt frightened of it, sick at the first recalling. It was the one event of his life he had always tried to forget. But Harold was linked to that memory, and the memory was riven to Harold. And now, suddenly and completely, he understood the meaning of the nightmare that had plagued his sleep in these past two years. The faces in his dream were real: they had an origin! And this boy, Harold, was here – but also back there, alive and grinning. He watched Harold, and his heart pounded, and he remembered a summer night in the year 1921.

He was working in San Pedro at that time, and he had found a pal in his boarding house, Paul Simmons, a longshoreman. Simmons was a local organizer for the IWW – a brawny, likeable, hot-talking, workers-of-the-world-unite man. They had beers together and talked capital versus labour and how to build the union move-ment. Simmons kept asking McKeever to sign a card and join the outfit and carry a banner among the oil workers, but McKeever never would sign. He was dissatisfied with the A. F. of L., and he liked the one big union idea of the Wobblies, but he had serious differences with them also. Paul's aggressive atheism always left him uneasy, and he had no belief at all in a coming revolution by the working man. He thought it was an impractical theory, and he had no use for it. Nevertheless, Paul and he were friends, and McKeever took great pleasure in their arguments. Sometimes he attended a Wobbly meeting if Paul was going to speak – or he bought a nickel pamphlet from Paul and marked passages with "Hell yes" or "Hell no" as he read it. And sometimes he attended one of the picnics by which the Wobblies raised a few dollars for their eternally barren treasury. These provided relaxation for a single man of forty-eight, and occasionally a woman with whom he could have some fun.

On this Saturday night in July, there was a beer party and dance in the IWW hall. About a hundred adults were there, half of them women, and a number of minor children who could not be left at home. At ten o'clock the phonograph was playing a snappy foxtrot, and McKeever was dancing as close as he could to a big-bottomed Swedish waitress named Millie. Without warning a shower of rocks cracked every window in the hall, set the women to screaming and the children to howling, and cut several people who were in the path of the splintering glass. Almost instantly the door burst open, and the local Ku Klux Klan joined the party.

About sixty men poured into the hall. They carried blackjacks and baseball bats and hatchets, and a few of them had revolvers. Some were drunk, and all were eager to do their Christian duty. Paul Simmons yelled, "Brothers, they're armed – don't start a fight." And from then on it was a sick nightmare.

McKeever had been reading the newspapers on the subject of the Wobblies, but he had never realized that he himself was a bastard of a Russian Bolshevik, a free-lover who wanted to tear down the American family, a stinking subversive and a yellow termite.* By obvious prearrangement, and under the direction of an efficient police sergeant who was using his night off creatively, the gang began to wreck the hall. They smashed every chair in the room, the two old desks, the wooden files. They threw the typewriters and the mimeograph machine out of the windows, tore the posters from the walls, smashed holes in the walls themselves. And meanwhile they yelled every foul term of abuse their tongues could command – not the least of which was the insistence that all of the women present were syphilitic whores. Their last act of destruction resulted in something appalling. The guests at the dance had herded around a long refreshment table on which there were salami sandwiches, doughnuts and cups of coffee. At an order from the police sergeant a flying wedge opened a path to this table and sent it crashing. Mrs Kenneth Black, a chocolate dipper in a candy factory, was a rather slight lady of fifty much given to aimless whining since her eldest son had died of influenza in the war just past. She was sent crashing down with the table. As she fell, she reached out for support. One hand caught the rim of an open pot on the stove in which coffee was boiling. It toppled over on her.

The Ku Kluxers left as her screams of anguish began. In the confusion they achieved their final purpose: they took Paul Simmons along. Not until a few minutes later was his absence discovered.

Mrs Black got well eventually: most of the burn scars were on her body, not her face. Paul Simmons also recovered from the effect of hot tar and feathers and went on in later years to become a minor Communist official whose name McKeever occasionally read in the Los Angeles newspapers. He had died some years back in an automobile accident. But after that night McKeever himself was not quite the same man. He had tried to forget the incident; but one part of him, perhaps the frightened part, never had. And finally now he could understand why an arthritic old man dreamt of lying helpless beneath a truck. As once the hot tar had been poured on Paulie Simmons, so choking oil poured down on him in his nightmare. And now he knew who the men were that squatted around the truck like buzzards and said "cockroach". He knew also why he was still afraid of them, as now he was stunned and sickened by Harold, and afraid of him. It was not a physical fear, but something worse: a fear that his life, as he had lived it and believed in it, was a fraud – a fear that men walked the earth like blind moles to a blind and aimless end, and that Simon McKeever might just as well have joined his wife forty-two years back. Standing over her grave, McKeever had needed desperately to understand the world, to feel it good despite its woes and to believe himself a useful part of it. He needed to believe that now, at seventy-three. A child was born on a farm and grew through hard years to be a man; an oil worker laid ten thousand miles of pipe – and buried his cold child like cold pipe in muddy earth; a man dreamt of being an engineer, but this dream also turned cold; yet, in spite of all this or because of it, and whatever he had held, relished or lost, he yearned and needed to believe that there was meaning to his life, and that there was a joy in being a Man – even a common, anonymous man – and that Men together were more than beasts in the field.

But at this moment he didn't know – he was tired and old and sick at heart, and he didn't know. He wanted to dismiss Harold as a crazy punk, but he couldn't. Harold was linked to the others, and *they* had not been crazy. And perhaps Harold was even right in his loony talk, a wild prophet in the desert – perhaps men had no good purpose on earth at all, and merely lived as the ants lived, the snakes or the wasps. And all of the work and the building – the accidents, the dying and the suffering, the striving and the thinking – were no more than the crawl of the snake or the sting of the wasp, and it was all garbage and empty motion, his life like all the rest. For if men could so easily lose their humanity, pass over into another existence of claw and fang, then perhaps the world was in truth a jungle, and it would never be anything else. And at this moment he didn't know.

Harold had stopped eating. He stood in front of McKeever, looking down at him with a grin. McKeever thought very sadly, "It's wrong, it must be. I'm tired an' I'm letting a loony get under my skin." His mouth worked and he said angrily, "It's wrong, you did wrong!"

Harold's face instantly became savage, as though McKeever's words had been a whip on his skin. His eyes blazed, and his teeth drew back from his lips, and he shouted viciously, "Jesus Christ, I could murder you. Oh my God, how I hate old men who lecture me about what's right and what's wrong! You're all liars – you're out for what you can get, you've pissed up the whole world." He flung the bowl and spoon on the ground. "You want supper from me? Why should I give it to you? Prove it!" He kicked the stewpot over; the contents poured out like a thick, white glue. "Lick it up with the ants, goddamn you."

McKeever started to get up. He dug his cane into the soft earth and used both hands in an effort to pull himself erect.

"Where you going?"

He didn't answer. Harold took a jackknife from his pocket and snapped open a blade. He said with soft lust, "Old-timer, if you don't sit down, I'll cut you open and let all the piss run out." He added furiously, "Sit down." McKeever obeyed. Every nerve in his body was dancing. Harold stood with his knife poised, and then he too sat down. He was a few feet away from McKeever, facing him, his features enraged.

For the second time a dog howled in the distance, and McKeever thought, "He howls for me."

Harold put away his knife. The rage in his face unaccountably began to give way to a look of pain. Then he suddenly gripped his head between his hands. His mouth opened – he sighed as though he were suffering intolerably. He cried out, "Someday I'll cut my own head off, I'll throw it in the river." He moaned with pain and ground his teeth so that McKeever could hear him. Then he got up and stumbled over to his duffel bag. He took out a small tin box. It didn't open easily, and in forcing it he cut his thumb on the sharp edge. He paid no attention to the cut or to the bright jet of blood that covered his finger. He took a cigarette out of the box, long and thin, in a brown paper wrapping, and lit it with a trembling hand. He drew smoke into his mouth, opened his mouth to suck the smoke deep into his lungs and then stood, holding his breath as long as he could. In silence he did this over and over again, and McKeever could see the furrows of pain gradually leaving his face, the forehead becoming smooth, the face young, clean and handsome again. Then, when the cigarette was half smoked, Harold burst out in a happy laugh. "Oh, the weed," he cried. "My pal, my buddy!" He drew on the cigarette, and then began to walk up and down before McKeever. Although he remained silent, he gestured occasionally – small gestures of great authority. He laughed, and he smoked. When the cigarette was down to a stub, he paused in front of McKeever, rocked back and forth on his heels and said, "What's your name again?"

McKeever told him.

"I wish you were my old man," Harold said joyously. "Oh, would I spit in your eye, would I make up for all that slapping around? I'm strong now, I've been in the Navy." He struck his thigh and said, "Bet he has every cop in Colorado looking for me now – bet he has. And the doctors, oh Christ how they're looking for me! And the nurses! I could've laid every one of them, every last one, but I didn't want to, dirty bags, diseased." He flipped his cigarette butt into the fire and gestured expansively. "Those doctors say it's habit forming. Why, I could stop it in a minute if I wanted." He snapped his fingers. "Like that. But why bother? We'll all be dead pretty soon. Atom bombs… bacteria. I see reality. Do you know who Aristotle is? I know his definition of time. Time is the measure of motion. Pretty soon – no motion, no time. Ha-ha. Aristotle and Plato and the other great thinkers – they all walk and talk with me, me and them are one." He noticed his bleeding thumb, wiped it on his shirt and opened the tin box for another cigarette. He lit up and smoked hard, and then, as the second cigarette added its narcotic effect to the first, he fell silent and began to stare at the fire. After a little while he sat down with his head thrust forward and his thin shoulders bowed. He smoked and stared moodily at the bright coals with their little tongues of flame. Then the muscles of his body began to sag, and he seemed to become smaller, to slump within himself. And after a little he sighed, and an expression of the most bitter and harrowing sorrow came upon his face. He began to cry, very softly, like a forlorn boy, the tears trickling down his thin cheeks. He said plaintively, as though the fire were a living creature to whom he was speaking, "Oh, Marty, Marty, Marty…" He paused and stared piteously at the fire. He was oblivious of McKeever's presence – a man in a state of trance. His voice took on a singsong quality, as though he were a priest reciting a familiar and hallowed litany. "Best friend I ever had… buddy and pal… brother and father… only father I ever had… Marty, my pal, Marty…" He sobbed, and his voice broke. And then, as McKeever watched in horror, he flung himself down by the fire, his body writhing convulsively, his head twisting from side to side. In hoarse, guilt-ridden tones, he sobbed out disjointed phrases, like a man who has been poisoned and who lies vomiting foam from his belly. "Threw you overboard, Marty… sold you out. Into the sea… the damn Coral Sea… You hate me now, don't you, *don't you?*… Nothing I could do, nothing, *oh nothing*… You pushed me… *I* didn't see it… You didn't *have* to push me… why didn't you think of yourself?…" He screamed suddenly. "There's your head in one place and your body in another and the fish eating both. Oh my God!" He sobbed in bitter misery. "Saved me twice… once when you pushed me… and once when

I grabbed that thing in the air and the shrapnel got it... Like a fountain of grape juice right out of your neck... And me with your head in my dirty hands. Oh my God! Into the sea... threw you overboard... into the damn Coral Sea..."

He sat up suddenly, his whole body quivering, and took the knife out of his pocket. He opened the blade and stroked the side of his neck gently with the blade, and the tears coursed down his face as he wept and wept.

McKeever watched him and was stunned with horror and compassion. He groped for words, for understanding – his brain whirled drunkenly, but he couldn't think or speak. Was it a new nightmare? Had the world split from too much suffering and too little done to put it right – and was it now the end, in a nightmare under a railroad bridge?

Harold stood up. Still carrying the open knife and bent forward like a hunchback, he crossed to his duffel bag. He picked it up and started away. He didn't look at McKeever, and he gave no indication that he knew anyone was there. He passed between the supports of the bridge, walking towards the open fields that lay in darkness beyond. McKeever watched him, watched the loose shirt flapping and the dull white gleam of his legs where he had rolled up his trousers like a high-school boy. And then he was gone.

A train whistle sounded in the night, and shortly a train crossed the bridge overhead in a majesty of thunder and flying sparks. McKeever lay back on the earth and watched it until it had passed. His whole body was trembling. He felt suffocated, as though he were lying in a swamp with a black muck covering his face. There was no shape to the world any more. It had split, and he was cast loose, alone in a desert waste. Alone and crawling the earth like a silly insect. And that was all – there was nothing else.

He groaned aloud and closed his eyes.

Chapter 14

McKeever slept, but he found no rest in sleep. Like an insect impaled on the point of a needle, he struggled and fluttered in a painful, exhausted swoon. His brain was on fire, and a thousand little tappets played, danced, beat in his body. Faces wavered before his eyes, spoke quick words, vanished as he awakened. He dozed again, and a stewpot fell over, and then a coffee urn toppled over upon a screaming woman, and then a cold voice said, "You'll pass over tonight: this is the last hunger and the last cold – this is the way a life always ends, in garbage and empty motion." He heard and felt anguished; his heart pounded, and he cried passionately, "You're wrong: there's more to it than that – I swear there is!" He tried to rise to his feet, but discovered that he could not, that his legs were weighted down. Then he saw with panic that during the night someone had fastened iron shackles around his legs. His brain asked in hurt confusion, "But why? Do I deserve it? I've always led an honest life!" He clenched his teeth and dug his cane into the earth, and suddenly leapt up.

He dreamt then that he was on a road, in the middle of a broad concrete highway. He was straining uphill towards a bridge, and in one hand he carried his cane, while in the other hand he bore a large book, like a Bible, that had a title stamped on it in gold letters: *The Dance of Life*. The iron shackles on his legs made it terribly difficult for him to walk, but he knew that he had good reason to carry on without fretting. He was certain that when he crossed the bridge he would find someone there with the right key to release him. Yes, indeed – on the other side of the bridge was his loving wife, Mary. It was she who would have the key.

He walked. It was inch by inch and inch by inch, but he ignored the terrible strain of it. And finally he was there, at the entrance to the bridge. It was an immense structure with two massive doors of corrugated iron, like the doors to a mattress factory. He located the bell and pushed it hard, and listened with satisfaction as it sounded high up on one of the towers like the whistle of a locomotive. Then he shouted loudly, "I'm on my way, so open up!"

Instantly a woman stepped out of a watchman's shanty by the side of the bridge. She was wiping her hands on her clean white apron, and she cried, "Why, Simon dear, Simon dear, my very best friend in the whole world – and what ever are you doing here, what ever now?"

"Open the doors, Ada," he replied joyously. "I'm on my way."

"What *are* you talking about?" she exclaimed in amazement. "There's a toll: it costs a dollar. Who ever heard of crossing this bridge without paying a toll?"

"It's *my* bridge, ain't it?" he replied with indignation. "I built it, didn't I? My own hands, my own skill, and reading the blueprints?"

"But you don't *own* it, do you?"

"I don't care who owns it," he told her with scorn. "Human rights before property rights – ain't you ever heard of that?"

"Oh la-la-la," she replied with a laugh. "What language to use! *Everybody* pays a toll."

McKeever listened to her brassy laughter and was suddenly frightened. He muttered forlornly, "But what's a man to do, Ada?"

"I don't know. It's no concern of mine."

He felt sick when he heard this: he felt like weeping bitterly. He cried out in sorrow, "Oh, Ada, Ada, were you an' me an' all the others born only to sting each other like black ants in a forest? There's more to it than that, ain't there?"

"I don't know," she replied fearfully, "I never thought about it. It gets me all confused to dwell on things like that."

"Damn it," he cried suddenly, "it's my bridge an' I'll cross it. Out of my way!"

"Harold... Harold!" Ada screamed. "He won't pay the toll!"

A young man burst out of the little shack by the side of the bridge. He carried a gleaming butcher knife, and his black hair flew in the wind as he charged up to McKeever. "You're under arrest!" Instantly McKeever found himself surrounded by a crowd of hostile men. He tried to drive them back with his cane, but they rushed him from all sides. They tore the cane from his right hand and the book from his left. Then they knocked him to the ground. He heard his own voice crying out in aching despair, like a flute note in the wind, "My book, don't tear it up, it's got my life in it." There were only jeers in reply, and he was dragged over the rough ground while a cruel voice shouted, "Over the cliff with him, he's garbage, he's pissed up the world enough already!"

Then he was hurled over into a void of cold and lonely darkness – he was falling, falling, falling, his bowels cramped with fear. He heard a voice call "Sentence him", and again "Sentence him", and still once again "Sentence him". He opened his eyes and saw that he was in a courtroom – an immense, vaulted cave of a room, forbidding and gloomy, with great shadows upon the cold stone walls.

"Sentence who?" he asked.

"Why, you, of course!" the judge replied. McKeever looked up to the bench and was horror-stricken by what he saw. There was no one in the judge's chair at all – it was empty – but on the wide desk in front there was a living head with hot, bright eyes and a grinning mouth. "Why, you, of course," the head repeated amiably, "you!"

"Damn it, I ain't even been tried yet," McKeever replied with anger. "How come I'm being sentenced already? What's the charge? I never saw a judge like you anyway. Where's the rest of you?"

"Oh, if it's a trial you want, you can have *that*," the head replied with a derisive grin. "It'll all come to the same thing in the end. Prosecutor, what's the charge?"

"He's garbage," Harold yelled with anger. "Why was he ever born?"

"Then I'm ready to pass sentence," the judge announced coldly. "Guilty! Cut off his head with a pocket knife. Throw it in the stew."

McKeever broke out in a clammy sweat. The shackles on his legs became so heavy that he thought he would faint. But in the next moment he was swept by a great anger. He cried out, "Damn it, you *can't* sentence a man without a trial. It ain't right."

"Right?" asked the head on the desk in sudden fury. "Who knows what's right? I'm a head without a body, can't you see that? Do you think that's right?" His white teeth chattered with anger, and he fixed McKeever with hot, unblinking eyes.

"Answer that, why don't you?" Harold cried. He suddenly twisted his own head off his neck. He tossed the head in the air while a fountain of hot berry juice spurted from his neck. "Answer this, too, you cockroach!"

"Oh yes, answer, you must!" a woman's voice called piercingly. McKeever turned around. He saw with astonishment that there were rows and rows of wooden benches behind him, and that they were filled with people he knew – his family and his loved ones and his friends. Seated in the very first row was Mary, his wife. She was holding out her hands to him, and her face looked so sad and white, her eyes so stricken, that McKeever felt as though his heart would shatter.

"Oh Mary, my dear, my own heart's darling," he called to her with pity and longing, "what is it you want me to answer?"

"The things I don't understand," she replied with tears, "the living and the dying and the thread that's snipped in two without rhyme or reason. Oh, answer me, Simon – I turn and twist each night in my coffin."

When she said this, a sudden moan burst from the people on the benches. They wept and flung their arms about; some cried aloud and others began to run this way and that, blindly and aimlessly, like moles who have been smoked from their burrows and are lost. "Oh, yes, answer!" they called. "Testify." And then he saw that along with the others it was his own father who was calling to him in this way. His father was kneeling on the ground under a cold sun, digging stony earth with his fingers. He raised his head and howled like a hurt dog, saying, "Testify." McKeever saw his mother there also; she was seated in a rocker, and on her lap there were five little waxen dolls. She fondled the dolls and looked at him with bruised eyes, and her lips framed the word, "Testify." He watched her in wonder, and then understood that she was keening for the five little babies she had borne, all of them dead after one season like sad little butterflies. He began to weep with his pity for her, and he cried out "Mother!", but she wouldn't answer him: she only shook her head and whispered again, "Oh, testify." Then, through his tears, he saw a host of others calling to him. And among them was the youth, Harold. He was sitting on his seaman's bag with his head under his arm, and the head was weeping tears of blood. He cried in astonishment to Harold, "But why are *you* among the mourners? Ain't you my prosecutor?" And Harold replied, weeping, "I am here and I am there."

McKeever shrank back from this crowd of wounded people. He cried out in protest, "Why do you ask *me*? It's upside down. Don't you understand that *I'm* the one on trial here? It's you who should be testifying for me."

"How testify?" asked Marcus Peake. He came forward timidly, bearing a pretty little cake that was covered with penny candles. "I'm your friend, but how can *I* help? Would you like some cake?"

"Why, just tell the judge I'm not guilty," McKeever implored eagerly. "Won't you do that for me, Marcus? Just tell him I lived a good life."

"Oh, I couldn't do *that*," Peake replied regretfully. "What's there to testify about in this world? You get born an' you grow old an' you end up like garbage, like the lice that a hard rain shakes off a tree. It's all confused, it's a dream an' a mystery to me."

"But there's more to it than that, ain't there? Ain't I lived in a man's way on this earth? Ain't I followed the path an' jigged the dance?"

"Oh, I wouldn't know that either," Marcus replied sorrowfully, "I ain't heard any music in years. I'm not so sure there *is* any."

"Me neither," said Percy Fuller, who was standing behind him. "It ends up in a silly room with mirrors, *you* know that. What's there to testify? There's no music at all."

"Ha-ha!" the judge screamed suddenly. "You've got no witnesses, and you've got no case. I'll sentence you now, by God. They'll roll you into a muddy ditch like a cold pipe."

McKeever knew then that he would have to testify without help from anyone. He felt stunned and betrayed. He thought with self-pity, "I'm the loneliest man in the world." But as he stood there and gazed upon the people all about him and listened to their cries of sorrow, a sudden knowledge came to him. He saw with utmost clarity that he was no more alone than they. A feeling of exquisite relief entered his heart, and he wondered why he had been so long in understanding it. Each man and woman alone and groping in the universe... and yet not alone, but striving together. And he knew suddenly that in spite of everything he still heard the music, and he still believed there was a good path to be trod. Strength flowed into his veins. His body pulsed and shivered and beat. He held out both arms in an agony of rapture and shouted, "I believe!"

A brooding, fateful silence instantly gripped the courtroom. And in the silence McKeever felt the passion of his seventy-three years, like the wings of a white bird, beating in his heart. He cried loudly, "I believe what a man lives for!"

"Hah? What?" the judge asked with chattering teeth.

"And the wars?" Harold demanded in a piercing voice. "The fish and the flies that nourish on the boys named Marty?"

"And the greedy ones?" Percy Fuller cried. "My tool shed and my house and my only-one-more-payment-on-the-mortgage? Lost, lost – the old men on the highway and no one caring, lost?"

"Like lice from a dead tree," Peake groaned. "Am I sixty-five yet, Simon, am I?"

"And the sorrows?" added his wife, weeping. Her tears fell like winter rain upon the stones. "The bitter accidents? The flesh of my Emily that was burnt and shrivelled? She twists and turns each night by my heart. What *can* you believe?"

"Oh Mary, my wife, my darling," McKeever replied, "there are cruel mysteries... but there's more. There are sorrows... but

more. There's the lice on the twig and the crawl of the snake...
but there's more."

"What more?" she asked forlornly. "Oh Simon, tell me now,
what more?"

He opened his arms wide and held them out to her. She came to
him, and he embraced her. "We'll go now," he said tenderly, "and
we'll lie down in the sweet-smelling grass, and there I'll tell you."

"But you have to testify," she protested. "You're on trial."

He smiled at her and replied, "It was only a nightmare. It's over
now. I'm light and strong again. The lameness is gone."

"But there's Harold."

"Only a poor boy. One of the cruel sorrows of the world. But
he's gone away. I'm ready to wake up now. It was only a dream."

She put her arm through his then, and they moved out of the
darkness towards the sunlight on the hill. He felt inexpressibly
good and strong, purged and at ease. And as they came out of
the cave, he saw with pride how rosy her cheeks were, and how
tenderly her eyes glowed when she looked at him. They lay down
in the clover, and he held her throbbing heart close to his. They
listened to the bird cries, to the shouts of children at play on the
slag heap of a coal camp down below along the river. He kissed
her lovingly on eyes and cheeks and mouth, and then he said with
exultation, "See how it is, my darling. We'll have a child, and we'll
do for it as best we can. But I've seen it now for seventy years, I
know at last. Some get tired and some lose their way. Some are
ground down by others and some get turned mad. But the earth
still turns, and only a man has the power to dream. Up from the
apes by his own doing, and that's the bright glory of it."

"Ah yes," she said with tears of soft relief. "That's how it must
surely be."

"Oh, it shakes the sky," he continued joyously, "it turns the earth.
Each generation with a dream like a bright North Star to guide
it through sad and bitter. Oh, I believe it, there's no doubt in me
any more. It's why Lincoln and Jesus lived and died."

"Ah yes," she said contentedly, "yes, my dearest, yes."

"Suckling the children and washing the dishes and raising the new generation. It's the good dance, Mary. Working the earth and changing it. Building a bridge or building a union. Losing the way sometimes and then finding it."

"And what will the way be for us?" his wife asked. "For you and for me and for the child, our Emily?"

He answered firmly, without sadness, "Not for you to know of me or me of you. But to know the big thing only – the turning earth and the generations up from the apes, walking the path, striving and standing up, shouting and singing. I believe it, Mary, it aches in my heart. And all by the doing of people like us, it's the fine wonder of it."

She was silent and at ease at last, pressing her face to his chest and weeping quietly. "I'll turn in my coffin no more. I'll rest quiet now."

"And I'll be going on," he said tenderly. "The clover is sweet, and you need to rest, but I'll be going on. My lunch pail's packed, my path leads over the bridge to Glendale."

"And what's for you there, Simon?"

"Who knows? But it's the right path, and surely I have to walk it. There's a dream at the other end."

"Goodbye then, dearest. Go."

He left her with a last look at her sleeping face. He strode off in the bright sunlight towards the bridge. He saw that the marble columns were strong and beautiful like the milk-white throat of a woman.

He opened his eyes and knew at once that he had been dreaming. A round, bright moon was high in the sky, and its rays fell in misty shafts through the ties and struts of the railroad bridge. He stared and wondered why the bedroom looked so strange. Then he remembered. He raised up on an elbow and saw the ashes of the fire, the overturned stewpot.

The dream still gripped him. The blood was pulsing hotly through his body, and he felt wondrously alive, good, content.

What had happened to him? How had this deep feeling of peace and exultation come to him? He didn't know, and he found that the crowded events of the dream were rapidly fading, the voices becoming half-tones, the figures blurred. But the ease in his heart remained. He murmured aloud, "What time is it, I wonder?" And then he murmured, "I'm thirsty." And then he thought, "Oh, it's a good trip, it's surely right, an' I'll get there."

He closed his eyes. He heard a dog bark far off in the night, and he fell asleep.

Chapter 15

McKeever awakened to the metallic thunder of a freight train crossing the bridge above his head. He lay watching it through gummy eyes – train going to Fresno to Bakersfield to Los Angeles. The night before he had felt wretched at the sight of a highballing train, but his reaction was different now. He murmured with satisfaction, "Well... had a hell of a wild night last night, didn't I? Some trip! What time is it, I wonder?"

When the train passed, he saw that the sun was high in the sky. He sat bolt up in a fret of irritation at having wasted the morning... and then almost toppled over with dizziness. He waited, hands pressing the earth, until his swimming head cleared. He murmured aloud, "What's the matter with you this morning?" A series of physical tabulations gave him the answer. His mouth was parched and he was dreadfully thirsty; his stomach cried out with the pain of hunger; his body was stiff and aching and weak all at the same time. "Oh my," he muttered, "bad business."

Two yards away from him there was a greyish white mess on the earth, the foul remains of the fish stew. Ten million ants were racing around its edges in lines and squads and columns. Flies, beetles, wasps, bumblebees also had swarmed to the feast. McKeever couldn't help laughing at the disgusting sight – Harold's stew was nourishment for the hungry after all. Poor, sorry, loony Harold.

He tried in vain to recall the night's dream. It had become a vague blur in his mind. But there had been a magic in it, that he knew: he felt its balm in his heart. It was quite wonderful and very odd... as though the dream had been a mountain he needed to climb... and he had climbed out of a swamp and up the mountain to solid ground and clear air. And now he felt fine in spite of his aches and pains, in tune with the universe somehow, eager and ready to be going about his business.

He grinned cockily and wondered how far he was from Glendale. He calculated for a moment and then decided that it was about two hundred and eighty miles. "*Hm!* Not bad!" he murmured with satisfaction. And Madera only a stretch away. He would hitch into Madera and canvas the welfare agencies for a bit of a loan. Jerusalem, Jerusalem – it was time to rise and shine.*

He turned on his side to begin the operation of standing up. First he knelt and then he dug his cane into the earth. He bore down on it with both hands. By the time he had struggled to his feet he was dizzy again and a clammy grease had welled out from the pores of his unwashed face. The white mess of the stew was shimmering before his eyes; the ants seemed to be rioting in an idiotic dance. "Oh my," he muttered a second time, "bad business." He breathed deeply and blinked his eyes and wiped his forehead with his sleeve. And then, as the vertigo departed, he chuckled faintly. "*Dance of the Bugs*," he murmured with weak gaiety. "That Havelock feller forgot it." He picked up his Gladstone bag. He turned his face to the path, to the mountain, to the precipice that led to the highway above.

A rattletrap auto, pulling a luggage trailer, was slowly approaching the dip in the highway under the railroad bridge. The auto was a business coupé designed to seat three people, but this one carried the entire Cooley family – husband, wife and six small children. A nursing infant lay on the mother's bony lap; the two girls were squeezed in by her side; a fourth child sat amiably on the floorboard; the two biggest ones, nine and ten, lay at full length on the shelf behind the seat. With the exception of Aubrey, the eldest, the family was passing the time by making up verses to the tune of 'Fly's in the Buttermilk'.* Aubrey had grown bored with singing, and had retired to the solace of shooting wild game in Africa. With his nose touching the car window, he held his elephant gun at the ready and plugged any lion, squirrel or panther that happened along. So it was that he suddenly stiffened and his head swivelled and he cried, "Pa, there's a dead man."

No one heard him. They were singing heartily,

> ...if you can't have whiskey,
> Buttermilk will do...

"A dead man!" Aubrey yelled. "A dead man by the road." His father heard and laughed and was not surprised. An hour earlier Aubrey had seen a rhinoceros.

> ...skip to my Lou,
> My dar... ling.

Aubrey began to beat his father on the shoulder. "I saw him!" he screamed. "A dead man."

His father stepped on the brake; the singing faded. "What'd you see?"

"A man... layin' on the ground... in the grass!"

"How do you know he wasn't asleep?"

The boy shook his head violently. "You never saw anybody sleep like *that*. He was flopped over something, I couldn't see, but his head was down an' his hind end was up... who sleeps like that?"

Cooley Senior frowned, but he was aware that he would have to return. Waste of time or no, he knew his Aubrey. He exchanged a tolerant smile with his wife and asked, "How far back, sonny?"

"Before we went under the bridge."

The car started back. The nine-year-old punched his brother in the ribs, enquired eagerly, "You see much blood?"

Aubrey considered it, yearned to remember the smallest trickle of blood, but replied firmly, "No blood."

"Oh, he's not dead," said his mother. "Don't be silly."

"He's dead all right!" Aubrey retorted. "Poisoned, maybe. That's why there's no blood."

"Raped, too," the nine-year-old murmured reflectively.

The parents guffawed. "Keep your eye peeled," said the father as they emerged from under the bridge.

"Near here... Slow down," Aubrey commanded with shrill excitement. "There!" He almost lost control of his voice.

"You *see* – do you *see* him?"

"Lester, there *is* a man," the mother said. "And he can't be sleeping."

Cooley stopped the car. He peered out at McKeever's awkward figure in the grass by the road and then said with sharp authority, "Nobody get out! Let me find what's doing first." He picked up a tyre iron from the floorboard. He stepped out quickly, but when he reached the shoulder of the road he advanced with caution, the weapon ready.

"Hey there!"

There was no reply. McKeever was sprawled out grotesquely. He had managed the arduous climb up the path, but at the end he had become dizzy again. He was still wearing Percy Fuller's overcoat, and he had tried to take it off. With one arm free of it he had toppled over in a faint. Since the Gladstone bag was in front of him, he had sprawled over it, head down, rump in the air. He had fallen only a few minutes before Aubrey saw him, and he was already beginning to stir back to consciousness. He sensed Cooley's hands as they lifted him off the suitcase and placed him on his back. His eyelids began to twitch and flutter.

Cooley felt the beat of McKeever's heart and then called to his wife, "He ain't dead. He's an old geezer, must've had a sunstroke. You got any water in the trailer?"

"No, but there's a bottle of milk."

"Get it."

The family piled out of the car. While Mrs Cooley, with the infant in her arms, ran back to the luggage trailer, the children gathered around McKeever with gaping mouths. Aubrey said authoritatively, "I told you, Pa, didn't I? He was *almost* dead."

"Dead?" McKeever echoed weakly. He opened his eyes. "I ain't dead, don't go burying me." He blinked in confusion at seeing the assembled Cooleys. "What? What's happened? Oh my, did I faint?"

"You had a sunstroke, I guess. My kid saw you."

"Me," said Aubrey.

"Ain't been in the sun... couldn't be that," McKeever argued weakly. His mouth worked, and he paused in shame before muttering, "No starch... ain't had anything to eat for a while. Oh my, never fainted in my life."

"Ma – can you find that milk?" Cooley shouted.

His wife came over with it after a moment, and Cooley whispered to her. She gave Aubrey the infant to hold and ran back to the trailer. Cooley knelt by McKeever's side. "I'll raise you up an' you drink some of this." McKeever nodded. He drank slowly at first, a mouthful at a time, but then he turned avid. He tilted the bottle with his own hand and gulped the precious, refreshing liquid. When he had swallowed half of the bottle, he sighed deeply and paused for a rest. He saw the children gaping at him as though he were an oddity in a zoo. He grinned back at them to hide his cruel embarrassment and muttered, "Better than Irish whiskey, thanks."

"Finish it."

"Thanks. McKeever's my name."

"Cooley."

McKeever nodded, but then paused and said, "What am I doing, stealing your baby's milk?"

"Forget it. We can buy some in Madera."

"I found a banana an' half a box of raisin crackers," said Mrs Cooley, running back to them. "We ate ourselves out last night. How're you feeling? I wish we had something better for you."

A lump balled up in McKeever's throat, and he lost his embarrassment in the face of their open-hearted kindness. "This is just fine," he told her emotionally. "I sure thank you people." He helped himself to a cracker, chewed its sweet nourishment with relish and grinned affectionately at the kids. He was suddenly in love with the Cooleys. Only a part of it was their decency to him.

Mostly it was the magnificent, comical sight of all eight of them grouped around in a blond and bony semicircle. There seemed no variation whatever to the Cooleys. Father and mother and every one of the children were tall and blond and bony, lean and strong, with freckled, bony faces and white, snaggy teeth – except for the infant, who kept puckering his lips over some inward secret and had no teeth at all. He was crazy about them: it was the family life he had missed – it moved the world. "Guess I can sit up by myself now," he said after a while. He felt greatly restored, and he wondered whether he ought not to be polite and refuse the banana.

Cooley helped him up. "You live around here?" He took the banana from his wife, peeled the skin half down and handed it over. McKeever lost his resolve. With his mouth full of the slightly overripe fruit he explained about his trip to Los Angeles, "Couldn't be you'd hitch me into Madera, could it?" he asked hopefully. "I'll be dandy once I get there."

Cooley shook his head. "We're packed in like sardines. We can hardly get all our kids in as it is."

"Well you've done plenty for me, don't worry," McKeever said heartily. "I'll get a hitch. I wish I could pay you right now for the eats, but I'm strapped. If you'll give me your name an' address, I'll sure send it to you. I got money coming to me first of next month."

"Forget it."

"Oh no," McKeever said earnestly, "I mean it, I'd like to." He fumbled in his jacket for his notebook and pencil stub. "What's your first name?"

"Lester Cooley. I can't give you an address, though. We're pickers – we live out of a tent."

"No address at all?"

Cooley looked over at his wife with a delicate grin. "Nope. We keep shifting around the Valley."

McKeever caught the grin and didn't like it. He had worked the Valley himself during the Depression – a man always used one post office or another for his mail. The lie was intended to be friendly, he knew, but it was also patronizing, and it rubbed him the wrong way. He said politely, "Then I'll send it to the Red Cross in your name."

Cooley laughed. "OK, do that." He held out his hand. "Good luck, Dad." McKeever shook hands and felt paper against his palm. It was a folded dollar bill. "Oh no," he said instantly, "I'm fine, an' you got a raft of kids."

"Forget it."

"Oh no. I mean it! Not unless I can pay it back."

"Forget it. C'mon, everybody."

"I mean it! I mean it!" McKeever cried harshly. His pleasure in the Cooleys had abruptly soured. The man had no damn right treating him as though he were a panhandler.

Cooley didn't reply. He was shepherding his kids to the car. McKeever struggled to his feet. "Here now," he called vehemently, "I mean it, I won't have it." His voice was shrill – it cracked unpleasantly from the depth of his feeling.

Cooley turned around and came back. "Suit yourself," he said mildly, a bit coldly. "I can use it."

McKeever gave him the bill and felt awful. "You don't understand," he said with a stammer. "It ain't that I'm not grateful."

Cooley nodded and turned away. His manner indicated that he wanted to be done with the matter.

"I just don't take money I can't pay back," McKeever cried after him. "I'm no pauper, you know. But I'm grateful!"

"OK," Cooley called back mildly, "keep your shirt on, Pop." He swung into his car and started the motor. Mrs Cooley waved, and McKeever, still feeling unhappy, waved back – and then they rolled away.

"Oh, God damn it," he muttered aloud. They had been so decent to him – he hated to think of their leaving in anger. But it was a terrible thing to treat another man like a beggar. Cooley needn't have been so stubborn.

He saw a car and raised his hand and watched it pass. Then he bent down and picked up the container of milk and the few remaining crackers. He was a bit hungry still, and a bit disgruntled also, but on the whole he was feeling... elegant. His strength had returned; his legs were loosening up in the hot sun; he felt heartily ready for another day, God bless the Cooleys. He would send a dollar to the Red Cross in their name.

A moving van passed him by, a Greyhound bus, an oil truck. He discarded the empty container of milk and the empty cracker box. He wished that he might wash and shave and change his socks, but such pleasures would have to wait for Madera, A boy in a jalopy raced by, then a couple in a roadster. He took out his pipe and rubbed the bowl against the wings of both nostrils; he stuffed it with Finney's brown cabbage and lit up. A second oil truck; a tomato-red convertible; a slow-moving station wagon with an elderly couple. The station wagon passed fifty yards beyond McKeever, stopped and commenced backing up. A lady was driving, and a white-haired man by her side peered out at McKeever through yellow sunglasses. When the car was abreast of him, the man called out in a voice so light and thin that it seemed to float on the air like a feather. "Do you want a hitch?"

"Oh my God, yes!"

"Where are you going?"

"Los Angeles. But any place is fine, Madera, Fresno – I need to make a town like the very dickens."

"Well we're going to Los Angeles, too, and we have plenty of room."

"Oh my God," McKeever cried, "my golden hitch, I can't believe it!"

The couple began to laugh, and the man said, in his feathery voice, "Why not? Why not believe it?"

Chapter 16

In the hours that followed, McKeever decided that he was being wafted to Los Angeles on a magic carpet. It was not only the golden hitch that made him feel that way: even more, it was the character of the couple who had picked him up.

From the point of view of fact and science McKeever didn't believe in omens any more than he believed in goblins. Yet, as he became acquainted with the old couple, there burgeoned in his heart a conviction of success and a vision of triumph that could only mean he had been granted a "sign". Or something. He really didn't care, and he refused to be sober about it.

The name of the pair was Cochran. The woman was small in stature, neatly turned; her round face was freckled and placid, her trim figure was firm; she appeared to be in her middle sixties. Her husband was slight and not much taller than she was; his thin, tanned, angular face was lined with fine wrinkles; his white hairs were sparse; the years had reduced him to false teeth. Yet, when they paused to buy gas for the auto, McKeever observed that he walked to the comfort station with an elastic step, his head erect, his back straight as a plank. He found it impossible to judge the man's age.

Both of the Cochrans were pleasantly cordial to McKeever and frankly curious about him. Their questions began the moment he was seated. Mr Cochran kept turning around to peer at his guest through yellow sunglasses and exclaim with interest, "Is that so?... Think of that!..." Or, very frequently, "And then what?" Mrs Cochran, who was a cautious driver, never turned around, but she asked as many questions as her husband, and McKeever noticed that from time to time her eyes would flick up to study him briefly in the rear-view mirror. Yet somehow their direct, uninhibited curiosity was sympathetic rather than offensive, and McKeever found it quite gratifying to tell them at length about his trip. From their appearance and their clothes, and from the workaday look of the station wagon, he assumed at first that they were farmers. As they drove along, however, he observed that neither of them had the knobby, work-worn hands of the trade and neither of them spoke like a farmer. They were, in fact, an unusually garrulous old pair, and their small talk with each other was odd and fetching. Even while making enquiries of McKeever they engaged steadily in a guerrilla warfare with each other. One of them would ask McKeever a question, and he would reply – and then Mr Cochran might say, "Go on, what happened after that? Don't stop!" And then his wife would interrupt to say, "Let the man catch his breath, Edgar" – and then they would be off in a skirmish.

"He can breathe for himself, keep your two cents out of this," Cochran would tell his wife. "You're a busybody, Margaret."

"I'm not a busybody." (Her voice placid and comfortable.) "What about you? Don't you realize you're a nag? Mr McKeever's not on trial."

"And then what, Mr McKeever?"

Each of these combats was indulged in casually, Mrs Cochran's manner retaining its serenity, Mr Cochran regarding her with raised eyebrows and a delicate grin. And McKeever, laughing at them quietly, answered a question, ducked their blows, then answered another – until finally the Cochrans knew why he was on the highway and how he came to be without funds; how he had slipped away from the Booger, and all about the woman in the drugstore. And not only his immediate history, but what he had done in his life, and even the things he had aspired to do.

"Quite a trip," Mr Cochran said finally in an admiring tone. "Say now, we've got a farm up by Marysville. You might look in on us sometime. What do you say, Margaret?"

"Oh yes. Provided you do your own cooking and wash your own dishes. Edgar keeps inviting people and expecting me to serve them. I won't – have my own work... What are you going to do when you get cured, Mr McKeever?"

"I got one or two leads on jobs already," McKeever replied boastfully. "I'll get something, I'm a good worker." And then, because Los Angeles was drawing nearer each moment, he lost his usual reserve and told them about his big project, his book. He described its content and listed some of the thinkers to be included. "The path of the common man," he explained eagerly, "it's never been presented like that, has it? An' the shaping of the world – that's never been told either, the big purpose of it. All those razor-sharp thinkers in one book, piling all their good thinking together... Oh, it's a useful project if I say it myself... I'll never know how it came to me." He paused, and his mouth worked and then he suddenly became shy and silent.

The Cochrans were silent also. The man turned around to peer at McKeever; his thin lips were pursed; there was an odd expression on his sharp face; and Mrs Cochran studied him closely in the rear-view mirror. McKeever swallowed and felt keenly embarrassed. He knew it was a good idea, but it was a blunder to expect others to understand it in advance.

"You know," Mr Cochran murmured at last, "that's a good project. I hope you do it."

McKeever cried sceptically, "You really mean it?"

"Certainly I mean it. What do you think, Margaret?"

"Oh, I agree," she replied with hearty warmth. "It's solid, it's got bones. I'd call it an anthology *about* the common man *for* the common man. Right? I wonder why no one ever did it before?"

McKeever soared through the heavens. He blushed and stammered, "Well now... it ain't done yet, it's only an idea. I'm not educated, I don't even know if I can handle it so that a book company will put it out. It's just that I have strong opinions on the subject."

Mrs Cochran, who was absorbed in passing a truck, said haltingly, "The best work... comes from... strong... opinions."

Her husband's feathery tone suddenly went up in pitch. "Car coming. Move over, Margaret. Don't you see him?"

"I see him... better eyes... than you have, Pokey."

She moved over into the right lane and said placidly, "Backseat driver. *The Path of Man* – that's a first-rate title."

"Reminds me of *The Dance of Life*," her husband added.

"It's better."

"No, it's not better. Don't butter the man."

"Yes, it is, Edgar. It's more sensible. Havelock had a weakness for the arty. Life's not a dance."

"What a lump you are."

"Why did he wear that beard? It was an affectation."

"You're dotty."

"Say now," McKeever interrupted, "have you folks *met* that writer?"

"He was a friend of ours, but he's dead now," replied Cochran. "He got my wife under the mistletoe one Christmas, and she wouldn't kiss him. He died of a drooping libido."

"You're so clever today, Pokey."

"What do you think's in my suitcase? It's that same book. You knew him, eh?" He stared in wonder at his hosts. A man in a sport shirt and a pair of old slacks; a woman in a gingham dress, a kerchief on her head. Who were they that they joked about a writer in this manner and could be friends with him? He asked, and a door opened upon the shining world he once had hoped to possess for himself.

"Why, we're scientists," Cochran answered.

"Scientists – what kind?"

"Biologists."

"You mean chemistry... serums?"

"Margaret's field is plants, mine is bees."

"An' what do you do? I mean, what kind of work is that?"

"You do research and write about your findings and teach students."

"Teach?" McKeever's tone became heavy with awe. "Are you professors?"

"Margaret was principal of a high school. I was professor of Biology at a university. We're both retired now, but I'm a consultant to the Department of Agriculture."

"You advise on bees?"

"The breeding and improvement of the honey species."

"When did you retire from that teaching?"

Cochran turned around with a smile. "You really want to know how old I am, don't you?"

McKeever nodded eagerly.

"I'm eighty-two, sonny. I'm one hell of a tough mule."

"Oh, that's wonderful! An' you're still at work?"

"Why, sure. We have a farm up at Marysville – it's our laboratory. Margaret's writing a textbook for students, I'm doing this and that."

"You mind my asking... how's your health?"

"Great," Cochran replied with manifest satisfaction. "I had to cut out my cigars, however – used to be a heavy smoker. Get a little constipated now an' then. I have old man's prostate, of course. You have that, don't you?"

"Not me," McKeever replied vainly. "There's my lameness, but once I'm over that I'll be sound as a bell. Got a strong constitution; I eat like a horse – used to do a handstand easy as breathin'."

"Fine," Cochran replied gently.

"Oh Lord, I'm so damn glad you folks picked me up!" McKeever burst out happily. "Aside from the hitch – and that's wonderful – you don't know what it means to be meeting you. Everybody telling me to lay down an' throw in the sponge... I knew they were cockeyed. Now I can tell them about you folks. Oh, I wish I'd gotten an education – how I wish I had a trade like yours! The oil line is great, you understand – only, it gives out... you need a strong back for it. Say, are you two headed for a vacation in LA? I can tell you where the zoo is, the planetarium, the history museum, a lot of things."

"We're not staying. We're going on a trip."

"Free boat ride," said her husband. "I do love boats. A boat, a moon and Mrs Cochran. Got all our children that way. Watch yourself this trip, Margaret."

"We have three boys, Mr McKeever. One of them is in science too – anthropology. A foundation is sending him on a field trip to Brazil, and we're tagging on."

"For how long?"

"For the summer. Until October."

"Oh my! You taken other trips like that?"

"Ten or twelve."

"Not all on boats though," said Cochran. "Some of them had to be on camels. It kept down the size of our family."

"Stop it, Pokey."

"My God, that's what I wanted to be," McKeever exclaimed with envy, "a scientist or an engineer."

"You've had a useful life of your own, haven't you?" asked Mrs Cochran. "Seems to me that's what your book is about. There are limitations in our field too."

McKeever sighed, and loved her for the remark, and felt wonderful. And he thought with rapture that if this old feather of a man could go gallivanting off to the jungles of Brazil at eighty-two, what music and shouting might not lie beyond for Simon McKeever? It was the good omen, the fine promise, the twenty-four-carat guarantee. It was the final inspiration he needed to walk in and see that doctor.

It was a day like a happy dream, the one day in a thousand, like lying with his Mary in the sun-drenched clover above the flowing Monongahela. They paused for lunch in the early afternoon, and Mrs Cochran came up with a picnic basket. There were fresh cucumbers and ripe tomatoes and celery; there was cottage cheese and fruit and lemonade. They sat in the cool of a pepper tree, and the Cochrans talked about trachoma in Egypt, about the milkweed as a source of rubber, about the function of the earthworm in the soil... and squabbled, battled, pecked and scratched at each other with abiding affection and pleasure. Then, while Mr Cochran took a half-hour nap, his wife drove McKeever to a service station down the road. He shaved and washed, changed shirt, socks and shoes, and emerged feeling like a king.

At sunset they reached Lebec, high on the mountain ridge between Bakersfield and Los Angeles. He asked Mrs Cochran to pull up for a moment and explained that he had worked there once. She did so, and he stared hungrily at the refinery buildings, the pumping station. In his mind's eye he could see himself in jeans and helmet, wrench in hand, shouting for the hell of it, "Where's Emil? Where's that useless, goddam helper of mine?"

And Emil, kneeling at his side by a steel strut, yelling out to the hills, "Where's that black Irishman, where's that goddamn, blabbermouth McKeever?" That was the day before Emil fell from a catwalk and broke his leg; it was a week before they finished the job and had a beer party at high noon, everybody drunk as a lord in the sun. And it had all been thirty years ago – but not gone, not lost, clear to his eye and written on the hills.

"A six-month job putting this up," he murmured softly to the Cochrans. "There's places all over this state got my fingerprints on them. Other states too."

The Cochrans nodded and were silent in the understanding of the old for the treasures of the past... and then they moved on.

It was almost ten at night when they arrived in downtown Los Angeles. McKeever, who knew that he should be weary, found that he was quaking with excitement. He said gaily, "Just drop me wherever you want, folks. An' I'm awful obliged to you."

"Do you have a place to stay for the night?" asked Mrs Cochran.

"I ain't worrying about that," he replied with a happy grin. "Now I'm here at last, all I got my mind on is seeing that doctor."

"But you can't see her until tomorrow, Mr McKeever."

"The night's young yet," he replied slyly. "What you don't know is I got her *home* address."

"Do you have an appointment?"

"She got a letter about me – she sure expects me. So I'm hell-bent to see her tonight if I have any luck with hitches."

"Well then," said Mrs Cochran, "we'll drive you there."

"But that's in Glendale, take you twenty minutes."

"It'll take you much longer."

"That's nice of you, but you already treated me to a fine dinner an'—"

"Oh, pooh! Shut up!"

They found the street with some difficulty, and not without stopping to ask directions. It was in a residential area, the cottages close together, with small patches of green lawn and ugly palms and gay little flowerbeds before each house. "Might even have her office in her home," McKeever murmured happily. "Some doctors do." He thought of his friends up at Santabello, of his long hours by the roadside, of the complex of events that had led him to this moment of triumph. He thought of Harold Malone weeping under the railroad bridge, of his dream and the dance of his life. "Jesus Christ," he burst out, "I'm so excited I'm rattling to pieces."

As the car stopped, Cochran said earnestly, "Mr McKeever, I've been thinking. Margaret and I have a student fund. It's not much, but we keep it circulating. Right now there's very little in the kitty, only ten dollars. But we'd be happy to let you have it as a loan. There's no interest required."

"But listen, I ain't a student, you know that." He laughed softly in wonder at the notion.

"You have this idea for a book. That's what I had in mind. It's a scholarly job."

"My goodness…"

"Don't be an old pokey," said Mrs Cochran. "We expect it back."

"You'll sure get it back."

Cochran gave him the bill and shook hands. He said with a grin, "Good luck, sonny."

"I don't know how to thank you folks. But it's surely your kind makes the world go round."

Mrs Cochran picked up his suitcase. "I'll go to the door with you. Just to be sure she's there."

There were no lights in the front of the house, but the number over the door was illuminated. When they were on the porch, they saw a small brass sign, AMELIA BALZER, M.D. McKeever rang the bell. His throat began to feel tight and a bit parched.

For a few moments there was no response. He rang again. Then the porch lights switched on. A coloured woman in a house dress opened the door. He said eagerly, "Is the doctor in?"

"You got an appointment?"

"Ain't she in?"

"She don't usually have appointments at night. Is it an emergency?"

"Sort of. It's been arranged for me to see her. She got a letter."

"Well... come in, then. I'll tell her. What's your name, please?"

"Mr Simon McKeever, from Santabello. She's heard of me."

The maid walked back into the house. Mrs Cochran said softly, "Goodbye." She squeezed his arm and gave him his suitcase. "I do wish you the best."

"Don't let that man of yours get you down," McKeever advised with an exultant grin. "An' don't get lost in the jungles of Brazil."

She smiled and nodded and left him. He wished he might have kissed her. He thought suddenly of his Mary and remembered her from the dream of the night before, and heard her piercing cry to him, "Oh yes, testify." And he answered her in his mind without realizing it, saying, "Rest easy, my darling." Then he walked into the house.

Chapter 17

He stood in the small foyer and thumbed the edge of his soiled panama and gazed at his face in a wall mirror. His hair was a bit tousled, and he smoothed it down with a nervous palm. It was an old face, he had to admit it. It was bone-thin, and weathered-looking like a cut of shale in the desert. But the skin was firm and tanned, the eyes had a lively sparkle. "Eyes show the inner man," he thought comfortably. He wondered what she would charge for the injections, and whether she would wait for full payment. He straightened up and ran his tongue around his dry mouth and felt nervous and happy. He knew it would turn out well, but he couldn't help shivering a little. It was, after all, a crucial moment.

A door opened at the rear of the foyer, and a woman in a purple house robe came towards him – a large, broad-shouldered woman, almost as tall as he was, full-fleshed but not stout, vigorous in stride. She wore her iron-grey hair with masculine severity, drawn tight over her large head. Her face was broad, and her features all were large: the clear, grey eyes were large and long-lashed; the cheekbones were high, the nose fleshy and strong; the mouth was thick-lipped, wide and firm. She looked capable, intelligent and iron-willed, and McKeever felt instant confidence in her knowledge and skill... and a bit wary of her. He asked rather shyly, "Are you the doctor?"

She nodded briefly. "My maid told me it was an emergency. What's wrong?"

He felt encouraged at hearing her voice. It was warm and richly timbered, and it denied the severity of her appearance, as though the person who owned that voice must surely be a sympathetic individual.

"I wouldn't exactly say it was *that* kind of an emergency," he explained eagerly. "But it *is* an emergency. Or else I wouldn't've come – I know it's late. But you expected me, didn't you? You got a letter about me? McKeever's my name."

"A letter from whom?"

"Why... why from that woman in the drugstore, a patient of yours, you cured her."

"What woman? What's her name?"

For a moment McKeever lapsed into a state of helpless confusion. In all that talk with the woman in the drugstore he had never thought once to ask her name. It was the doctor's name he had been after. And now, quite clearly, the woman had forgotten her promise to write down about him. He said anxiously, "I thought you knew about me. I'm from Santabello, an' I'm lame from the arthureetis. Didn't she write you about me, a woman you cured – she came to you on crutches?"

The doctor frowned. She said quite crossly, "I'm afraid I don't know what you're talking about. Why *won't* you tell me her name?"

"I don't know it." He saw her frown again, and he burst out hastily, "But look, it's no fake – she gave me your address, that's why I came here. I can sure describe her to you – small an' fat, a high colour in her face, blond hair, dyed I think, cut short... an' you took down her blood pressure, too, she said. Her husband was in the liquor business, they—"

The doctor interrupted him with a quick, annoyed gesture. "Yes, I know the woman – Mrs Lees."

"Thank God for that. At least you won't think I'm an idiot or something. So that's why I've come to you. I'm sure aching to be cured the way you cured her – you're a lovely sight to me, doctor."

She asked with cold annoyance, "How long have you had arthritis?"

"Started on me four years ago."

"Then it's scarcely an emergency, is it?"

"Well, ma'am—"

"I don't have office hours nights, Saturdays or Sundays. Call up my nurse on Monday and wait your turn with my other patients. And in the future, please remember that doctors are human beings: they get tired, and ten thirty at night is not the time to come to their homes with a case of chronic arthritis."

The doctor's angry face blurred a little before McKeever's eyes, as though she had suddenly slapped him – as she had. Yet it was not the slap that he felt most keenly, but the sour truth of his whole situation – it moved in his belly like a viper. For four days he had wrapped himself in a shining cloud of fantasy, but now a hard wind had blown him naked, and he was left shivering. This was not the kindly, gentle doctor who would take his arm and smile with merciful power and say, "Why, of course I can cure you, we'll start our injections right away – why, you'll be working again in no time." This was a real doctor, tired after a day's work – hard-faced, annoyed, with appointments and office hours and other patients. This was a doctor who had looked him over and knew already how little he could pay, and who said flatly, "Wait your turn... next week, the week after, what difference does it make to me?" This was a doctor who lived, like the Booger and everyone else, on a raft in the great, big economic ocean – and why had Simon McKeever been such a wet-eared simpleton?

He bent down and picked up his overcoat and Gladstone bag. Without glancing at the doctor he began his slow crawl to the door. His mind was already turning, slowly and dully, on practical things, a place to sleep for the night, food for the days to come. How would he manage? The bag felt frightfully heavy in his hand, like a cast-iron weight. But he knew that this, also, came from the humiliation in his heart.

Dr Balzer opened the door for him. He couldn't help glancing at her on his way out. She said to him, "Walking comes hard, doesn't it? I'm really not an alligator, you know." There was a twist of a smile on her firm lips. "But I *was* in bed, and I *am* tired and it *isn't* an emergency. I can also do a better examination in my office."

He nodded and forced a smile in return. He muttered hoarsely, "I'm sorry, made a mistake. I'll call for an appointment." His mouth worked, and then he stopped walking. "I'd like to say one more thing to you, though."

She nodded.

He raised his head and gazed at her stubbornly. "Just so you'll know I ain't an idiot. I don't like people thinking I'm an idiot. When I met that lady you cured, I couldn't figure anything but coming right down to get your injections. Only, I couldn't come by airplane, couldn't come by bus. I may as well admit I was temporarily out of money. It's taken me three days hitching on the road. Guess I barged in on you like this because I felt like a man let out of prison... an' you were my only relative. Guess the people I was with tried to tell me it was late, but I didn't listen. I'm sorry."

The doctor said crisply, "Come back in. I've changed my mind."

"There's no need for that."

"I've changed my mind, I told you."

"I was only trying to explain – I wasn't asking any favours," he replied sternly. "I'll wait my turn, I'm no better than anyone else. Goodnight now."

Dr Balzer grasped his arm with a strong, insistent hand. "You're a mulish old bastard, aren't you?" she asked amiably. "Now come in before the neighbours think I'm running a whorehouse."

"Oh my God," he said with a happy laugh, "I've found somebody more stubborn than I am. Sure I'll come in. I'm crazy to come in."

She laughed and took his overcoat and bag. She set them down in the foyer, opened a door and switched on the lights of the room beyond. "Go in there," she said briskly. "I'll get my instruments."

He walked into a small sitting room. The walls were lined by low bookshelves and covered with a decorative wallpaper. He found a straight-backed chair and sat down on it. He took out his pipe, but he didn't smoke. He thought of Professor Cochran, who was gallivanting off to the jungles of Brazil at eighty-two. He heard the plumbing groan at the back of the house, and shortly after that he heard kitchen noises, and then she returned. She was wearing a white physician's jacket over her purple dressing gown, and she carried an instrument bag.

"I'm making some coffee. We'll have it after I look at you." She took a cigarette case from her pocket. "Smoke?"

"Thank you kindly." His mouth trembled a little. "I sure appreciate this, doctor."

She held a match for him and lit her own cigarette. She switched on a standing lamp and moved it so that he was within its light. Then she sat down in an easy chair. "How old are you?"

"Sixty-two. I ought to say three, maybe. My birthday's next month."

"The arthritis started four years ago?"

"That's right. I was strong as a bull till then. Worked my full day, never was sick before."

"Just answer my questions," she interrupted crisply. "We'll make better time that way. It started with stiffness in the joints?"

"That's it. My hips when I bent over, they felt locked."

"Any pain?"

"Not at first. After about six months I took to aching when I walked."

"Do you have pain now?"

"No ma'am. That proves it ain't serious, don't it?"

"Pain for about a year and then it more or less stopped. Is that right?"

"That's just right. I had a lot of pain the second year – it made me quit work, damn it. Then it went away, but the lameness got worse."

"And it was the same with your hands, knees and feet?"

"Why, yes," he replied eagerly. He felt a surging wave of affection for this keen, capable woman. It was a wonderful feeling to know that he was in good hands at last, that she knew so much about his illness she could anticipate his answers. And it was an added pleasure to him that she was a woman. He had always believed that few women got a chance to prove their abilities in this world.

"Did you ever have syphilis?"

"No ma'am."

"Gonorrhoea?"

"Dodged that too."

"Are you positive?"

"Why, sure, I never did go to hoores. Not after the first few times, I mean. I didn't feel—"

"We'll skip your sex life," she said with a little grin. "Rheumatic heart disease as a child?"

"No ma'am. I been awful healthy. Got all my own teeth, keep my bowels—"

"Nodules on your feet? Bumps?"

"Little ones, rosy."

"You're a factory worker?"

"No, ma'am, not me. The oil line – I'm a pipe-fitter... that's skilled work."

"Work out of doors?"

"All my life. It's the out of doors that's kept me so healthy."

"In all sorts of weather, I suppose?"

"Why, sure – rain, cold, snow, it never bothered me."

"Close to the ground?"

"Some of the time. Laying pipelines."

"Use your hips and hands a lot?"

"Why, yes, but that never bothered me. This lameness started in the mattress shop where I last worked. It was awful damp there. That damp rusted me the way it does a piece of iron."

The doctor reached over and put a hand on his knee. With the other hand she moved his leg up and down, feeling the crepitation of the joint. She repeated the operation with his other knee. Then she carefully probed both hips with her strong fingers.

"Jiminy, I need oiling, don't I?" he said with an eager smile. "I'm your man, doctor. You just shoot your stuff into me. A lot of it."

"Ever have an injury to your knees or hips?"

"Never had any breaks, but I been banged up here an' there. The oil line is rough work."

She nodded and made no comment. She moved a hassock, set his legs upon it, unlaced both shoes and peeled off his socks. She scrutinized his feet, felt the nodules on the big toe joints. McKeever was relieved that he had washed his feet and changed his socks only that afternoon. It would have been humiliating otherwise, especially before a fine woman like this. He watched with interest and curiosity as she held one hand upon his instep for some moments, to what purpose he didn't know.

"Unbutton your shirt." She stood up, crossed to the door and switched off the overhead lights. She returned and opened her instrument bag. She watched his fingers fumbling with the buttons of his shirt, but she made no attempt to help him. When he was ready, she raised his undershirt and put a stethoscope to his chest. Her head was bent down and her tight-drawn, iron-grey hair had a healthy, attractive sheen to it in the glow of the lamp. McKeever suddenly wanted to stroke her hair. And, feeling this, he had an intense, flashing hunger to be forty again for one night, strong and lithe as he had been when he built the refinery at Lebec, lusty and virile so that he could hold a strong woman like this strongly in his arms, cover her firm mouth with his and feel her go soft against him, female and responsive.

She took her stethoscope from her ears, and he said, "I got a good heart, ain't I? I've always been told so."

"Fine. It belongs to a man of sixty." She rolled up his sleeve in order to take his blood pressure. "Ever have sinus trouble?"

"No ma'am. I have a wonderful constitution. Used to do a back somersault easy as breathin'."

When she had taken his blood pressure, she switched off the lamp. In the darkness she examined his throat, nose, sinus chambers. Then she said, "Look over towards the door." She examined each eye in turn with an ophthalmoscope.

"What's that for?" he asked curiously. "I ain't got arthureetis *there*, have I?"

"The eye is a place where we can see the condition of the arteries."

"How are mine?"

She didn't answer until she had switched on the lamp again. "Fine. You can dress." She put away her instruments and said, "Now we'll have some coffee."

He waited for her to return with a smile of satisfaction on his lips. She had turned out to be a sympathetic woman after all. He was certain now that she would let him pay gradually for the injections. His heart and arteries were Grade A, as he had known in advance they would be, and they were the foundation of good health. Life was turning very rosy after the two years in prison at the Booger's.

> Whatever be thy fate today,
> Remember, "This will pass away!"

It was a verse for a man to keep fixed in his mind.

The doctor returned with a tray. There was a bottle of Scotch on it as well as the coffee things. She said briskly, "Will you have a whisky?"

"Why, ma'am, thank you. You're being awful good to me. I will."

She poured the coffee, helped him to cream and sugar, poured his whiskey, gave him a cigarette. She was silent throughout, her eyes preoccupied. McKeever began to worry a little lest her silence reflect concern over money. He drank his whiskey, murmured appreciatively "That sure hits the spot" and then said, "You know, I've got my old-age insurance. It comes in regular every month, so I expect to pay you for my treatments. An' I've got a fine job lined up for October."

The doctor nodded. She fingered her firm throat, then asked quietly, "Didn't you ever go to a doctor before me?"

He answered with scorn. "Why sure, at the clinic in Santabello, but I didn't get no help there. Those young interns, what do they know? They don't want to bother with an old man, just a charity patient to them, a 'terminal case'. I wouldn't trust them – I didn't even listen to *them*." She remained silent, and his voice rose in

pitch. "They don't care... they don't know... they ain't a specialist... they ain't got injections like you."

She said quietly, "If you came into my office next week, I
could do a urinalysis, take some X-rays, give you a metabolism test. But I wouldn't learn anything I don't know already.
You can't walk properly because of bony outgrowths in your
hips and knees. They interfere with the free movement of your
joints. The condition is called 'degenerative arthritis'. So far
as we know, it doesn't come from dampness like other forms
of rheumatism – at least not primarily. It seems to be a disease
of old age, Mr McKeever. Elderly people get it, particularly
labourers or mechanics who have kept using certain joints in
their work over many years. It also seems to affect those who
have been exposed to the weather through outdoor work... like
you." She fingered her throat and added quietly, "And there's
no cure for it."

His limbs turned to sponge, and he cried out in harsh protest,
"But your injections – you cured that woman... what are you
telling me?"

"I didn't cure her of arthritis. I gave her injections three times a
week, but do you know what was in them? Water. She's a hysteric.
The only thing *wrong* with her was high blood pressure, and even
that came from nervousness. She got sick and walked on crutches
because she wanted to avoid a sex life with her husband. She had
four children and didn't want any more. I made her believe she
was cured because I dominated her and bullied her and sympa-
thized with her and fooled her. I also got her a diaphragm so she
could have intercourse without getting pregnant. She happens to
be a stupid, hysterical woman, and when she was living down in
Los Angeles I prevented her from sending me patients. Now I see
she's begun again. I'm sorry, Mr McKeever, I'm terribly sorry, but
there are no injections at all that can help you. Gold injections
won't help and vaccines won't help. There is nothing known in
medicine now that can either prevent or cure your condition. It's
the work you did, and your age."

He was silent, and he looked at her face and heard the echo of her words. He listened to them and chewed them over and tasted their harsh bile in his mouth. He was suddenly back in a saloon in Pennsylvania, a fly crawling on his hands and his wife and child cold in a graveyard. He wanted to say something to the doctor, but there was a paralysis in his throat. He rubbed his fingers over his face and eyes. His mind fought to keep him proud before this stranger, and he thought, "Say something." And then he thought, "It's the very dickens, connected this way to my work." He rubbed his face and eyes again. "It sure is the dickens," he murmured aloud. Then he swallowed and said, "Well now… a life without happiness wouldn't be a good life at all, would it? But I guess a life without disappointment wouldn't be real. No… *hmmm.*"

The talking didn't help, and he fell silent again. And then he asked, "Will I get worse?"

"I don't know. You won't get better. If the disease arrests itself, you'll stay the way you are. But it may get worse."

"Is it possible I'll get worse till I can't walk at all?"

"Yes, it is."

"End up in a bed, you mean? Helpless?"

"Yes."

He was silent, and then he stood up and reached for his cane. She said, "Will you have another whiskey?"

"No, thank you, ma'am… How much will it be?"

"There's no charge."

"I can pay. I got a loan of some money just before I saw you."

"You've had quite a trip for nothing, and I'm somewhat the cause of it. I'll feel better if you don't pay me. Do you have a place to go tonight?"

He didn't reply for a moment, and then he said, "Why, yes, ma'am, I do. Got some relatives here. I'll stay with them. Will you be good enough to phone for a taxi?"

"Yes, of course."

She watched him as he crawled towards the foyer. "How old are you really, Mr McKeever?"

"If I don't pass over before the tenth of next month, I'll be seventy-four."

"I knew you weren't sixty-two, but you did fool me."

"I always did have a strong constitution, ma'am. I wanted to encourage you."

"Why don't you sit down here till your taxi comes?"

"Well... if you don't mind, I'll sit out on your porch. That way you can go to sleep an' I can think a little. I got some thinking to do."

"All right. There's a rocking chair out there."

She carried out his bag and overcoat and held the rocker while he settled himself in it. "If the taxi takes a while to come, don't care. They do at night."

"Don't worry about me."

"Goodbye then." She held out her hand. He shook it and smiled a little and said, "I'm much obliged to you."

"That's all right." She turned around and the door closed.

He took out his pipe and stuffed it with the Finney tobacco and lit up. The porch light was on, but beyond its brightness the street lay in quiet night shadows, the moonshine clean and silvery upon the houses where people slept, the old men growing older and the young children dreaming of adulthood and the vigorous couples locked in warm embrace, joining their seed for the new generations to come. He rocked quietly, and after a while he rested his head back on the hard frame of the chair and closed his eyes. He began to taste his defeat. "It's sure the very dickens," he murmured aloud. For the second time that night an image of his wife flashed through his mind, and he heard her piercing cry, "Oh yes, testify."

And where was his Jerusalem now?

He sat on a park bench in downtown Los Angeles and pondered the question. When the taxi driver had asked where he wanted to go, the name of this park had come to his mind. It had seemed as good a place as any for a man who had no destination and who needed to think. And perhaps it was a better place than most, because even now, at 1.30 in the morning, there were echoes of the daytime stir that had always pleased him about this park. It was small and dirty and overcrowded, but it also was green and pulsing and gay, and it existed in bright defiance of the concrete city that surrounded it. There was a small lake here, and occasionally he had come of a weekend to row a boat, to feed the white ducks that paddled the water, to watch the excited, bright-eyed children on an outing with their parents... white children and brown children of Mexican stock, black and coffee-coloured Negro children and shy, yellow-skinned, Chinese children... and all of them beautiful to a man who had no child of his own. This afternoon's peanut shells littered the pavement at his feet; the empty Cracker Jack boxes* floated lightly on the still water. And tomorrow this park would stir again with boats and healthy, scampering legs and pigeon wings beating the sunshine... the earth turning and the people coming and going.

Only, where would he go? He didn't know. For the first time in his life, he felt utterly empty inside. And that was something new to comprehend.

His initial shock had largely passed. The doctor's sentence of life imprisonment had stabbed into the soft pulp of his heart – but he was no longer bleeding, he realized that now. The sun had risen and set so many times, the earth had turned, and that was all. Now he was old... really and truly old... and prepared to admit it. Twilight had come rather sooner than he had calculated, but what of that? In a way, it was even satisfying to know that his illness was the harvest of his work rather than an accident. A man could accept that, because it was the bad along with the good. Even his eventual confinement in a bed had a different meaning now... if that was the way it would turn out – and perhaps it wouldn't. But he felt sure he could accept that too.

What he could not accept was the vacancy that was now his life. His mind faltered, and he felt like weeping at the bleak prospect of it. There was nothing left to him now except empty hours in a rocking chair. Perhaps that would do for others, but it would not for him. He had suffered many disappointments before, but none so awful as this.

He sighed and stared at the murky water, at the peanut shells by his feet. He bent down and picked up one of the shells. He twisted it between his fingers, pressed it and listened to the split and crackle. What happened to old peanut shells? They were swept up and put into trash cans. They floated out to the sea eventually or were fed to pigs as garbage. A child had eaten this peanut, and it had given him nourishment – it was energy for racing legs, and one day those legs would be tall and muscular and would dance the earth in proud activity. It was a good dance, and he could testify to it: that it was a fine, proud thing to be a man, and that even now, at seventy-four, he had no regrets. Only, he did have an emptiness in his heart. And he could not deny it.

He stared at the water. He had been sitting on this bench for over an hour. He felt dull and lost and forlorn. What to do? Where to go? How to pick up again? The deep thread was lost.

He sucked his cold pipe and closed his eyes and heard Mrs Cochran say, "It's solid, it's got bones... it's a fine title, Mr McKeever." He heard her husband's voice. "I hope you do it." They were professors, he thought sorrowfully, they had sound judgement. And surely they hadn't been stringing him along – not those people. Now that activity was denied him, now that freedom and independence were gone, if he could only be at work on his book, he would be content in a rocking chair, even in a bed.

He sat and tasted the sour bile in his mouth. He gazed at the still, indifferent water and wondered why the dice had rolled this way for him. And then, suddenly, he sat erect and laughed. And then he cried out, "You're a damn idiot, McKeever." In one tempestuous burst, a magnificent thought had come to him. He began to shiver with pleasure at the size of it. He felt as though the wings of a bird were beating in his chest.

What was a book? It was not a pipeline. It was not put together by steel or bolts, by the turn of a wrench, by a man's hips or feet or muscles. A book was the sap of mind and heart... it was the yeast and ferment of study and years and strong opinions. And why couldn't a work like that be created in a rocking chair, even in a bed?

McKeever bit down so hard on his pipe that he could hear a warning crack in the stem. He snatched it from his mouth and muttered aloud joyously, "Take it easy, lad, sort it out, figure it calm."

Why couldn't he do this book? For two years he had delayed work on it – but why? Because of a notion that now seemed terribly mistaken. And it *was* mistaken, by God. Since he needed a library as his tool, he had taken for granted that he would have to wait until he had a job and was cured of his lameness – until he could walk and use a pencil and get around like a normal man. But why, really why? Couldn't the books he needed be brought to *him*? And, for that matter, why the hell couldn't he still work in a library himself, if somebody would transport him there?

But who? The question sobered him. Not the Booger. Why should the Booger go to that trouble for him? Why on earth should the Booger or anyone else spend twenty-five cents a week on gasoline to borrow books for Simon McKeever?

A second question: suppose he got the books – what then? He still had the damn problem of his hands. Writing was no easy matter these days. His fingers cramped, the words sprawled like chicken tracks... It would get worse, perhaps. And even *his* kind of book couldn't be handled without some writing... notes to put down and pages to mark and things like that. There would also be the whole plan and outline of the project to be written down clearly, so that a publisher would understand it. It might even have to be done with pen and ink in order to look professional.

But still, he argued instantly, if he had a friend, perhaps a good friend like Percy Fuller, who had been a clerk and could write a fine hand... perhaps the friend would be willing to help him?

The bird wings beat furiously again. He felt a stir of such keen optimism and strength that he wondered if he were possessed by some spirit. Why, my goodness, he thought boldly, it would be like Eugene Debs running for president when he was in prison. "Oh lad, do it, do it – give it a whirl," he muttered fervently. "Take a whack at it! You've lost two good years already – don't waste any more time."

A warning phantom shimmered in the water before his eyes. He saw the weak, scared, greedy face of the Booger, the pale, penny-pinching eyes. Once again his rapture cooled a little. He knew too well that he would never find a willing ally in the Booger.

What to do? Carefully, very soberly, he began to estimate the possibilities that were open to him. He might try to remain in Los Angeles. There were homes for the aged here, and the public library was better than the one in Santabello. Yet there was a problem in that. The library was in the business section of town – he had gone there often. Whatever home he found was likely to be a considerable distance away in a residential district or a suburb. In that respect there would be a definite advantage in returning to the Booger's. The Booger had a truck, and he drove into town every morning. The truck would guarantee the books he needed... provided the Booger was willing. Furthermore, he had his good friends up at Santabello – he would have Percy Fuller to do a bit of writing for him.

Only, how could he control the situation? How in hell could he squeeze a promise from the Booger that would stick? There was no use pretending that he could always leave if things didn't work out: that would be kidding himself. He could leave now – but what about a year from now? What he had to have was an airtight plan that would guarantee the situation even if he was confined to a bed. He needed to return on *his* terms, not on the Booger's. He needed to know absolutely that the Booger would keep his word...

His thoughts broke off as he heard footsteps approaching his bench. He turned around... and instantly went cold inside. Out of long memory of the Depression years, of other benches in other parks, he waked with automatic resentment and hostility.

The young policeman surveyed him for a moment and then said, "On the bum, old-timer?"

"I should say not." His tone crackled. "Can't you tell a working man from a bum? I got money in my pocket right now."

The policeman noted the Gladstone bag, the incongruity of a winter overcoat on a warm May night. "Don't think I'm dumb. If I catch you trying to sleep in this park, I'll run you in."

"Women being raped," McKeever replied acidly, "children dying of consumption, politicians grafting, racketeers an' labour spies getting paid off – an' all you got to do is arrest old men for sleeping in the park. What a profession!"

The policeman said thickly, "One more snotty remark like that an' I'll pound your head."

McKeever pushed up to his feet. He stood very erect, swept by hot rage, and said sternly, "Pound away. It's your kind has kept Ireland in slavery – you've been tramping on the rights of the labour movement for a hundred years."

"Oh my God!" cried the policeman. "A world full of squirrels!" He walked off laughing and swinging his billy.

McKeever watched him with contempt. Then he took out his wallet and counted his money. "God bless the Cochrans," he murmured softly. He had not quite nine dollars, enough for taxi and bus fare. He might even have the price of a last taste of loin of pork. There would be no more of that once he returned to the Booger's.

"But you need a plan, lad," he muttered sternly. "If you can't go back right, don't go back at all." His mouth worked for a moment and then he added with determination, "Leave it wide open. For all you know, you'll be hitching on the road again tomorrow."

He picked up his suitcase. His mind began to grope for a plan.

Chapter 18

Shortly after four o'clock the next day a Greyhound bus stopped at Harry Kilgore's service station near Santabello. The driver went to the rear of the bus in order to open the luggage compartment. By the time he returned to the front exit, McKeever had conquered the steps and was waiting for him on the gravel. "This is yours, I hope," the driver said pleasantly. "Sometimes we get the checks* mixed."

"It's mine." He took the Gladstone bag and said, "Thank you for the nice ride, young feller – you're a careful driver."

"Why, thanks, Pop. I appreciate that."

McKeever watched the bus until it was once again roaring down the highway – bus going to Santabello, to Marysville, to San Francisco – and then he made his way to the office of the station. He found young Kilgore inside, absorbed in reading a comic. Kilgore said hello and then looked surprised. He asked, "Ain't you from the Finney place?"

"That's right."

"Here the other day, weren't you? You went off to Los Angeles?"

"That's right."

"Boy, the fuss you caused! Finney split a gut when he got here."

McKeever said drily, "To think I missed it!... Will you do me a favour?"

"What?"

"Will you telephone him? Tell him Simon McKeever's here. Tell him to drive down an' see me."

"I'll do that. What's up?"

McKeever extended a nickel without replying, and Kilgore crossed to the wall telephone. He made the call, and McKeever heard Ada Finney's brassy voice come on at the other end.

"They have to call him," Kilgore said. "He's outside."

McKeever chuckled drily. "Cuddling his flowers. That's the second time this week I've busted in on his horticulture. I'm tearing down his life."

"What's this all about anyway?" Kilgore asked curiously. "I never did get the whole story."

"Well, now… guess it ain't ended yet, son."

They waited in silence for a few moments, and then Kilgore turned back to the phone. McKeever could hear the Booger's voice and his surprised "What?" – and then an explosive "Goddamn!" He smiled thinly.

Kilgore said, "He'll be right down."

"Thank you, son. Is that Half 'n' Half in that case?"

"Yeah."

"I'll take three cans." He thought of Pavlovsky and added, "Two of those candy bars also."

"That's forty-eight cents."

McKeever gave him a half dollar and thought with satisfaction that even if he didn't remain at the Booger's, he would have these presents to leave with his friends. He said briskly, "I'll wait outside if you don't mind."

Kilgore's eyes were sharp with curiosity, but McKeever's tight face rejected questions. He murmured "Sure" and returned with regret to his comic.

McKeever pushed outside and made his way around to the rear corner of the office. He wanted to keep an eye on the road that led to the Home, and he wanted privacy when he saw the Booger.

He dropped his cane and lowered himself to the ground. He rested his back against the wall of the station and stretched his legs out flat. He felt quite weary, and the warm sun was pleasant and soothing. He had napped for brief periods on the bus, but most of the time he had been too busy and concerned to sleep. There had been a dozen strategies to invent and analyse and discard before he found the one that satisfied him.

He closed his eyes and recalled the face, the crisp voice, of Doctor Balzer. He sighed a little without knowing that he was doing so. He thought of the Cochrans, and wondered if their boat had sailed as yet, and how they would fare in the jungles of Brazil. His mind drifted back to a grocery store in Brownsville, Pennsylvania, to a girl who had sat fanning herself there, to her voice and her milk-white throat. She was still there somehow, bearing another name, with another young man standing before her, gazing at her face with delight.

McKeever smiled a little. And then, at the sound of tyres in the distance, he looked up to see the Booger's pick-up truck.

He remained where he was. The truck rolled up to the gravel of the service station. Finney stepped down and walked towards the office – but then, seeing McKeever, he paused. He didn't say anything, and McKeever also kept silent. Finney's plump face turned red, and his loose mouth parted to accommodate his rapid breathing. It was evident to McKeever that he was full-blown with gas and fury, and he thought, "No good!" And then he added, "To hell with him. I'll start right back to Los Angeles."

"Well!" Finney said indignantly. "*Well!*"

"Nice day," McKeever replied calmly, although he didn't feel at all calm. "How are your flowers behaving, Tom?"

Finney moved closer. He gripped his hip bones with his big hands and burst out cholerically, "You're a fine gent! You sure pulled a fast one on me! What do you want now? To come back, I suppose? I'm supposed to say, 'Howjado, Simon, ol' boy, glad to see you, hope you'll come back with us, a nice gent like you, never cause no trouble…' Oh Jesus, I'm mad at *you*!"

McKeever remained silent.

"Well… well?" Finney shouted indignantly. "What if the police had picked you up? It could've ruined us. We're supposed to take care of our old folks. We get our licence because we're *responsible*."

"That's right," McKeever agreed coldly. "You're supposed to be responsible."

"Then why'd you go off like that – hey? Tell me, damn it. An' why you back now? You got tired of park benches like we said – is that it? Our place seems pretty good to you now?"

"It's got its points."

"Oh, it has?" Finney retorted with boiling sarcasm. "You admit it finally?"

"I always said so."

"An' what now? Are you back to make trouble or will you behave yourself an' stay put?"

McKeever said evenly, "It could be I've got a subpoena in my pocket. Could be it's ready to be made out to you."

"*What?*"

"Bring you into court maybe, on a charge of stealing from a pensioner."

Finney's plump cheeks drained of all colour.

"I've got witnesses, too, you know," McKeever said relentlessly. His blue eyes began to glitter with excitement as he measured the Booger's reaction. "Wouldn't even do you good to offer to pay me back. From what I found out in Los Angeles, it sure looks like you'll end up with the State Welfare shutting down your Home."

Finney stared at him with uncertainty, with fury, with bitter terror. He bent down on one knee so that he could peer into McKeever's face. When he spoke finally, it was in a husky whisper.

"Why would you want to do a horrible thing like that?" He ran his tongue over his lips. "It ain't true – you know it ain't: it's a lie an' a slander. My God" – his manner turned beseeching – "I know *you*. You wouldn't turn thirty-two old people out on the road? You're not that kind. Not over a little spat. Hey?"

"Depends," McKeever replied sternly. "I'd have no reason to do a thing like that unless you made me."

"I? Why should I do it?" He flung out his arms in a gesture of misery and bewilderment. "Jesus, this whole deal is topsy-turvy. Why should I do it to my own business?"

"I can't guarantee how *you'll* act," McKeever replied sharply. "But *I've* got to have a place to stay, right now an' for the rest of this month, an' permanent."

"You mean a home?"

"Sure I mean a home."

"But I thought... You went down to get cured. What happened to that?"

McKeever swallowed, then answered calmly, "I can't get cured. I've got old-age lameness. I'm incurable."

Finney's bitterness overcame his anxiety. "Goddamn it – I told you that in advance, didn't I?"

"Yes, you told me."

"But you had to go off anyway, didn't you? All this damn mess for nothing."

"What mess?" McKeever asked sharply. "*I'm* not in a mess. *You* are! All I got to do is find me another home."

"Another? Why another?"

McKeever paused, took a deep breath. "You've filled my place already, haven't you?" he asked with clear disinterest.

"As a matter of fact, we haven't," Finney burst out eagerly. "Why, you can come back with me now, right this minute."

"Can't say as I want to."

"Why not?"

"I don't think I'll be treated very decent at your place any more. I think you've got it in for me now."

Without realizing it, Finney got down on his other knee like a man about to pray. "Why, that's crazy, Simon. I've always liked you. We've had a spat or two, but I don't carry hard feelings – I'm not *that* kind of man."

"That's fine, but I'm not coming back to your place unless we settle a couple things first an' put 'em down in a contract."

"A contract?"

"That's what I said. A legal contract, with witnesses."

"A contract?" Finney muttered thickly. "Saying what? What things?"

McKeever paused. The wings in his chest beat so hard he was afraid he would groan aloud with excitement and nervousness. "First of all, I want some different smoking tobacco. Or else the money to buy my own."

"Now wait a—"

"You wait a minute! That manure you give us can't be smoked. I don't know how much you pay for it, but it won't cost any more to get another brand."

"That's what you say!"

"I know – I'm a smoker, you're not! You just let me shop around."

"Provided it don't cost a penny more."

"Agreed. Will you put that in a contract?"

Finney licked his lips. "OK. What next?"

"What does my lunch cost you?"

"That's my private business, ain't it?"

"Thirty cents?"

"That's a laugh. You been in a grocery store lately? Food's sky-high."

"Then you've got another deal. I need cash, I owe some money to three or four people. I'll skip my lunch an' you'll give me thirty cents every day until I've paid off my debts."

Finney jumped to his feet. "The hell I will. That's no deal. We buy in bulk."

"What'll you offer?"

"One dime, no more."

"My, wouldn't that look fine in a report to State Welfare?" McKeever asked with a cutting laugh. "Three dollars an' twenty cents to feed thirty-two people lunch. You'd sure lose your licence over that."

"All right, damn it, I'll make it fifteen. But that's the absolute limit – absolutely."

"Will you put it in the contract?"

Finney was silent.

"Will you?" McKeever demanded.

"OK, OK." He wiped his forehead with his sleeve and muttered plaintively, "Why does there have to be money in the world anyway? It's the root of all evil. Oh, how I hate to be quarrelling always... Well, is there anything else?"

"You're damn right there is. It's the most important of all. It's the one thing that makes me feel a home right in Santabello would suit me a lot better than your place."

"Now, how can you say that?" Finney asked pathetically. "Just when we're getting together – an intelligent man like you. Why, you need the fresh air an' quiet. You want to live on a dirty street with noise day an' night?"

McKeever said slowly, with momentous emphasis, "There's one thing I need more than fresh air. I need a library!"

"A book library?"

"That's right, the public library. I need to be able to go in there once a week."

"What for? We get books an' magazines from that church, you know that."

"Those books ain't what I want. I got a piece of work to do. I need *special* books."

"Oh my God! You mean what you told us the other day – you're serious?"

"Sure I'm serious."

"Simon McKeever Shakespeare – ha-ha-ha."

"You can just go to hell," McKeever said furiously. "Beat it, get out of here."

"Now, wait a minute! Keep your shirt on! You can't blame me for being surprised. It's your business, of course. But who ever heard of a man like you writing a book? What on earth do you want to bother with it for?"

"To agitate the minds of better men than you, you numskull!" McKeever burst out indignantly. "To move the world one inch forward. Does that mean anything to a creature like you?"

"Creature? Who you calling a creature?" Finney retorted excitedly. "What do you have to get so nasty about? Ask anybody

– it's the agitators cause the trouble in this world. You ought to be ashamed, at your age, to talk about 'agitating'!"

McKeever struggled to his feet. "Why, the princes of the earth have been agitators, you idiot," he thundered. "Jesus... and they nailed Him to a cross for it – people like you, no doubt. St Paul, an' Thomas Jefferson,* an'—"

"I?" Finney sputtered. "I nailed Him? I'm a Christian, a peaceable man – I love flowers. Why do you insult me like that?"

"Goodbye," McKeever said wrathfully. "There are better homes than yours, an' better libraries too."

"Now, wait a minute, don't lose your temper," Finney implored, grabbing his arm. "After all, I don't care what kind of a book you write. That's your business. I won't interfere."

"But will you take me to the library?" McKeever demanded. "I need to go there once a week."

"Well, shucks, of course I will. Why, I go right past the library on my way to the market. I'll take you there any time you want."

"Will you let me stay all day?"

"On Wednesdays an' Fridays I can."

"Will you put that in the contract?" McKeever asked hoarsely. "With witnesses?"

"Why, sure, absolutely. Why not? It's no skin off my hide."

"An' suppose I get so crippled I can't walk any more," McKeever added fiercely. "Will you go to the library for me, will you get the books I want?"

"Why, sure, if it don't cost me nothing."

"Will you put that in the contract, too?"

"Why, sure."

McKeever closed his eyes and took a deep breath.

"Is it a deal? Are you coming back?" Finney asked eagerly.

"Under those conditions – the library an' the tobacco an' the lunch money... with a contract an' witnesses – under those conditions, I guess I will come back."

* * *

He pushed slowly down the corridor that led to his old room. It was the dinner hour, and from all over the house there came the low murmur of conversation, the clink of tin spoons on crockery. He had not seen anyone as yet, and he was glad of it. He had insisted upon stopping off in the Booger's office. There, with Finney pecking at a typewriter, he had dictated their agreement. Now it was in his pocket and presently it would be signed before witnesses. And now he was ready to greet his friends again.

He paused at the door and put down the Gladstone bag and the overcoat. He thought idly, "I'll die in this room." But it was only a passing thought, easy, without dismay or resentment, and he added to himself with satisfaction, "But not yet. Got a lot to do before I pass over." And then he thought, "I bet this world will be a wonderful place some day. It sure will be. First they'll have to fix up the economics of things, of course, an' then they'll put the best brains to work on rickets in kids an' the plagues that old men get an' a lot of things like that. But it'll take time. Yes. *Hm...* a lot of disappointments before then, a lot of long trips for nothing... *hm...*" He was sad for a moment, and then he thought: "Why... tomorrow is Sunday, I clean forgot – that nurse is coming to visit me with her boyfriend. I wanted to send her a postcard and I never did. What luck!" He smiled in pleased anticipation of their visit, a pretty girl like that, so like his Mary with her strong, chunky figure. He would have to tell her she was like his wife. And then he thought, "I can begin work on Monday morning."

He opened the door. They were all on their cots – Percy Fuller and Stan Pavlovsky and Marcus Peake; Hanbury, the farmer, was listening to the radio as usual; and Timothy Wright, in cowboy boots and ten-gallon hat, had his nose in his soup. He saw the stunned surprise on their faces as they looked up... and then the good, heart-warming friendship and pleasure in the eyes of his friends. He said gaily, "Why, hello there, everybody. What have you goddamn lazy coots been doing these past few days?"

Note on the Text

The present volume follows the text of the first edition of the novel, published by Little, Brown and Company in May 1949. The spelling and punctuation have been standardized, modernized and made consistent throughout, as well as anglicized where necessary, although some American forms have been retained, in order to preserve the distinctively American character of the text.

Notes

p. 5, *Epigraph*: The epigraph is taken from *At the Bottom* (better known in English as *The Lower Depths*), a 1902 play by the Russian writer Maxim Gorky (1868–1936), in the translation by William L. Laurence (1888–1977), published by Samuel French (New York) in 1930.

p. 7, *a Jack London novel*: A reference to the American novelist and journalist John Griffith Chaney, better known under his pseudonym Jack London (1876–1916), author of famous works of fiction such as *The Call of the Wild* (1903) and *White Fang* (1906), set in Alaska and the Yukon during the Klondike Gold Rush at the end of the nineteenth century, but also politically and socially engaged works such as *The Iron Heel* (1908) and *Martin Eden* (1909). Like McKeever, London was a self-taught man, having dropped out of college at the age of twenty-one.

p. 18, *Whatever be... "This will pass away!"*: The last two lines (ll. 35–36) of 'The Old Man's Motto', a poem by the American poet John Godfrey Saxe (1816–87). "This will pass away!" is the refrain of the last four stanzas of the poem.

p. 26, *There is nothing... pay to try...*: From 'The Little Black-Eyed Rebel' (l. 43), an 1876 poem by the American poet Will Carleton (1845–1912).

p. 41, *The Cry for Justice by Upton Sinclair*: *The Cry for Justice: An Anthology of the Literature of Social Protest*, a collection of writings by philosophers, poets, novelists and social reformers edited by the writer and political activist Upton Sinclair (1878–1968).

p. 49, *Tom Mix*: The American film actor Tom Mix (1880–1940), a star of early Western films.

p. 52, *his Western Stories*: *Western Story Magazine* was a pulp magazine devoted to Western fiction that ran from 1919 to 1949.

p. 52, *Pinkertons*: Private law-enforcers working for Pinkerton's, a detective agency established in the United States in the mid-nineteenth century by the Scottish cooper Allan Pinkerton (1819–84). They were often used as strike-breakers.

p. 57, *pie-card*: A labour-union member.

p. 57, *the A. F. of L.*: The American Federation of Labor, a national federation of unions in the United States.

p. 58, *July Four*: The Fourth of July, a national holiday in the United States commemorating the Declaration of Independence of 1776.

p. 64, *a jitney*: A nickel, a five-cent piece.

p. 73, *a Pilgrim's Progress if ever there was one*: An allusion to *The Pilgrim's Progress from This World to That Which Is to Come*, a 1678 Christian allegory by John Bunyan (1628–88). Narrated in a series of dream sequences, the book charts the journey of Christian, an everyman character, from his hometown, the City of Destruction, to the Celestial City.

p. 74, *There is a saying... Can ever come to naught*: The first four lines of 'Spes Est Vates', a poem by John Godfrey Saxe (see note to p. 18). The Latin title can be translated "There is hope, poets".

p. 75, *blue-balled*: A humorous jibe alluding to a supposed discomfort ("blue balls") attributed to prolonged, unreleased sexual arousal.

p. 76, *baloney*: Bologna sausage.

p. 77, *Teddy Roosevelt*: Theodore Roosevelt (1858–1919), later president of the United States from 1901 to 1909, who formed, together with Army Colonel Leonard Wood (1860–1927), the First US Volunteer Cavalry Regiment (the so-called "Rough Riders"), which was involved in some skirmishes in Cuba during the Spanish–American War of 1898.

p. 86, *Wheatena*: An American brand of toasted-wheat cereal.

p. 92, *Billy the Kid… Wild Bill…*: Billy the Kid was the nickname of the American Old West outlaw and gunfighter Henry McCarthy (1859–81), alias William H. Bonney. Wild Bill was the nickname of another notorious American gunfighter, James Butler Hickok (1837–76). For Tom Mix, see note to p. 49.

p. 94, *Sittin' Bull*: Sitting Bull (1837–90) was a Lakota chief who led his tribes in a fight of resistance against the US government.

p. 97, *Gladstone bag*: A small portmanteau suitcase named after four-time UK prime minister William Gladstone (1809–98).

p. 104, *WPA*: The Work Projects Administration, an American agency that hired unemployed labourers to carry out large public works projects.

p. 105, *the Meat Trust*: In the early 1900s, five companies had an effective monopoly on the US meat market. Between 1913 and 1921, President Woodrow Wilson's (1856–1924) administration enacted a series of measures to crack down on the big five's anti-competitive practices.

p. 105, *Upton Sinclair… in his book*: Sinclair's novel *The Jungle* (1906) was an exposé of the terrible conditions in America's meat-processing industry.

p. 107, *Old Harry*: The Devil.

p. 125, *a jerkwater town*: A small, insignificant town.

p. 125, *dick*: Guard.

p. 129, *percentage*: Advantage.

p. 131, *Debs*: The trade unionist and political activist Eugene Victor Debs (1855–1926), one of the founding members of the Industrial Workers of the World (IWW), an international labour union founded in Chicago in 1905.

p. 131, *Whitman*: The American poet Walt Whitman (1819–92).

p. 132, *Abraham Lincoln... so many of him*: This quotation, often with some variations, is ascribed to Abraham Lincoln (1809–65), the 16th president of the United States.

p. 138, *Churchill*: The British politician and statesman Winston Churchill (1874–1965), who served as prime minister of the United Kingdom between 1940 and 1945 and from 1951 to 1955. At the time in which the novel is set, Churchill would have been the same age as McKeever.

p. 139, *Justice Holmes*: The American jurist Oliver Wendell Holmes, Jr. (1841–1935), who served as an associate justice of the US Supreme Court from 1902 to 1932.

p. 146, *"To them that hath... taken away"*: See Matthew 13:12: "For whosoever hath, to him shall be given, and he shall have more abundance: but whosoever hath not, from him shall be taken away even that he hath."

p. 155, *But mice... long year*: *King Lear*, Act III, Sc. 4, ll. 130–31.

p. 156, *The Dance of Life*: A 1923 work of popular non-fiction by the English-French scientist, writer and social reformer Havelock Ellis (1859–1939). In this book, Ellis studies the constant development of the self through a variety of arts, including thinking, morals and dance.

p. 156, *John D. Rockefeller*: The American industrialist and philanthropist John D. Rockefeller (1839–1937).

p. 160, *Jerusalem, Jerusalem*: An allusion to the Christian hymn 'Jerusalem, Jerusalem' by Lina Sandell (1832–1903), with music by Charles H. Purday (1799–1855). The last four lines read: "My goal is fixed, one thing I ask, / Whate'er the cost may be, / Jerusalem, Jerusalem, / Soon to arrive in thee." Jerusalem is seen as a metaphor of the Kingdom of Heaven.

p. 164, *Travelers Aid or the Community Chest*: Two charitable organizations providing financial support to travellers or the community at large.

p. 165, *Protagoras*: Protagoras (*c.*490 BC–*c.*420 BC) was a pre-Socratic Greek philosopher associated with the Sophist school.

He famously affirmed that "Of all things the measure is Man – of the things that are, that they are, and of the things that are not, that they are not". The quotations are again from Chapter 1 of Havelock Ellis's *The Dance of Life* (see first note to p. 156).

p. 165, *"The Art of Dancing"… "The Art of Thinking"*: Chapters 2, 4 and 3, respectively.

p. 167, *IWW*: Industrial Workers of the World, an international labour union founded in Chicago in 1905. Their members are nicknamed "Wobblies".

p. 174, *a yellow termite*: That is, a cowardly saboteur.

p. 192, *it was time to rise and shine*: See Isaiah 60:1: "Arise, shine; for thy light is come, and the glory of the Lord is risen upon thee."

p. 192, *'Fly's in the Buttermilk'*: An old American partner-stealing dance accompanied by a song, usually known under the title 'Skip to My Lou'.

p. 220, *Cracker Jack boxes*: Cracker Jack is an American brand of molasses-flavoured, caramel-coated popcorn and peanuts.

p. 225, *the checks*: The counterfoils.

p. 232, *Thomas Jefferson*: Thomas Jefferson (1743–1826), one of the authors of the Declaration of Independence of 1776, served as 3rd president of the United States.

CALDER PUBLICATIONS

EDGY TITLES FROM A LEGENDARY LIST

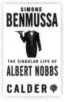
SIMONE BENMUSSA — THE SINGULAR LIFE OF ALBERT NOBBS — CALDER

ALAN BURNS — BABEL — CALDER

ALAN BURNS — BUSTER — CALDER

ALAN BURNS — CELEBRATIONS — CALDER

ALAN BURNS — DREAMERIKA! A SURREALIST FANTASY — CALDER

ALAN BURNS — EUROPE AFTER THE RAIN — CALDER

WILLIAM BURROUGHS — DEAD FINGERS TALK

MICHEL BUTOR — CHANGING TRACK — CALDER

COPI — FOUR PLAYS — CALDER

MARGUERITE DURAS — MODERATO CANTABILE — CALDER

MARGUERITE DURAS — THE GARDEN SQUARE — CALDER

PAUL ÉLUARD — SELECTED POEMS — CALDER

SYDNEY GOODSIR SMITH — COLLECTED POEMS — CALDER

GERHART HAUPTMANN — THE HERETIC OF SOANA — CALDER

SADEQ HEDAYAT — THE BLIND OWL AND OTHER STORIES — CALDER

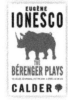
EUGÈNE IONESCO — THE BÉRENGER PLAYS — CALDER

GEORG KAISER — PLAYS VOL.1 — CALDER

GEORG KAISER — PLAYS VOL.2 — CALDER

ALBERT MALTZ — THE JOURNEY OF SIMON McKEEVER — CALDER

ALBERT MALTZ — THE CROSS AND THE ARROW — CALDER

ALBERT MALTZ — A TALE OF ONE JANUARY — CALDER

ALBERT MALTZ — A LONG DAY IN A SHORT LIFE — CALDER

LUIGI PIRANDELLO — SIX PLAYS — CALDER

RAYMOND RADIGUET — CHEEKS ON FIRE — CALDER

ALAN RIDDELL — ECLIPSE CONCRETE POEMS — CALDER

www.calderpublications.com

EVERGREENS SERIES

Beautifully produced classics, affordably priced

Alma Classics is committed to making available a wide range of literature from around the globe. Most of the titles are enriched by an extensive critical apparatus, notes and extra reading material, as well as a selection of photographs. The texts are based on the most authoritative editions and edited using a fresh, accessible editorial approach. With an emphasis on production, editorial and typographical values, Alma Classics aspires to revitalize the whole experience of reading classics.

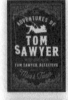

For our complete list and latest offers

visit

almabooks.com/evergreens